▪ NEVER LET THEM
SEE YOU SWEAT▪ ▪ ▪

Ron smiled. "Bet you guys thought I'd never pull it off, didn't you?"

Tony shook his head. "We knew you would, Ronny. Why the hell you think we made the deal?" Tony was starting toward the car. "Come on, Ronny," he said. "Time to get a little payback, ain't it?"

DeCicco laughed. He took a step in Tony's wake, then felt an arm circle his throat, and he tried to squirm free. What the hell was this? he wondered. This wasn't any time for horsing around. Something sharp jabbed against his spine, just above the belt. He tried to ask what the hell was going on, but the thick arm crushed the words in his throat. He heard the gunshot for just an instant, then went numb and slumped to the ground. The second bullet went through his forehead, but there was no need for it. Ron DeCicco was already dead.

Also by Philip Baxter

CRITICAL MASS
DOUBLE BLIND

Available from HarperPaperbacks

POWER
TRIO

PHILIP BAXTER

HarperPaperbacks
A Division of HarperCollins*Publishers*

This is a work of fiction. The characters, incidents, and dialogues are products of the author's imagination and are not to be construed as real. Any resemblance to actual events or persons, living or dead, is entirely coincidental.

HarperPaperbacks   *A Division of* HarperCollins*Publishers*
10 East 53rd Street, New York, N.Y. 10022

Cover photograph by Herman Estevez

First printing: August 1994

Printed in the United States of America

HarperPaperbacks and colophon are trademarks of HarperCollins*Publishers*

❖ 10 9 8 7 6 5 4 3 2 1

POWER TRIO

- ONE- - -

THE HEADLIGHTS PICKED OUT THE SIGN, ATTACHED to a rusting chain-link fence. In big, hand-painted block letters, it read DeCicco's Auto Salvage. Smaller letters beneath the name in wavy script added *Peter DeCicco, Owner*. The red lettering was chipped, peeling away from the white background. He remembered when they'd painted it, he and his brother, and it seemed a long, long time ago. The script was Pete's, and Ron had cursed him out for it, telling him how hard he'd worked on the sign, only to have it ruined by ego. That was the thing about Pete, he could never leave well enough alone. Now, letting the station wagon roll to a halt, its tires crunching on the gravel in front of the gate, Ron wondered if that's what big brothers were like, if their mission in life was to torment their younger siblings.

But time was getting even with Pete. The junkyard, because that's really all it was, was hanging on, and Pete with it, by his fingertips. Even through the windshield of the station wagon, he could see the film of grease clinging to the warped wood, the way it clung to Pete's entire life. Ron tried to remember the last time he'd seen Pete with greasy overalls, a thick black half-moon of crud under every fingernail that hadn't been chewed to the quick.

The whole thing, peeling paint, rusty fence, and beyond it, acres of rusting hulks and weeds flourishing among the wrecks, was a mess. It was Pete's life, and it was a fucking mess. And Pete didn't even seem to realize how pathetic it was. He was actually proud. "I'm in business for myself," he told people. But when they asked what it was he did, he got evasive, changed the subject like a skier negotiating the gates in a giant slalom. Pete didn't realize it, but even that meant he was going downhill.

"He can have it, man," Ron whispered, opening the door of the station wagon. "He can have the whole fucking mess."

He walked to the gate, already reaching into his sagging pocket for the key to the heavy padlock. The key felt like it was made of lead, and he hefted it once in his palm as he lifted the thick rubber pad under which the lock rested, its chain a rusty arc with the lock at its center.

Once the lock was open, Ron rolled the big metal gate aside, nearly slipping on a greasy pool where the bluestone had long since been crushed into the dirt. He cursed, gave the gate an extra shove, and heard it clang against the stopper, wondering if one of the guide wheels had jumped the track, like it usually did. Even the goddamned gate to this shithole doesn't work right, he thought, peering into the shadows along the fence. He couldn't tell for sure, but he'd deal with it later, muscling it back on track if he had to.

He walked back to the station wagon, climbed in, and pulled the door closed, throwing the wagon in gear and listening to the crunch of the tires change to a hiss as it passed through the gate. Now he was on dirt, dirt so black with oil and grease that on sunny days it reflected enough light to hurt your eyes.

The alleys among the hulks were wide, but ragged. Cars were dropped wherever they'd fit, according to some scheme that only Pete understood. Some of them were nothing more than bodies and frames, the doors, hoods, trunks all gone. Even the seats were removed. Others, their hoods gaping as if for a dentist, spewed wires and hoses. The smell of old oil and grease was thick in the air, and the musty stink of rust gave it an edge.

DeCicco reached into the back of the wagon to pat a cardboard carton, stroking it the way a hunter does his favorite dog. The box held his future, or part of it, anyway. No more small-time gigs, hustling for a few bucks here and a little there. He was on his way now. He'd show Pete what you could do if you weren't willing to settle for peanuts. He was like the old man, something his brother couldn't, or wouldn't, understand. Only he was going to make it all the way.

The alleys were rutted, and the Ford wagon rocked and rolled over the oily bumps. His headlights picked out a new Porsche, its front end crumpled like a cigarette pack. The windshield was a web of cracks, and in the bright light of the headlamps, a smear of blood glowed dark red on the inside of the glass. He remembered reading about the crash, some politician's son, no license, blood alcohol of .15. But this was one jam the kid's old man wouldn't get him out of, not by a long shot. DeCicco smiled at the wreck as the Ford rolled past.

Turning left, he slowed a bit. The headlights picked up the blue panel truck where the rest of his future was waiting, in five more cardboard cartons just like the one beneath his anxious fingers. He smiled again, this time cackling with perverse pleasure. "Whoomp, dere it is! Whoomp, dere it is!"

He backed off the gas and let the wagon roll into the empty space beside the panel truck. He killed the lights, then the engine, and reached over the seat back to shove the carton toward the rear door on the driver's side, then climbed out. Pocketing the keys, he walked to the rear of the panel truck, opened the back, and peered inside. He could see the blocky shadows of the other five cartons, hidden under a tarpaulin, and smiled again.

Walking back to the wagon, he tugged the heavy carton free, and finally, he had the last box under his arm, and it felt heavier than the others. Maybe, he thought, it was knowing that it was the last one. Maybe all the pressure of the last two months was getting to him. Maybe . . . hell, he could go on forever, a litany of maybes and possiblys and probablys. It was the last goddamned box, and that's what counted. He lugged it to the panel truck, dropping it with an echoing thump on the truck bed. He shoved it inside then climbed in after it, yanked away the tarp, and tied the carton down, using a thick woven cord to lash it down, just like the others. When the tarp was back in place, everything was just about perfect.

He nearly bumped his head jumping out, cursed again, and slammed the doors harder than he'd meant to. The slam echoed from the sheet-metal walls of a low shed at the back edge of the property, coming back so loud, he actually turned to see whether someone had closed another door. He was edgy, and talked to himself, trying to calm his nerves. Fumbling in his shirt pocket, he pulled out a joint, fat but bent. "A mighty spliff, mon." He laughed. Fishing a lighter from his pants pocket, he sucked the joint into life, held the smoke in his lungs for several seconds, then choked it loose. He'd have preferred coke, but didn't have the money. Not yet. In an hour, everything, even that, would change.

He leaned against the back doors of the panel truck, sucking the grass down to a chubby roach, then pinched off the light and tucked the stub into his pocket. "Waste not, want not," he said, wondering if his grandmother had marijuana in mind when she used to tell him that. The thought made him chuckle again. The very idea of that ancient crone of a grandmother, always dressed in black, and still smelling of the graveyard twenty years after her husband had been buried, toking, made him hysterical. He slipped down the truck's back, rested on the bumper, then slipped off and landed hard on his ass. "Waste not, want not, in Babylon, mon," he said.

Grabbing the bumper to haul himself up, he slid along the side of the panel truck, his hands squeaking on the cold metal. Opening the driver's door, he climbed inside, slapped his knees, and took a deep breath. "Ready to roll, breaker breaker, one-niner . . . whatever the fuck that means. Pedal to the metal, dude." He was giddy, knew it, and tried to stop it, but deep down, he didn't give a damn, and he knew that, too. He was too fucking close to the end of the rainbow now, little leprechauns ready to hand him his pot of gold.

He glanced into the back of the truck. It was impossible to pick out the shapes of the six cartons, but he knew they were there, and they were full of gold, maybe more than gold, maybe platinum. All he knew was that in one hour he was going to have more money than he ever dreamed of. He could get his own Porsche, get himself a Rolex, and kiss off his stinking job. Good-bye New York, Hello Florida. Get down and get brown, that's what he wanted to do, lie on the sand with a broad on either side of him, tits so big he'd have to sit up to look down the beach.

The good life, he thought. The best fucking life money could buy, which was the only kind of life worth living. He jabbed the key into the ignition and cranked up the engine on the old Dodge. The panel truck shuddered and trembled, its muffler coughing and barking before settling into a steady rumble.

He backed out of the tight space, so close to the Ford wagon that their bumpers clashed, and the wagon rocked as the panel truck finally got free.

He took it easy going back the way he'd come in. He could see the tire tracks left by the wagon, the little pools of oil squeezed out by the tires glistening in the wash of his headlamps. It looked like light was seeping up out of the ground, or as if the earth were cracked, revealing a well of illumination in some underworld beneath the junkyard.

He pulled through the gate, the old brakes squealing. Must be rust on the drums, he thought, been so long since anybody drove this damn thing. He climbed out of the truck, started to pull the gate closed, and as he'd thought, found that one wheel had jumped the guide rail. He cursed once more, stepped back through the fence, and leaned against the gate, hauling upward with both hands at the same time. The gate bumped back into its track, and he sighed, then started to pull the heavy wire mesh, closing the opening, leaving a gap just wide enough for him to slip through to the outside. Turning, he leaned into the gate until it clanged home, then he pulled the chain into place and slipped the padlock through, ramming it home with the heel of his hand. The heavy click as the lock snapped shut felt good, significant somehow, as if his future had just been ratcheted to another level.

He was nodding his head as he climbed in behind the wheel, closed the truck door, and shifted into first. The gears were whiny, grinding a little, but that, too, was probably a legacy of disuse. He'd been saving the panel truck for months, slowly adding to his cache. He'd start it up once or twice a week, sneaking down late at night, when he got off work, just to make sure that it would be ready when he was.

Now, rolling out of the gravel lot onto the road, he could hardly believe the moment had actually come. He reached for the radio knob, turned it on, and winced as a blast of static crackled from the twin speakers. Turning the dial, he found WBGO, some funky organ shit, probably Jimmy Smith or Brother Jack McDuff. He liked the bottom, the way they used the pedals to keep the groove going. Rolling to a stop at the first light, he tried it himself, beating a bass line with heel and toe, but his legs got tired and he lost his rhythm even before the light changed. Bastards must have strong legs, he thought.

The organ was cooking, the guitar chops behind it bluesy, but using some subtle chords, probably Kenny Burrell. The light finally changed, and he rolled across the intersection. It was a mile to Route 17. Three miles north to Mahwah. From there, he'd have his choice, he could stay on 17 or pick up the thruway. He liked the idea of speed, and the thruway gave him that. All those dinky towns on 17—Suffern, Sloatsburg, Tuxedo Park—they had one cop and he stayed in the bushes, waiting for some asshole to ignore the posted limits. It would slow him up going that way, but maybe it was better. There was always some junker of a pickup or van clattering along 17.

Nobody would pay him any mind, and as long as he paid attention to the speed limit, he'd be home free.

The meet was set for 2:00 A.M., and he could already smell the stacks of new bills, feel the stiff paper under his fingers, that slightly gritty coating that only new money seemed to have.

As he got closer to Harriman State Park he slowed, knowing there was an entrance, and not quite sure where, on 17. When he found it, he shifted down for the turn and left the truck in second for the winding road. There were trees all around him, hills sloping up on both sides, and his headlights kept picking out boulders, some of them the size of freight cars, all covered with this gray-green stuff that wasn't old paint, but looked like it.

The slopes on both sides of the road were covered with dead leaves, like brown snow. He knew where he was supposed to be, and when, and he was getting close to both time and place. He wondered what would happen if he was late, and felt his palms begin to sweat on the steering wheel. Once more, he reached behind him to pat one of the cartons, reassuring himself that his cargo was still there.

He was looking for a little picnic area, a place he'd been to only once, and was beginning to worry that he'd made a mistake coming in from 17 instead of the Palisades Parkway. He couldn't believe there could be so much forest so close to New York City, but here he was, smack in the middle of it. He started to imagine Indians behind every boulder, maybe even cavemen, or saber-toothed tigers watching the truck with greedy amber eyes. There was something primeval skittering along his spine now, some instinct he hadn't known he possessed.

And then he saw the first picnic table through the trees, and the dead black water of the lake behind it. Another table, then a third, and the little jug handle popped up. He slammed on the brakes, and as he made the turn he saw the car, already there, two men standing beside it.

He negotiated the sharp turns into the small parking lot, coasted in alongside the Buick, and killed the lights and the engine. The two men walked toward him, and he started to open the door of the truck.

One of the men lit a cigarette, and in the glare of the match, DeCicco recognized him. The other was just a bulky shadow. On the ground again, Ron felt giddy, his head swimming just a little.

The one he recognized, Tony his name was, said hello. "Ron, how you doin'? You get all the stuff?"

"I think so."

Tony sucked on the cigarette, his face turning red for a few seconds. "What do you mean, you think so? You got it all or you don't—"

"Yeah, yeah, I got it all."

"Let's take a look. How many boxes?"

"Six. They're pretty big, and they're kinda heavy."

"Let's see."

DeCicco walked to the back of the panel truck and jerked the handle on the door. It ground open, and he swung the door wide.

The other man, the one Ron didn't know, pulled a small flashlight from his jacket pocket and trained it on the cartons. Then he glanced at the Plymouth van parked beside the Buick.

"Think it'll all fit, Butch?" Tony asked.

Butch grunted as he straightened up. "Fuck yeah. It'll all fit."

"Good."

Ron smiled. "Bet you guys thought I'd never pull it off, didn't you?"

Tony shook his head. "We knew you would, Ronny. Why the hell you think we made the deal?" Tony was starting toward the car. "Come on, Ronny," he said. "Time to get a little payback, ain't it?"

DeCicco laughed. He took a step in Tony's wake, then felt an arm circle his throat, and he tried to squirm free. What the hell was this, he wondered? This wasn't any time for horsing around. Something sharp jabbed against his spine, just above the belt. He tried to ask what the hell was going on, but the thick arm crushed the words in his throat. He heard the gunshot for just an instant, then went numb, and slumped to the ground. The second bullet went through his forehead, but there was no need for it. Ron DeCicco was already dead.

- T W O - - -

ALL THE WAY HOME FROM THE AIRPORT, PAUL
Desmond felt empty. The car seemed huge, bigger
than a wide-body jet. And he was handling it the
same way, sluggish turns, drifting as if the air were
pushing the Oldsmobile off course. It took him a
while to realize why—it was empty, as empty as he
felt, and it would be empty of everything but him, for
three weeks. Audrey and the kids were such a big
part of his life, when they were absent the world
wasn't big enough to fill the void.

He kept glancing at the passenger seat, expecting
to see his wife grinning at him that crooked way she
had. The backseat, too, was a vacuum. Without Sally

and Maria to fill it with their chatter, it was just a vast, silent space, colder than the emptiness beyond Pluto. Or maybe, he told himself, with his own wry version of Audrey's grin, I just plain miss them.

He missed them all right, but he didn't envy them. Three weeks was a long time to be without his family. But three weeks in Florida was an eternity. He couldn't imagine himself there for more than two or three days, unless someone held a gun to his head. The unrelenting sun, the acres of pastel doubleknit in every mall, the tons of sagging flesh barely contained by mile upon square mile of wrinkled skin. Maybe that was it, maybe it was the fear of getting old that held him back, the thought of being trapped with a million reminders of how his own flesh would soften and droop like the jowls of some cartoon puppy, his skin get unnaturally dark, turn to thin leather, brittle as old paper and about as attractive.

He knew all the wonders of the state, the Everglades and Okeechobee, the Keys, the marlin and tarpon leaping high, trying to spit out the hooks, the alligators and the manatees. But those things were not for him. He didn't like air-conditioning, and liked less the idea of moving from one artificially cold cell to another, looking out at the brilliant sun that might as well be a moon, for all the good it did him.

Absently, he reached over and patted the seat, thinking he could feel Audrey's forty-one-year-old, but still youthfully firm thigh, under his lonely fingers. Glancing at the rearview, the way he did when Sally was giving Maria a hard time, he saw only his own pale blue eyes, staring back at him as if he were a stranger. He saw that his hair needed cutting, that it was a little lighter than he remembered, and a little thinner. But his cheeks were still solid, there was no wattle beneath his chin. He was getting old, but he wasn't there yet, not by a long shot. Florida fodder he wasn't.

The monotony of the thruway lulled him a little. He watched the sheer rock walls crowding the edge of the asphalt, some of them fronted by walls of artificial stone, others by walls of bluestone behind wire mesh. It was evening, and he knew that when he got far enough north, there would be deer in the meadows on either side of the road, or on the hillsides, at the edge of the trees, ignoring the cars, bobbing their heads to pull at the grass or nibble a little bark. Dead ahead, a wheeling hawk caught his eye through the windshield, and he used the spritzer to clean the glass and get a better look.

He wished he could have afforded to take some time off. A vacation would do him good, and if he had had the time, they could have gone someplace they would all have enjoyed, maybe Cape Cod. It was November, and the Cape would be all but deserted, the way he and Audrey liked it. And Boston was nearby, full of music and bookstores, not to mention clam chowder and baked beans. The Red Sox were just a memory now, and would be for six months, but there were Celtics and Bruins to watch. But there was a lot of paperwork, and so he was alone, boring a hole through the Hudson Valley, heading home, for work and more quiet than he could probably stand.

Desmond leaned forward and clicked on the cassette player, fumbling for one of the Ornette tapes he'd brought along for the ride. He found the one he wanted, *Change of the Century*, shoved it into the machine, and punched the play button, his hand poised over the volume knob, waiting for the first notes of "Ramblin'" to come blasting out.

The line, played in unison by Ornette and Don Cherry, made him smile the same way it always did. When Ornette broke into his solo, his horn fighting the stumbling rhythm until he found a bluesy groove, Desmond cranked it up full bore. He turned on the rear speakers to get the full impact of the rhythm section, Haden and Higgins listening to the horns with sensitive ears, always ready for the mercurial shifts of Ornette's alto.

By the time "Free" started, Desmond was tapping the steering wheel, desperately trying to follow the shifting tempo and the breakneck twists and turns of the melodic line. Jazz was the one thing that could ease the pain of separation, not filling the temporary hole in his life, but at least plastering it over so no one would notice. No one but him, anyway.

At Exit 18, Desmond got off the thruway and headed through New Paltz, wondering if maybe one of the bookstores was open, then decided that he had enough to read sitting on his desk. He cruised slowly through the little town, until he got to the junction with Route 208, then headed north. The sun was just about down now, sitting on the tips of the Shawangunks like a drop of molten gold. It seemed to quiver like an egg yolk. The mountains themselves were dark bruises under the oozing gold light, not quite blue and not quite purple.

He was tired and he was hungry, and he leaned back in the seat, letting his mind drift through space, his eyes plugged directly into his hands on the wheel, driving by instinct while he listened to "Bird Food," the boppish, Parker-like line a perfect tribute to Bird.

By the time he reached the last turn before the long, tree-lined country road leading to his home, he was ready to turn around, drive back to Newark, and get on the next plane to Daytona. It made him feel weak, vulnerable in a way that he wasn't used to and didn't like, and he slapped the steering wheel hard. He could hear the slightly amused tone of his old Company mentor, Allen Burton, and gave it voice. "Discipline, Pavel, discipline. That's what you lack. You will never be completely self-sufficient until you learn to master your feelings."

The old man was right, but that didn't mean it didn't hurt to acknowledge it. Once more, he glanced at himself in the mirror, saw the crinkled skin at the corners of his eyes just barely breaking into a smile.

He shook his head, partly in annoyance at his own vacillation and partly in amusement at how readily the fabric of his life could be reduced to tatters. He was one step removed from the mumbling winos on city streets, verbally tilting at personal windmills, evening scores no one else kept, indicting the world for personal failures. He watched the sun set behind the trees, their black spikes almost like Oriental calligraphy against the darkening sky.

He passed a huge meadow, its tall grass sweeping

up and away toward a line of trees, and spotted a dozen deer, maybe more, loping across the hillside. He slowed to watch, pulling off onto the shoulder after glancing in the rearview to make sure no one was behind him. Stopping on the side of the road, he rolled down the window and leaned on the sill, resting his head on his forearm. The small herd followed the trees, then started downhill and vanished one by one. When the last deer was gone, he sighed heavily, cranked up the window, and pulled back onto the road.

The last two miles seemed an eternity. He wanted to be home, to surround himself again with the things that mattered to him, and he had to fight the urge to sit on the gas, pushing the Cutlass too hard for the curves. Only when he could see the house through the pines did he relax.

When he pulled into the winding drive, he caught a glimpse of color through the jungle of dark trunks, and slowed. It looked like company, and he wasn't expecting anyone.

Letting the Olds roll uphill, giving it just enough gas to keep it moving, he broke through the trees and saw a sky-blue Porsche in front of his garage. Under the floods, it looked impossibly bright. He could see the silhouette of a man at the wheel and watched him closely as he pulled in alongside the Kraut iron.

The man at the wheel reached for the door handle and climbed out of the Porsche as Desmond killed his own engine. Desmond turned off the ignition and set the parking brake, something he did only when distracted.

"Mr. Desmond?" the visitor asked, leaving his door open, and resting one hand on it.

Desmond nodded. "Yes. Did we have an appointment? If so, I'm afraid I—"

The man cut him off. He was dressed tastefully, his clothing obviously expensive, but not ostentatious. "No, no, I'm sorry to come unannounced, but I have something urgent I need to discuss with you. Something . . . sensitive, I guess is as good a word as any."

Desmond closed his car door and approached the visitor, tensing just a little, watching him closely, ready for the first tensed muscle to betray the man's intentions, whatever the hell they were.

The visitor stuck out a manicured hand, and in the light from the garage floods, Desmond could see the glitter of a watch he took to be a Rolex under the neatly pressed white cuff. "Warren Resnick, Mr. Desmond."

Desmond shook the hand. "Pleased to meet you, Mr. Resnick . . . I guess."

"I'm sorry, I know this is rather unorthodox, and maybe just a little rude, but I have a serious problem, and I've been told that you're someone who can help me."

Desmond raised an eyebrow. "Oh? And by whom were you told?'

Resnick hesitated. "Not exactly told, I . . . look, maybe this is a bad time. Maybe I should come back."

Desmond shook his head. "You're here now. You might as well come in and tell me what this is all about."

Resnick smiled. "Thank you, Mr. Desmond."

Desmond led the way up the stone steps to the front of the house. Unlocking the door, he held it for Resnick to enter, still not quite sure it was a good idea, and then led the way to his office.

He clicked on the light, indicated a leather chair beside the desk, and said, "Have a seat, Mr. Resnick. Can I get you something to drink?"

"Seltzer would be good, if you have it."

Desmond grinned. "Sure. Somehow, though, I didn't take you for a sparkling-water type."

"Oh, and what type did you take me for?"

"You look to me more like a Jameson's man, or maybe bourbon."

Resnick shook his head sadly. "Not anymore, I'm afraid. My thirst for liquor, which I used to think was insatiable, cost me a marriage and two children, and very nearly cost me a job into the bargain."

Desmond walked to the small refrigerator behind his wet bar. "Perrier all right with you?" he asked.

Resnick nodded. "Fine, fine."

Desmond grabbed a bottle of Perrier then a can of diet Coke for himself, opened both, and walked back to his desk. After handing Resnick the bottle and a glass, he sat down and took a sip of the soda straight from the can.

Leaning back, he said, "Now, why don't you tell me how you happened to end up on my doorstep, Mr. Resnick?"

- THREE- - -

WARREN RESNICK SEEMED NERVOUS. HE KEPT
fidgeting in the chair, his eyes searching the room for
someplace to land comfortably. Anyplace, apparently,
but on Desmond's face would do.

Desmond was used to this kind of anxiety. He'd
give Resnick a little time before prodding him. He
watched as Resnick got to his feet and walked toward
the stereo cabinet, resting one hand on a shelf as he
ticked a nail against a row of CDs.

Without looking at Desmond, he said, "You're
pretty eclectic, I see. It isn't often you find Bartók's
Mikrocosmos on the same shelf as Anonymous Four

and Bob Dylan." He turned around then, smiling uncertainly. "I guess you don't know who I am . . ."

Desmond smiled reassuringly. "I figured we'd get around to that eventually."

Resnick laughed. "I get so used to . . . well, anyway, that doesn't matter. I guess we should get right to business."

"It would let us both get to bed before dawn," Desmond said.

"I'm the CEO of Griffin Records. When Mitsugi, the Japanese entertainment conglomerate acquired Griffin about two years ago, they brought me in to run the American operation. I'd been at CBS Records when Sony acquired it, and I was familiar with Japanese management style. I guess they wanted someone they could be comfortable with." Resnick stopped again, realizing that he was running on. His voice was detached, almost as if it were being piped in from another location, and he cleared his throat before walking back to the chair and dropping into it with a sigh of resignation.

"You said I was recommended to you," Desmond prompted.

Resnick nodded. "Yes, you were." He smiled. "Very highly, I might add."

"Would you also add by whom?"

Resnick chuckled. "I'm sorry, Mr. Desmond. I suppose I must seem just a little addled. And I suppose I am."

"Take your time, Mr. Resnick. But I think it would help both of us if you were to tell me what this is all about. Especially if you start from the beginning. Maybe if I ask a few questions . . . ?"

Resnick seemed relieved, as if Desmond's offer was what he had been hoping for. "By all means, yes, ask me whatever you want to know."

Desmond sipped his soda before asking his first question. "Who recommended me?"

"Valerie Harrison, from Northamerican Insurance. You had done some work for her, and the results were more than satisfactory, as I understand it. She didn't give me any details, understand, but she did say that you had succeeded beyond her wildest dreams. She couldn't stop singing your praises."

"Did you approach her about your problem?"

"Yes." Resnick bobbed his head, repeating, "Yes. I did."

"Personally or professionally?"

"Both, I suppose. I mean Northamerican was interested in our business, and she was part of the management team in the negotiations. We wanted to upgrade our coverage of all sorts of things—manufacturing plants, recording studios, archives, artists, and so on. As it happened, we were in the middle of an inventory, preparatory to concluding the negotiations, and that's when we discovered the missing material."

"What's missing, Mr. Resnick?" Desmond felt as if he were coaching a quiz-show contestant, trying to pry information out of someone who knew it, but was too agitated to focus on just what it was he knew. "Something that belongs to Griffin Records? Or to you personally?"

"Griffin," Resnick said, reaching for his bottle of Perrier and taking a long slug. He looked like a man who was trying to drown himself in booze, and the water wasn't going to do the trick. "It belongs to Griffin."

"Can I ask why you came to my home, instead of contacting me and having me visit your offices?"

Resnick finished the Perrier. "Can I trouble you for another one of these?" he asked, holding the bottle out to Desmond.

"Would you prefer something a little stronger, Mr. Resnick?"

Resnick sighed. "I suppose I would, yes."

Desmond smiled. Getting out from behind the desk, he patted the back of Resnick's chair. "Relax, Mr. Resnick," he said as he moved past. "Relax."

At the bar, he got a couple of ice cubes, put them in a tumbler, and poured a couple of fingers of Bushmill's, swirling it once to chill it before heading back to the desk. He sat on the corner of the polished wood, handed Resnick the tumbler, and waited while the nervous executive tossed it down in a single swallow.

Setting the glass on the desk with exaggerated care, Resnick rubbed his palms on his thighs, flattening the razor-sharp creases of his slacks, and rocking like a davening Hasid on a subway seat. He looked up at Desmond, his face torn between hope and despair. "You've heard of Colin Yeats, I suppose?"

Desmond nodded. "Naturally. I don't imagine there's anyone under fifty in this country who hasn't. He one of your artists?"

Resnick laughed. "You could say that, I guess. If he's anyone's. But I'm not sure he is. I don't know if you have any idea just how significant he is, not just culturally, which just about everyone knows, but economically. He was named by *Life* as one of the hundred most significant people of the twentieth century. He has sold more albums than Elvis Presley, the Beatles, and Bob Dylan combined. And most music critics think he's more significant than all of them, revolutionized popular music not once, but three times, and he's likely to do it again anytime he gets the notion. One album alone, *Bitter Harvest*, sold more than thirty million copies worldwide, more than any single album in history. And I do not exclude Michael Jackson's *Thriller*."

"I had no idea he was that successful."

"Few people do, Mr. Desmond. He's so elusive, shuns the limelight, as I'm sure you know. One might almost call him a recluse. A recent article in *Rolling Stone* called him rock and roll's Salinger. I don't know but what that might be going a bit too far, but he cherishes his privacy, has done ever since his first marriage went on the rocks."

"And I gather you're not telling me all this just to pass the time, Mr. Resnick. What's the connection to your problem? Or is Colin Yeats your problem?"

"No, it's not Colin . . . at least, as far as I know, it isn't."

"But there is a connection?"

"Yes . . ."

Desmond slid off the corner of the desk. "You'll excuse me for a moment, Mr. Resnick? I have to get my smock."

Resnick looked baffled. "Smock?"

Desmond nodded. "Yes. And my pliers. Do you prefer gas or novocaine?"

Resnick looked more baffled still. "I . . . uh . . ."

Desmond shrugged. "Look, Mr. Resnick, if I'm going to have to pull teeth, I want to dress the part. And I don't believe in inflicting unnecessary pain, so you can have your choice of anesthetic."

Resnick took a deep breath. Desmond watched him, ready to jump in as soon as the record executive began to turn blue. But after a long moment Resnick expelled the air. "I'm sorry, I guess I'm not really making this easy, am I?"

"No, you're not, Mr. Resnick. And I'm running out of patience, in case you didn't notice."

Resnick rubbed his chin. "All right, you're right, let me try to explain."

"Good," Desmond said, sitting back on the corner of the desk.

"When we did the insurance inventory, which was completed yesterday, there were items missing, as you can expect. Griffin and its subsidiaries have been in business for a long time. We are the third largest producers of recorded music in the entire world. Larger than Philips and Deutsche Grammophon. We've recorded everyone from Caruso on. You name it—John McCormack, the great Irish tenor from just after the turn of the century, to rap and industrial. The first recordings in the vaults were done on cylinders, for Christ's sake. Covering that much time, and with so many little companies coming and going, it was natural that the inventory would be incomplete. And as far as I can determine, it was the first complete physical inventory of our archival holdings ever done."

"So what's missing, Mr. Resnick? It must be something more than you would have expected, more than routine, or you wouldn't be here. Am I right?"

Resnick nodded. "Yes. We're missing a substantial amount of Colin Yeats material."

"How substantial?"

"Several hundred hours."

"Tell me about it. I assume there must be copies."

"No, no copies. These were studio tapes. All kinds—the old three-quarter-inch stuff, cassettes, digitals—covering his whole career with us. And whoever took them—"

Desmond interrupted. "You're sure they were taken?"

Resnick nodded. "Oh yes, there's no doubt about that. Whoever took them knew exactly what he was doing."

"How can you be sure of that?"

"All the material taken was unreleased. In some cases just alternate takes. In others, songs that have never been released in any form whatsoever. The vaults were cherry-picked, Mr. Desmond. Nothing that has been released is missing. Everything that is missing is unreleased. Whoever is responsible displayed an intimate knowledge of Colin's career. He knew what was worth taking. The released material exists in other forms—masters, digitized tapes, and so on. And he took the trouble to substitute blanks so that the theft would not be so obvious. In fact, had it not been for the physical, I don't think we'd know about the theft yet."

"It almost certainly was an inside job, then," Desmond suggested.

"I don't know. I suppose it would have to be. But the point of all this is that no one but our chief of accounting and the head of our library knows about it. And no one *can*. We are in the process of negotiating an extension of Colin's contract. The existing contract expires in six weeks. And as part of the celebration around his resigning, we are planning a massive retrospective, something on the order of Dylan's *Biograph* or *The Bootleg Tapes*. We wanted to cull the best material from the unreleased recordings, but now . . ."

"And naturally, if Yeats learns that you can't keep your own house in order, he might not resign, is that your worry?"

"Part of it, yes. It will cost us untold millions of dollars. But I'm afraid it's even more complicated than that. It could cost us other artists, either unsigned at all, or who might otherwise have changed labels to sign with us. Others may choose to leave when their existing contracts expire. Those losses could be incalculable, because we might never know whether an artist we were unable to sign chose to go with another label because of this. And there's still more possible fallout."

"Which is?"

"Bootlegs, Mr. Desmond. If those tapes fall into the wrong hands, someone could manufacture illicit CDs, tapes, and LPs. Neither Griffin nor Colin Yeats will ever see a penny from the sales of those unauthorized recordings, and we could potentially be sued, since Colin's contract gives him the final say over what material gets released. The tapes were in our custody, and if he chose to, he could sue the pants off us if somebody starts bootlegging that material."

"What other reason could there be for taking the tapes, if not bootlegging?"

"There is a huge underground market, collectors of all kinds. Some of them are driven by passion, of course, but others by greed. Even in the collectors' market, those tapes are worth a fortune to whoever has possession of them."

Desmond stood up, turned for his soda, and drained the last of it. "And you want me to recover them, is that it?"

Resnick nodded hesitantly. "Yes. We'll pay you well, of course."

"Of course."

"But it's imperative that no one know you're looking for them. I know that will make your job more difficult, but the need for secrecy is the reason I'm here. I can't go to the police, for obvious reasons."

"I can't very well go around looking for something without asking people where it is, Mr. Resnick."

"I know, I know," Resnick said. He looked as if he were about to cry, and Desmond felt sorry for him, but he still found it amusing.

"Let me think about it, all right?"

— FOUR— - -

ROY MITCHELL EXAMINED HIMSELF IN THE MIRROR, scraping a patch of dried shaving cream from his scalp with a fingernail. His skin was bronzed, as usual, but not, as most people thought, by nature, but by a bank of tanning lamps. He still couldn't believe how easy it was now to maintain the healthy-looking tan. In the old days, he used to hang a single sunlamp from a hook on the bathroom door and, more often than not, managed only to mottle his shaven scalp with red blotches. But, like he preached, he had practiced, and practice does make, if not perfect, then close enough, at least when you're preaching to people desperate to believe.

He popped in his brown contacts, each one blotting out the washed-out blue of his natural eye like a drop of ink. He blinked once, then again after each lens was inserted, just to make certain they were properly seated. He remembered the first time he'd worn contacts, how his eyes teared until he thought he was going blind. It had felt like someone were rubbing a piece of sandpaper over each cornea. They were cheap lenses, all he could afford, and they had driven him crazy. When he took them out the first night, he dropped them into the toilet, flushing them away with a curse and without a second thought, swearing never to put anything in his eyes again.

But those were the old days, when he still was Roy Mitchell. Since then, he had managed to make himself over from head to foot, changing the color of his skin, changing his name, changing the color of his eyes, changing his past, and unless he badly miscalculated, changing his once-bleak future into a paradisaical retirement in Hawaii. But that would take some time. There was still a lot to do. He stood looking at his image slowly disappearing under a sheen of steam.

He stepped back from the mirror, then leaned forward to wipe at the steam with the flowing sleeve of his saffron robe until his image was clear again. Then he adjusted the robe, tugging it down around his broad shoulders until it hung from them the way it was supposed to do.

He had a busy morning ahead, and that idiot Bobby was making everything messy. He practiced a disapproving scowl, licked his lips, and reached for the light. When the bathroom went dark, he saw his image shimmering in the mirror for a few moments, slowly disappearing as the mist collected on the glass again until an even sheet of condensation blotted him out as surely as he had blotted out his past.

"A miracle," he whispered, "just like they expect. I am the magic man." He laughed then, closed the bathroom door with a flourish, and crossed the deep-piled blue carpet, his sandals whispering on the soft wool tickling the sides of his feet.

He closed the bedroom door behind him, heading down the long hall to his study, where, no doubt, Bobby was pacing back and forth, tapping his fingers on his thighs and coughing nervously, just like he always did. Bobby was starting to look like a weak link. He hadn't thought so at first, but the more he observed the kid under stress, the more he wondered.

Gandar, one of his body guards, who had also changed his name, from Pete Grogan, stood at the other end of the hall, his massive arms folded across his steroid-inflated chest.

When Mitchell reached that end of the hall, he looked quizzically at the huge man, and Gandar nodded. "He's inside."

Mitchell crooked a finger, and Gandar smiled broadly, then pressed a button in an open control box set in the wall. Almost immediately, the sound of a sitar sprang up, seemingly out of the very walls, a sweeping glissando as Ravi Shankar began one of his sometimes interminable ragas. The volume was kept low so that the sound seemed to seep into the rooms rather than blare at them. Mitchell reached for the knob, turned it, and yanked the door open. The sudden vacuum sucked incense into the hallway, and Mitchell bowed to Gandar before gliding on sandaled feet into the next room.

The door closed behind him, and he stood motionless for several seconds, scanning the room, knowing where Bobby was, but not yet looking at him, letting the kid stew a little. It was like cranking up the heat under a pressure cooker, waiting for the safety valve to start its staccato clatter.

Bobby bowed, the sleeves of his own robe, a muddy brown almost capuchin, sweeping the carpeted floor. "Master Primasanha," he said, as if speaking to the floor.

"Robert," Mitchell said.

Only then did Bobby look up, his eyes darting from one corner of Mitchell's face to the other, never quite making solid eye contact.

"Well," Mitchell said, using the resonant voice he reserved for his appearances before his disciples, who did not know him as Roy Mitchell. Nor did they know he was from Jersey City. The official biography listed "Primasanha's" birthplace as Lahore, in India.

Bobby gulped. "Soon, Master," he said.

"You have been telling me soon for quite a long time, Robert. I am beginning to think that soon does not mean to you what it means to me."

Bobby gulped again. "Time is water, Master. You always say that. It flows where it will, when it will. The sun comes up when it will. But it does come up."

"You seem to have a good memory for everything but promises, Robert."

"Tonight, that's when I make the pickup."

"Are you sure?"

Bobby nodded. "I'm sure. It's all arranged." He started to say something else, but Mitchell waved a peremptory hand, then canted an ear toward the sitar, now accompanied by the faint throb of tablas. Mitchell grooved on the music for several minutes, all the while keeping one covert eye on his anxious disciple, watching the sweat bead on his forehead and upper lip. Only when Bobby wiped his brow with the handkerchief he kept tucked in the knotted hemp cincture around his waist did Mitchell speak again.

"Don't disappoint me, Robert. I have already waited far longer than I had planned. I am losing patience with this entire project and, especially, with you and your incompetence."

Bobby nodded. "I know, and . . . and I'm sorry. It'll be all right after tonight, I swear. I'm leaving in an hour."

"And there will be no connections? You will sever the chain, as you have been instructed?"

"Yes."

"Alone?"

"Yes," Bobby stammered, possibly lying. But Mitchell knew that pressing him harder now wouldn't solve anything.

"Very well, then."

Mitchell waved a hand, and Bobby bowed again, backing toward the door across the huge room, his bare feet scraping the carpet with every backward stride. He bumped into the wall, straightened, and reached for the doorknob a couple of feet away. He left swiftly, pulling the door closed with such force that the plumes of smoke from the censers began to flutter like flags in a stiff breeze.

Mitchell shook his head, looking at Gandar then at the door. "Asshole," he whispered. "You better not fuck up."

The Strat was heavy, not as heavy as a Les Paul, but it still had heft. The neck was rock maple, white as bone, even under the yellowing lacquer. The body was battered, looked, in fact, like it had been through a war, and maybe it had. It had been used by Jimi Hendrix, rewired by the man himself. The paint was chipped, and the body showed through the black like the filling of a broken Oreo. It had cost twelve thousand dollars at auction, and if the auctioneer had known who was bidding, it probably would have cost twice that much. But the auctioneer hadn't known, because the buyer was smart enough to use a stand-in. And now it belonged to him.

It still had an aura, like it radiated something, something trapped in the heavy wood, like it had soaked up the essence of Hendrix, the way a piece of iron will soak up magnetism, as if the very cells of the wood had reoriented themselves under the influence of some powerful electric field.

Colin Yeats plugged the Strat into the Fender Twin, an amp even older than the guitar in his hands, tube-driven, small, just two-twelves, but powerful. One note, the A string, bent a little, and it burned. A chord, A minor, then an E-minor-seventh chop.

The strings seemed to hum as his fingers approached them slowly, the way an old woman approaches a bank of votive candles in a church, halting, uncertain, the pinched dime trembling in her gnarled fingers.

A run then, racing up the neck, thirds mostly, using a diatonic scale, almost Japanese, but really the blues. Then back down the neck, the way Otis Rush does it, ending in a flurry of bass notes twisted almost beyond agony into something more articulate than speech or music, a voice subhuman maybe, or metahuman, but glorious. Then a fast shuffle, the toe tapping, alternating chops and runs, Magic Sam maybe, then the sweetness of Albert King.

Yeats bent over the guitar now, his pinkie cranking up the volume a little, then hitting the pickup selection switch, looking for more treble, more bite. The tubes were burning now, a slight burr, the fuzziness of a juke joint at 2:00 A.M. any Sunday morning. His head was bobbing, his fingers no longer under its control. They had a life of their own now, and the music came from somewhere else, another planet, another universe, but it filtered through the Windy City on a cold winter night, when the hawk was out, and the snow was two feet deep, still clean, still untouched by the plows, still unchurned by early traffic into winter city muck.

He heard the phone, but he didn't care. That's why they had machines. And besides, he was talking to somebody else already, never mind who, maybe Stevie Ray, maybe Chaucer. He glanced toward the phone, thought about answering it, but shook his head as if someone had asked him a question, stuck his tongue into the corner of his mouth, and ripped off a run he didn't quite believe, then slid into a white-hot "Crosscut Saw," letting the words come from the same place he found the music. He'd forgotten he even knew the song until he found his fingers reminding him, and the words seemed to coalesce in his brain like crystals growing at the speed of light.

He caught a glimpse of himself in the window pane, the glimpse swallowed almost immediately by the yawning darkness beyond it. He stared at his reflection, looking through it, into the trees on the hill. The machine clicked, and he could hear a voice now, vaguely familiar, but he wasn't sure why, and he knew it didn't matter.

He turned away, not wanting to be distracted by himself, not even a transparent image, no more substantial than a shadow on a negative, and especially not by what he thought of himself. That was poison. He was tired, tired of himself, tired of thinking, tired of worrying about thinking and thinking about worrying. The only thing he wasn't tired of was the music. That was what it was supposed to be about, making music, tapping the wellspring, ripping a few seconds of truth or beauty out of the night, spreading it out on the table like some magus reading entrails, then holding it up for everyone to see, to feel, and maybe, just maybe, to believe.

But that was so much bullshit. He knew that. They didn't hear, not really. To some of the fans he was a magician, a guitar slinger, fretting his hour on the stage so they could shake their heads in amazement, their moneymakers in ecstasy, and stomp their feet while they swilled their booze. To others, he was a prophet. They looked to him for guidance, as if he knew the answers when he knew, as they did not, that he didn't even know the questions. Not really. All he was doing was groping in the dark, a blind man without a cane, his twitching fingers stretching, trying to read the stainless-steel braille. That's all it was, man—a tentative, desperate, almost pathetic approximation. But they didn't know, because they didn't fucking listen.

It was all there. Every damn album was full of it, the tortured confessions of a man who kept making the same goddamned mistakes, and embroidered them on his sleeve for all the world to read. But they didn't read. They didn't go back to the source— Donne, Spenser, Milton. They didn't know about Joyce and they thought Homer used to work with Jethro. The real seers, the men who were plugged in, hell, hardwired—the ones like Blake, Whitman, Stevens—who saw everything, who used their nerves as antennae, let them thrum with the energy, God's fucking radios, those were the ones. But if you couldn't dance to it, nobody listened. And if you could, then they danced and forgot to listen.

And he was getting so damned tired of it.

Another run now, blistering, his fingertips flying over the strings as if afraid to touch them, as if they glowed in the night, gave off white light bright enough to read by. And still it came. He started toward the door, held one note, bending it, torturing the string with the expertise of an Argentine police-man as he reached for the doorknob, yanked open the door, and kicked open the screen, stepping out into the coolness of the night.

Behind him, the Twin sounded pure now, as if the cool night air filtered out all the impurities, gave him a perfection he could only dream of. He stared at the trees, and at the shapes of the trees spilling up the dark gray hillside, almost as alike as coal and its shadow.

And behind him, the music burned blue and white-hot. This was where he was supposed to be. This was where he would stay, until, somehow, it all came together, the way it had to, the way he would pray for it to come together, if only he could remember how. And then, almost before he realized how magical it was, the cool air got to the strings, threw the Strat out of tune, just a hair, but enough that he could hear it, and know that it was going sour. He stopped, damping the strings with his palm and cursing into the darkness.

Again.

FIVE

FOR AN HOUR AFTER THE ALARM WENT OFF,
Desmond stared at the ceiling, wondering what he
had gotten himself into. Resnick had been so desperate, there had been no thought of turning him down.
He was willing to pay, and Desmond knew that
record labels had money to burn. But money was not
the only thing that mattered.

He tried to put himself in the shoes of Colin
Yeats, wondering what he would think of the situation. But Yeats was hard to figure in the best of
times. Under these circumstances, trying to think
like him was about as useful as trying to pinpoint
an electron in its orbit around a nucleus. The

harder you looked for it, the more elusive it became.

After agreeing on a price with Resnick, Desmond had gone to the Tower Records store down near NYU and bought everything they had by Colin Yeats. He'd spent the night listening to the albums one by one, trying to construct a picture of the man from the concerns reflected in his lyrics. But Yeats was not easily pinned to a piece of velvet like some gaudy butterfly. There were deep and contradictory currents swirling through the music and, presumably, the man himself. And Desmond was only halfway through the catalog. It was not going to be easy to find the missing tapes, he knew that already. And the more he listened to Colin Yeats, the more he hoped the singer was not involved, because trying to second-guess him was like trying to predict Brownian motion.

But a deal was a deal, so he had agreed to accept Resnick's offer. And Desmond had to admit that he was intrigued. Keeping things secret, as Resnick had insisted, was not going to simplify things, but Desmond had explained that it wasn't very easy to find something unless you asked questions. The more somebody wanted it missing, the more questions you had to ask. In the end, Resnick had waived his insistence on confidentiality, with the understanding that Desmond would tell as few people as possible as little as possible, but that he would not be responsible if word somehow leaked out to the general public.

It had occurred to Desmond that if someone wanted to ruin the relationship between Colin Yeats and Griffin Records, news of the missing tapes almost certainly *would* leak out. But that might be helpful, because rumors were like slugs. They left glistening trails of slime behind them, and like a slug, a rumor often could be tracked back to its source. Find the source first; then, if you looked under enough rocks, at the end of the trail you also found the reason, more often than not self-interest. But Colin Yeats had broken a lot of eggs over the years, and he had as many enemies as he had records.

Desmond's cover was going to be that of freelance writer, working on a biography of the singer. It would enable him to visit the offices of Griffin Records, and be seen with Warren Resnick without raising eyebrows. It would also enable him to nose around, ask as many questions as he wanted of as many people as he thought relevant. Some of them would seem irrelevant to the more suspicious types, but journalists were not known to be focused thinkers, at least not the kind of journalist who poked around in the music scene, where oddballs and ax-grinders were as populous as army ants.

Enemies Yeats had made along the way would be only too happy to tell everything they knew. Friends would be more circumspect, possibly even hostile. But the truth Desmond was looking for was somewhere in that no-man's-land between friends and enemies, and he hoped he could eventually zero in on it. It seemed a lot like that childhood game he had called "Land." You drew a rectangle in the dirt, bisected it, and took turns with a friend, throwing a knife. Where the knife stuck, you drew a line, adding a piece of your opponent's land to your own. He did the same, and you traded control back and forth until one of you had too little land left to accommodate the knife. That man lost. What Desmond wanted to do was slowly pare away the nearly limitless terrain of Colin Yeats and his friends and acquaintances until he reduced the possibilities to one tiny corner. There, if he was right, he would find the missing tapes and the person who'd stolen them. Or so he wanted to believe. If he was wrong, he would have wasted a lot of valuable time to no good purpose, but it didn't seem as if there was any other way to proceed.

Climbing out of bed, he went to the kitchen, put on coffee, and went back upstairs for a shower and shave. When he was dressed, as casually as his somewhat limited wardrobe permitted, he went back to the kitchen for a cup of coffee and a piece of toast.

His briefcase was full of the journalist's paraphernalia—pads, pencils, small tape recorder, some blank micro tapes, and a handful of magazine articles on Colin Yeats, together with an unauthorized biography published three years before by an associate editor of *Spin*. He'd read the articles the night before and was halfway through the biography.

He had an appointment with Warren Resnick at Griffin headquarters at ten-thirty. After that, he would hit a few bookstores, starting with the Strand, trying to run down as many other books on Yeats as he could manage. He'd already done some looking in *Books in Print* and the library, and the biography he had in hand listed in its bibliography more than seventy other books that were devoted in whole or in part to Colin Yeats. It seemed that no one in rock, not even the Beatles, had attracted so many writers. But whether Desmond could, or could stand, to read all of them was an open question.

Already, he had a fix on the mind-set that Yeats affected. Whether it was genuine was debatable, but Yeats was undoubtedly an enigma, although whether by choice or nature it was far too soon to tell. Somewhere down the road, Desmond knew he would have to talk to the man himself, but it was far too early for that, and he had not even raised the possibility with Warren Resnick. Better to let Resnick get used to the idea that an outsider was poking around, not only in Griffin Records and its business affairs, but in the life of its single most valuable asset.

When the meager breakfast was behind him, Desmond grabbed his briefcase and headed for the car. It would take him an hour and a half to get to Manhattan, and probably another half hour to find someplace to park. Since it was already eight o'clock, that left him a rather small margin for error, at least by New York traffic standards.

On the way in, he listened to more of Colin Yeats, trying to get through the dense lyrical textures to the essence of the man who'd written them. Bob Dylan was the soul of scrutability in comparison. References to mythology from a dozen countries, most of the world's major religions, poets from Homer onward, and history from the Stone Age all the way to the modern era were layered, impenetrable as mortar, but glittering with an undeniable, if somewhat mystifying brilliance.

And under the lyrical tapestry was the essence of

modern American popular music—the basic quartet of drums, bass, guitar, and keyboard—sometimes a piano almost baroque, sounding like Glenn Gould on acid, and sometimes that churning organ sound from Dylan's "Positively Fourth Street" and "Like a Rolling Stone." Unlike a lot of his contemporaries, Colin Yeats was not interested in hiding his lyrics or tricking them up with layers of unnecessary strings or pedestrian horn charts or a braying chorus of backup singers. He was, apparently, a man who knew what he thought and was not afraid to say so. Whether anyone understood him precisely seemed less urgent a concern than that the statements be made.

And there was no arguing the fact that the music was as good as the lyrics. It was a solid, blues-based approach, with Yeats on guitar, playing leads that were somewhere between Mike Bloomfield and Magic Slim. But like Thelonious Monk, Yeats was a master at breathing new life into a form that seemed as much a straitjacket as the sonnet to less gifted composers. He occasionally used elaborate rhyme schemes to disguise chorus breaks, and his melodic lines were sometimes through composed. But underneath it all was the gut-wrenching power of the twelve-bar blues right out of Chicago's South Side, even if the song's superstructure couldn't have been further removed from Pepper's Lounge than a Haydn quartet.

When the first tape finished, Desmond was intrigued. He grabbed another, saw that it was titled *Slouching Toward Bethlehem*, an obvious homage to the singer's namesake. Desmond jammed it into the cassette deck and listened to the opening of the first track, a steamy slow blues in A, called "Manhattan Project." Yeats quoted from at least half a dozen guitar masters, without losing his own style. Desmond recognized the guitar techniques of Buddy Guy, Albert King, Magic Sam, Roy Buchanan, Mickey Baker, and Eric Gale before Yeats, in his raspy, world-weary voice, began to sing. The lyrics sketched a history of weapons and their use, starting with a fist and clearly building toward nuclear weapons, if the song's title was any indication.

Picking up the Palisades Parkway, Desmond was really getting interested, and by the time he reached the George Washington Bridge, he was a fan. It made him feel strange, and more than a little awkward to think that he was about to start digging around in the private life of a man who clearly did not want to be bothered with public scrutiny. Add the tinge of criminality, however tangential, and you had an explosive mix, and a single spark, never mind from where, might set it off. That it would be thunderous was almost certain, and when the smoke cleared, Griffin Records might be in ruins.

Desmond hated midtown Manhattan. You had to watch the sky in case some lunatic decided to loft a brick or paint can, or even himself, from the parapets. At the same time you had to keep patting your pockets to make sure your wallet stayed where you put it. In the car, the cacophony of horns, blown by cabdrivers from a hundred foreign capitals, honked in the universal language of frustration. It set his nerves on edge. On the street, you never knew when some rheumy-eyed schizophrenic might decide that you were the man who had been following him all his life. At best, he screamed at you and at worst decided to practice surgery with a kitchen knife.

Desmond had spent ten years in the field for the Company, every place from Saigon to Lebanon, but he never felt less at home than he did on Madison Avenue, where the streets were lined with galleries peddling overpriced lithographs of artists on the rise and glitzy warrens where professional liars were paid millions to convince you that your breath was bad, your clothing worse, and your car was a neighborhood laughingstock second only to your thinning hair in comic potential.

As he found a garage on Forty-eighth Street, under the Simon & Schuster building, Desmond was all ready to turn around and go home. But he sucked it up, tucked the metered ticket into his pocket, and grabbed the briefcase from the backseat of his four-year-old Cutlass.

Griffin Records was four blocks away, in one of the northernmost office buildings of Rockefeller Center. He did the walk at a brisk pace, checking his watch at every traffic light. He still had fifteen minutes when he climbed the broad steps, ducking the windborne spray from a fountain, its low stone walls lined with seated bag ladies and tourists, doing their best to ignore one another.

The lobby looked like an embassy, with security guards stationed at every one of the four doors. As he checked the building directory, a fifth guard, floating freely like a nickel back, drifted toward him. "Help you?" he asked.

"Griffin Records?" Desmond said, spotting it on the board at the same instant.

Cocking his head, the guard said, "Next bank of elevators. Last elevator only. They have six floors, but the elevator only stops at thirty-two."

Desmond thanked him and moved away from the board, conscious of the guard's eyes on his back even after he turned into the alcove where elevators serviced the upper half of the building. For a moment he imagined the shafts as stainless-steel tubes, threatening as missile silos, and pushed the thought aside only when a bell tolled softly, announcing the arrival of his car.

Inside, alone, he smelled lemon oil and saw his reflection in the polished marble across the hall as the door closed. He felt as if he'd left something behind, part of his personality or maybe his soul, smeared on the glistening wall. The car took off with a gut-wrenching swoosh, then all sense of motion vanished until it slowed for the thirty-second floor.

He stepped out into a thickly carpeted room, its center dominated by a semicircular desk that looked like a topless pillbox from the Maginot Line. A breathtakingly beautiful brunette looked at him quizzically as he approached, briefcase in hand, feeling like a new boy at school.

"Can I help you?"

"I have an appointment with Warren Resnick."

"Name?"

"Desmond. Paul Desmond."

She nodded, checked her calendar, then directed him to a small bank of elevators. "Mr. Resnick is on thirty-seven," she said.

Once more, Desmond climbed into an elevator. It was as if the desk were a space station, and freed of the pull of gravity, he were ready to leave earth orbit for the distant reaches of the solar system. She watched him, smiling brilliantly, until the door closed and he blasted off again for the short trip to the top of the building.

When the door opened, he was staring into space. A glass wall gave him a magnificent view of the skyline. He could see the rooflines of the hotels along Central Park South far below and, beyond them, the sereness of the park itself, most of its beauty rolled up and put away for winter. The Sheep Meadow looked sad and brown, the lake stone gray. Farther north, the reservoir looked like the hide of a huge elephant, choppy and dark behind the fence he could not see but knew was there.

To the left, a smaller version of the pillbox, this time womaned by a striking blonde with Indian cheekbones, severely cropped hair, and huge eyes bluer than star sapphires, served as the reception area. The woman smiled. "Mr. Desmond?"

He nodded.

"Someone from Mr. Resnick's office will be right out."

He moved across the carpet toward the glass wall and the leather banquette that ran from one end to the other, and sat down, looking back over his shoulder at the tops of the shorter buildings all around him. He felt a wave of nausea and wondered whether it was the height or the assignment. Then he wondered whether it made any difference which it was.

- SIX- - -

A DOOR OPENED TO THE LEFT OF THE RECEPTION
desk, and another blonde appeared, this one wearing
a business suit, with pants instead of a skirt, the way
so many young women lawyers did. She had a color-
ful tie decorated with butterflies around her neck, a
tight Windsor knot tucked under the button-down
collar of an oxford-blue shirt.

"Mr. Desmond?" she asked, crossing the carpet
toward him, her right hand extended.

Desmond got up, took the hand, and shook it.

"I'm Sally Parker, Mr. Resnick's administrative
assistant. Follow me, please."

She led the way back through the doorway and the

door closed automatically behind her. A long hall seemed to lead into the sky dead ahead. Polished wooden doors lined the hall on either side, but Parker bored on, turning left when it looked like she would step out into thin air. Another glass wall extended in both directions. Looking down on the traffic several hundred feet below, Desmond felt a little giddy. He followed the young woman as she made yet another left turn, passed through a large interior chamber, thankfully contained by four solid walls, each decorated with a large modern canvas, then on into another hallway. Ahead, Desmond could see an open office door and a sliver of sky beyond it.

Parker made an abrupt right, ducked into a comfortable office larger than any he'd seen so far, and sat down at a desk. "Warren's got someone with him at the moment. He sends his apologies. He'll try to get free in time for your appointment, but if he runs over, he wants you to wait. It's an agent," she said, wrinkling her nose as if there was something on Desmond's shoe. "And you know how they are."

"Actually, no, I don't," Desmond told her.

"Can I get you something to drink?"

Desmond shook his head. "No, thanks, I'm fine."

"You're writing a book on Colin Yeats, I understand."

Desmond nodded. "Hoping to, anyway."

"I didn't recognize your name. Have you published anything before?"

"No, I haven't."

She looked him over then, carefully, as if she thought he might suddenly turn into something even worse than an agent, as if such a thing were conceivable. "Kind of long in the tooth to start writing about rock and roll, aren't you, Mr. Desmond?"

"I'm young at heart, Ms. Parker."

"You don't dress like it, Mr. Desmond. If you don't mind my saying so."

Desmond knew she didn't give a damn whether he minded or not, so he said the polite thing. "Of course I don't mind. We are what we are, Ms. Parker. Even you. And you don't dress any too conventionally either, I might add."

Unexpectedly, she laughed. "That's true." She looked down at the suit, adjusted the lapels of the jacket, and looked back at Desmond. "Actually, this is an experiment. So far, I'd have to say it's not going well." She shrugged. "But you never know. . . ."

"It looks fine, just a little odd, is all."

If she took offense, she didn't show it. "You have a contract for this book, or are you doing it on spec?"

"Speculation."

"Magazine connections? I hope you at least have a hook for a couple of magazine articles."

Desmond shook his head. "No, actually, I don't. I thought I'd see just how many ducks I could get in a row before I tried to find someone interested in publishing the book."

Parker looked skeptical, but she said nothing.

Anxious to fill the silent void, Desmond decided to ask a few questions. "Have you ever met Colin Yeats, Ms. Parker?"

She chewed on her lip before answering, and when she did, her voice was brittle, suggesting something more than she was willing to admit. "Yeah, I know him."

"Well?"

"No one knows Colin Yeats well, Mr. Desmond. And if you think you can plumb the depths of that well, you'll drown like all the others that have gone before you. I have never met a more . . ." Then, as if she were on the verge of saying something she regretted, she took a deep breath and trailed off into silence.

Before Desmond could ask another question, a buzzer sounded on Parker's intercom, and she jumped at the chance to answer it. "Yes?" She nodded, looking at Desmond while she listened. When the party on the other end of the line was finished, she said, "I'll bring him right in, Warren." Hanging up the phone, she stood up, straightened her tie, and stepped out from behind the desk.

"Follow me, Mr. Desmond."

She led him toward the open door where the sliver of sky had now turned from blue to gray, stuck her head into the doorway, and said, "Here he is, Warren."

She gestured for Desmond to go on in, and he stepped through into the largest office he had ever seen. A deep blue carpet, overlaid with several exquisite Orientals, mostly Chinese, seemed to stretch all the way to the horizon, an effect heightened by the glass wall behind Resnick's massive desk, which was dwarfed by the huge room.

Resnick smiled. He stood up and walked around the desk to greet Desmond, then continued on past to close the door to his office. He seemed so much more relaxed on his own turf. It was hard for Desmond to remember how nervous and frightened he'd seemed just a couple of evenings before.

"Ready for the grand tour, Mr. Desmond?"

"Not yet, Mr. Resnick."

Resnick seemed taken aback by the response. He knit his heavy brows, and under the tan his face seemed to blanch for a fraction of a second, turning almost as white as his sun-blanched hair, before he regained his composure. "Problems?"

Desmond shook his head. "Questions, is all. Not many. Just a few things I thought I ought to ask before I look around." He patted the briefcase. "I've been doing a little research, and—"

"Research, on what?"

"Colin Yeats, of course. I hadn't realized he was such an industry unto himself. It seems there are more things written about him than about Shakespeare. And I'm not sure my cover is going to hold for very long, either. Your assistant, Ms. Parker, seemed somewhat dubious."

Resnick laughed. "Sally's dubious about everything. Don't let her bother you. She's invaluable to me, and I expect that you'll be seeing a lot of her. I can't very well spend much time escorting an unknown journalist around the premises, even if he is doing a book on our biggest moneymaker. That would raise eyebrows and hackles both. What are your questions?"

"I understand Yeats has spent quite a bit of time with a guru of some sort. Is that right?"

Resnick scowled. "Swami Rajah Primasanha," he said, the venom fairly dripping. "That crook."

"Crook?"

"You know how it is with these seekers, and Colin Yeats is nothing if not one of them. There has been a whole passel of these pseudomystics and quasipsychics on the fringes of the music world for a long time. Some of them are legitimate, I guess, and some aren't. The Beatles had Maharishi Mahesh Yogi, Carlos Santana and John McLoughlin had Sri Chinmoy. Hell, half the music business has been in and out of Scientology or any of a dozen clones, spin-offs, and imitations."

"I gather Primasanha was less honest than some."

"That's an understatement if I ever heard one. It's kind of like saying John Gotti is somewhat less honest than Mother Teresa. It's true as far as it goes, but it doesn't go half far enough."

"Tell me about distribution for Griffin Records."

Resnick leaned back in his chair. "What about it?"

"Everything."

"That covers a lot of territory, Mr. Desmond. If there's something specific . . . ?"

"All right. You don't have your own distribution, do you?"

"No. But I don't see that that—"

"I don't mean to imply anything, Mr. Resnick. But we are way up the creek, and neither one of us has a paddle. Warner has WEA to handle its distribution. That gives them some significant measure of control over their product. Several of the other major label complexes also have affiliates under the same corporate umbrella to give them the same kind of control. Griffin doesn't. I want to know why."

Resnick sighed. "So do I, Mr. Desmond, so do I. But the fact of the matter is, no one seems to know. We have a long-standing relationship with our distributors, however, and judging by our bottom line, it works just fine."

"That's not what I hear."

"Well, it's true."

Desmond nodded. "Have it your way, Mr. Resnick. But if you want me to find those tapes, I would suggest that you try to be a little more forthcoming."

"I don't know what you mean."

"What I mean is that your distribution is handled by Guarino Internationale, through a subsidiary, Mega Sound. Three of the principal officers of Guarino have, at one time or another, been indicted for a variety of things, including fraud, extortion, and violation of the RICO statute. To me, that suggests the potential for difficulty. The fact that there is money in distribution, a lot of money, tells me that from the perspective of maximizing your profits, if you could get out of your arrangement with Guarino, you'd do it in a heartbeat. But you haven't. Why?"

"I told you, we have a long-standing relationship. We have a contract, and Griffin is not in the habit of breaching contracts."

"But from what I have been reading, the Japanese don't like the deal. They have their own distributor that handles all of their labels except the American one. They have been putting pressure on you to terminate the arrangement with Guarino, but you haven't done so. As a matter of fact, Guarino was implicated in a piracy program that netted more than one hundred million dollars a year for several years running. And you tell me that you're afraid that the Yeats tapes might be prime candidates for piracy. You can see, I think, why I'm a little confused."

"I can see that you're suspicious, yes. And I suppose I understand why, but—"

Desmond cut him off. "We'll come back to Guarino later. Right now I think maybe I should tell you what I need, then I want to take a look at the vault."

Resnick seemed to relax, like a man walking a tightrope who'd finally made it to the opposite platform. "All right, tell me what you need."

"For starters, I want to know everyone who has authorized access to the vault. Are records kept?"

Resnick nodded. "There's a sign-in system. It's not ironclad, but it's pretty well enforced. I'll see that you get the records. What else?"

"I'll need your salary structure for everyone who could conceivably have access to the vaults."

"I don't see why."

"If money changed hands, Mr. Resnick, there is a chance that money burned a hole in the guilty party's pocket. One way to find the leak is to find somebody who owns more than he or she could normally afford. In this case, however, half the people with access probably make more than the president, so it won't necessarily give us the break we need. But I can't afford to ignore the chance, however slim. If money *was* a factor, the chances are it will be some lower-level personnel, people who need the money more than your top executives do. I'll also want a list of all your regular contractors and services, anyone who could come and go without attracting attention."

"Gordon Evans, our administrative vice-president, can help you with that."

"Does Evans know the tapes are missing?"

Resnick slapped his forehead. "Jesus, this is trickier than I thought. No, he doesn't. I'll get it for you. But it'll take a couple of days."

"Fine. Whenever. I might also need entrée to Guarino, if you can arrange it."

Resnick stiffened again. "Is that necessary?"

"Maybe."

"All right."

"Let's take a look at that vault now, if you don't mind. There will be some other things I'll need, but I have enough to work on for the moment."

━ SEVEN ━ ━ ━

DESMOND SPENT A COUPLE OF DAYS BONING UP ON
the record business, particularly distribution and
pirating. He didn't know whether the Yeats tapes
would end up in the underground business, making
their appearance piecemeal on vinyl and CD, or if
they were going to be held for ransom. But it seemed
unlikely that ransom was the probable purpose
behind the theft because Warren Resnick had not
been contacted by anyone. Generally, the ransom
demand was made immediately.

There was, of course, the possibility that whoever
had orchestrated the theft was not finished yet. They
may have started with the Yeats tapes the same way a

jewel thief goes for the big-ticket items first. Discovery is a possibility at any moment, and if you have to cut and run, the more you have in your pockets, the better.

But that question was all but moot now, since Resnick had instituted much more stringent controls on the Griffin vaults. In theory, at least, it was no longer possible to enter the vaults at all without appropriate authorization and a clear paper trail. Unable to obliterate footprints, a man would have to be a fool to try to get away with any more tapes, even if the operation were ongoing. Any sensible thief would bide his time, wait for the immediate concerns to subside and the controls to be relaxed, as they almost certainly would be in time. One day the wrong person would be annoyed by the security, someone with the clout to get things changed, and that would be the end of Resnick's plan.

In less urgent circumstances, Griffin could afford to sit back on its corporate hands and wait for the bootlegs to appear, then follow the trail back to the point of origin. But there was no time for patience. Colin Yeats was unhappy, likely to terminate his relationship with Griffin Records at any moment. And when that happened, those tapes had better be where they were supposed to be.

So, Desmond knew that he had to rip the manhole cover loose and slide down into the fetid slime under the glossy surface of the music business. And, as a rule, when you did that you found the slugs of organized crime. The record business, apparently, was far from an exception to that rule. The Mafia's fingerprints were all over the place. They controlled artists through management agencies, even owning some acts outright. They controlled a huge, and growing, piece of the pirate business. They had a significant chunk of the ticket-scalping business. Through organized labor, they were in a position to exact a high price for cooperation at major arenas all over the country, since most such places were at the mercy of half a dozen or so groups, whether it be custodial, security, or backstage unions. It just took one of them to balk to bring an entire operation to a screeching halt. But it was probably their ability to disrupt distribution that gave them their deepest penetration into the business. Not only was the transportation of product essential, which freight haulers could expedite or interdict, but also the wholesaling end of the business was at their mercy.

Average music fans, whether their taste ran to Narciso Yepes or Dwight Yoakam, didn't care how many intermediate fingers had handled a CD. They knew what they liked, and as long as they could get their own hands on it, nothing else mattered. But to the retailers, it mattered a lot. Access to recorded music was essential. Without it, they died a quick and painful, though unlamented, death.

But the books and journals Desmond had run down were dry, and they were probably out-of-date. He wanted to get a feel for next year, not last year, and for that he needed a Vergil, someone who could take him by the hand and lead him through the labyrinthine meanderings of the business and its less savory practitioners. And he knew just the man.

Stanley Collins was the recently retired head of the NYPD's Organized Crime Unit. He'd been exploring the mob's tangled affairs for more than two decades, and if anyone could tell him what he needed to know, it was Stan. He was working on a book that was part memoir and part history, but he could spare the time, and Desmond had an appointment for that afternoon.

Collins lived in a small apartment on the Upper West Side, on Eighty-sixth Street, just off the park. It took twenty minutes to find a parking place, and by the time he had, Desmond had seen more than a dozen blocks, from Central Park West to Broadway and from Eighty-third up to Eighty-eighth. He sneaked into a space by the Walden School, with just his front bumper sticking into the yellow zone, and hoped that the traffic officer on duty had gotten up on the right side of the bed.

He walked the three blocks to Collins's apartment building, passed muster with the burly Cuban doorman, and found that the elevator was out of order. He rode up on the freight car with the doorman, who had to lock the front. Unlike a lot of New York apartment personnel, the Cuban seemed affable enough, and explained that the elevator broke at least once a week because the landlord was too cheap to fix it properly, despite gouging the tenants for two or three times the legal limit in the rent-stabilized building.

Stan Collins was about as far removed from the typical ex-cop as New York had to offer. He met Desmond in the hallway, and the sound of Charlie

Parker bounced out of the apartment's open door and echoed from one end of the building to the other. It was one of a dozen versions of "Koko" Bird had cut, and the intricate line, taken at breakneck speed, seemed almost impossible to play.

The doorman returned to the lobby while Collins hooked an arm around Desmond's neck and gave him noogies. "You rubber Czech you, how the fuck are you?" he asked, finally letting Desmond go.

"I had a headache, actually, but it seems to have gone."

Collins twirled his fingers under Desmond's nose. "Irish know-how, boyo, Irish know-how."

Desmond shook his head while Collins laughed, a hacking cough interrupting him momentarily, but not really slowing him down.

"You all right, Stan?" Desmond asked.

"I've been better, Paul. But you get to be my age in this damn city and you start bringing up all sorts of things from your lungs, whether you smoke or not, and of course I do. Come on, tell me what I can do for you."

Desmond had worked with Collins for the first time more than fifteen years before, when the Company was contemplating getting into bed with the Mafia one more time and Desmond's boss at the time, Allen Burton, had sandbagged the ill-conceived affair before it got into gear. They had kept in touch over the years, and when Desmond had gone private, they had taken to lunching three or four times a year, just to trade information and to enjoy each other's company.

Once inside, Collins turned the stereo down, but left the Parker on. "You never turn off the Yardbird," he said. "You let him say what he has to say. When the record's over, the machine will shut itself off. Just the way God intended it."

He stepped into the small kitchen and grabbed two cans of diet Coke from the refrigerator, popping both lids and pulling a pair of straws from a canister on a counter beside the stove.

Desmond was already in the sunken living room, looking at the shelves full of jazz, mostly on vinyl. "Still Stone Age, aren't you, Stan?"

"Let me tell you something, boyo," Collins said, handing Desmond a can and straw. "Those assholes at the big labels don't know how to save the warmth. They digitize everything except the soul of the music. It's better on vinyl, nicks and all. Believe me."

He dropped into a worn leather chair, peeled his straw and stabbed it into the can, took a sip, and leaned back. "So, what's on your mind?"

"The mob."

"You come to the right place, me lad. But it's a big subject. Can you narrow it down a little for me?"

"Sure. The mob and record distribution."

"Aha! It's bootleggers you're after, is it?"

"I don't know, Stan."

"Can you be more specific, before this old Irishman shuffles off his mortal coil and goes to the great pub in the sky?"

Desmond filled him in, holding nothing back. He knew he could trust Collins, and the more he told the old cop, the more likely he was to get the advice he needed. Collins interrupted a few times with questions, more for clarification than anything else, but for the most part he just listened, leaning one cheek on an open palm, his elbow braced on the arm of his chair.

When Desmond was finished, Collins sucked the last of his soda from the can with a loud slurping sound. "So, boyo, you're going to take a little tour of showbiz, are you? Talk about a snake pit, that's it. I don't know this Yeats lad, but with a name like that, he can't be all bad, eh?"

Desmond laughed. "I'll let you know, if I ever get to meet him."

"Hiding out, is he?"

"I don't know. He's a strange bird, and from what I gather, it's not uncommon for him to be incommunicado for weeks at a time. Not even his agent seems to know where to find him. Or so he told Resnick."

"You've talked to the agent?"

Desmond shook his head. "Not yet, but I will tomorrow. I spoke to his office, and all I got was the cold shoulder. I had Resnick run some interference for me, and that may make things a little better."

"So you have no way of knowing whether this Yeats is hiding out from you, from his record company, from his agent, or from the mob. Or maybe the whole passel of you . . ."

"That's about the size of it. And there is one more wrinkle in the fabric. Yeats at one time belonged to some sort of religious group, a cult or whatever. It could be that that plays a role in his reluctance. But for the moment it's the tapes I'm concerned with.

They're the key. If I find them, then I've done my job, and Resnick can joust with Yeats and his agent until doomsday. But if the tapes surface before I get them, or if word of their being missing leaks out, then everything changes."

"Well, I can tell you a few things about the pirate record business, and about the distribution, but I don't know a goddamned thing about rock and fucking roll. It's all noise to me, Paul. You know that."

"It doesn't matter what kind of music, I'm sure the mechanism is the same."

"It is. You know, bootlegs of one kind or another have been around almost since the beginning. In the early days, it was simple. They used to record off a seventy-eight to make another master, then press their own. A lot of record stores were into that, putting the money in their own pockets instead of sending it to RCA or Okeh or Columbia, whoever. . . . Of course, that ripped off the artists as well as the record companies, but it was less of a problem in those days, because half of the people who made records got paid a flat fee anyhow. Fifty bucks to Robert Johnson, he sits down and plays guitar and sings half the day, and that was it. No royalties, either as artist or composer. Fifty bucks. Period. That happened to a lot of jazz and blues musicians, and also to the early country singers. Most of them weren't educated or sophisticated, and they didn't have lawyers in every pocket, so they got taken to the cleaners. The business itself was the same way. Turnabout is fair play, I guess."

Collins got to his feet, squeezing the soda can until it crumpled, then holding it out toward Desmond. "You want another one?"

Desmond nodded, sipped the last of his diet Coke, and handed the empty to Collins. "Yeah, I would," he said.

Collins disappeared into the kitchen and returned before the refrigerator door slammed, carrying two new cans. He gave one to Desmond and popped his own open as he collapsed back into the chair. "There's all kinds of bootleg stuff, too, Paul. Opera fans are real big on it. They like to have copies of live performances, and they can even get them on video now. Seems like the opera ain't over even *after* the fat lady sings. But the kind of thing you're probably lookin' at, the manufacture of popular music in illicit pressings, whether CD or LP, you're looking at the mob, and more than likely the Basciano family. Guido, the current don, is an opera buff himself. Maybe that's how he got started, I don't know. He's got a couple of kids in the business, too—one of whom went to Harvard, got an MBA. Another son went to Stanford, got a degree in engineering or some damn thing. Anyhow, pirate records is their thing, and they have the perfect cover. Old Guido is a smart guy, and a funny guy. Has a lot of charm. I met him more than a few times. But his kids, they're the real brains. They built one of the first CD-manu-facturing plants in the U.S. They were contracting out legitimate work for years before CDs got big. And they have a legitimate distribution company, too. Handles a lot of independent labels, folk music,

POWER TRIO - 67

that sort of thing, imports a bunch of stuff from France, Germany, and Japan. That's legit, too. They cut deals with foreign labels to handle domestic distribution and, in some cases, manufacture. The whole thing is under an umbrella, Guarino Internationale. The crooked stuff is folded in, buried so deep in SEC forms and computer printouts it's damn near impossible to find. Courtesy of the Harvard boy, I think."

"You're sure they're not completely aboveboard? I know about the indictments, but they were years ago, and the corporate officers got off with a small fine."

"I'm certain. But, see, it's the perfect cover. You run a legitimate business, and you have everything in place from one end of the pipeline to the other. What do they call it—vertical monopoly or some shit. Anyhow, they got everything from recording studios to warehouses and a fleet of fucking eighteen-wheelers. They can move pirate stuff with legitimate product, and who the hell would know? That's why it's so hard to nail them. They can mislabel shit, they can hide a ton of bootlegs in the middle of a shipment and nobody would be any the wiser. The fact is, that's exactly what they do."

Desmond nodded. "They just happen to be Griffin Records' distributor. Apparently legitimately, but I have a funny feeling."

"Doesn't surprise me. See, it could be working two ways. They could be using the Griffin business as a cover for their own stuff. Big label like that, you can hide a lot of stuff with it. Then, too, could be they got their hooks into Griffin. 'Course, the Japanese bought it a couple of years ago, but they got their

Yakuza, so they know about organized crime. If you're up for it, I can hook you up with somebody can tell you a lot more about it."

"Hell, Stan, I'm looking at a blank wall. I'll talk to anybody."

"Let me make a call."

- EIGHT- - -

COLLINS GOT UP, WALKED TO THE STEREO, AND changed CDs. As he walked into the bedroom, where the phone was, the opening piano chords of "Balcony Rock" welled up out of the speakers, filling the room. Desmond leaned back as his namesake began to spin, with effortless ease, an improvisational web, the horn richer, more resonant than usual, warmer, too, than the dry martini sound Brubeck's altoist generally favored.

The melodic lines, and there were two of them, played in alternation, swirled around each other, never losing the bluesy tint but sounding more and more like Bach as they grew more intricate. Desmond was on another planet now, a place of purple skies and blue sand, the hollows left by his feet the only sign of life.

Collins returned and stood on the steps leading into the living room, not saying anything, watching his younger friend drift on the melody. He leaned over to turn up the volume a little as the piano took over, Brubeck's hand more delicate than usual, almost Chopinesque in its lyrical exploration. But the blues were still there in the harmony as the chords grew thicker, blocks alternating with single-note runs, some suspended, tolling like funeral bells.

Desmond knew the long tune note for note, started humming now, his hands loping along his thighs, keeping time. He had first heard the record in Prague, on a school trip, and fallen in love with the music. It was, in some ways, the one constant in his turbulent life, and he had risked life and limb to collect the records at a time when jazz was outlaw music behind the iron curtain.

Only when the delicate theme returned, one the group would use later to close another song close to his heart, would Desmond open his eyes. Collins stood there grinning at him. "I still think Bird is better, but I understand what it is in Desmond that attracts you. That high lonesome feeling that makes poetry out of personal desolation."

"You're entirely too philosophical for an ex-cop, Stan," Desmond said.

Collins laughed. "It was the only thing that kept me sane all those years, Paul. You know that. Detachment, distance, perspective—the holy trinity."

He walked to the stereo cabinet and killed the music in the middle of "Out of Nowhere." "Get your coat," he said.

"Where are we going?"

"A record store. A friend of mine will meet us there. You have a car, I hope."

Desmond nodded, slipped into his leather jacket, and patted the pockets to make sure he had his cigarettes. Collins got his own coat from a hall closet, turned off the lights, and waited in the hall. When Desmond joined him in the dim light, Collins closed and locked the door. "We'll walk down. No point in dragging Jimmy off the door."

He led the way to an unmarked door in the middle of the hall, pushed it open to reveal battleship-gray stairs lit by a bare bulb that spilled shadows of the iron railing down to the next level. As Desmond started down the steps he felt as if he were entering an Escher print. The conflicting patterns of lines and bars, real and shadowed, extended ahead and stretched out behind him. It made him dizzy, and he shook his head to restore his balance.

Only when they reached the lobby seven floors below was he able to shake off the vertigo.

On the way to the car, Desmond asked, "Who are we meeting?"

"Dan Brennan, fellow who took over my job when I finally cashed in my chips. He can tell you what's been going on the last three, four years. And he knows more about the kind of music your boy Yeats makes than either one of us." He shook his head in mock dismay. "Kids today, I swear."

When they were in the car, Desmond asked, "Where to?"

"Twenty-third Street, between Seventh and Eighth. Place called Tin Pan Alley."

Desmond dropped a cassette of John Coltrane into the deck and pushed the play button, then started the car. Collins patted the leather seats. "Nice car. If you like cars. I never cared for them. I liked the idea of getting around without having to depend on a machine."

"Where I live, you have a car or you don't get around."

"How are the kids?"

"Fine."

"And Audrey?"

"Good. They're in Florida for a couple of weeks, soaking up the sun."

"I'd like to see them again."

"Come up in the spring. Audrey can show you her garden. Sometimes I think she takes more pride in her flowers than she does in her paintings."

The traffic was heavy, but moving, and Desmond drove with the reckless abandon of an Afghan cabbie. Collins leaned back and closed his eyes, listening to the music or napping, Desmond wasn't sure which.

When he turned into Twenty-third Street, from Seventh, he slowed. Collins, sensing the shift in motion, sat up. "It's on the north side, closer to eighth, but grab a space wherever you can."

Desmond found one in front of a double-parked truck, and backed in like a pro. He killed the engine, and Collins climbed out of the car, stretching and looking around. He pointed toward a hand-painted sign suspended on chains a few doors ahead. "There it is. Now, where the hell is Danny Brennan?"

As if in response to the question, someone shouted from across the street, then a car door opened, and Desmond saw a big redhead waving with his left hand. The car door slammed hard enough to rock the Chevy on its springs, and Dan Brennan bounded across the street, grinning from ear to ear.

"Stanley, Stanley, Stanley, ain't you something? Finally seen the light, did you? Want to quit listening to that moldy jazz of yours and give a listen to what's happening now?"

He grabbed Collins in a bear hug, lifted him off the ground, and grinned at Desmond over Collins's shoulder. One beefy hand stuck out and Desmond, not knowing what else to do, grasped it and shook it. "Dan Brennan," the big man said, finally setting Collins back on the pavement. "Come on, I told Saul we'd be here fifteen minutes ago. He's closing for lunch, so we'll have a chance to talk."

Brennan was nearly six feet six and probably weighed two sixty or so, Desmond guessed. And the hand he'd shaken felt as if it had been carved from granite. Brennan herded them along the street, his light jacket open despite the chill, and he towered over them, the way a scoutmaster towers over his charges, coaxing them along with his arms spread wide.

The record shop, as Brennan said, was closed, a cardboard sign with a small clock face showing it would open again at two o'clock. But Brennan rapped on the glass and Desmond could see some-one moving toward the door. A moment later a short man with a salt-and-pepper beard and the twinkling eyes of a fun-loving elf opened the door for them.

Brennan took charge immediately. "This is my friend Saul Whynman," he said. "You want to know anything about popular music, you ask him. You want to find a record that nobody's seen in thirty years, he's probably got it in the basement. That includes jazz, by the way, Stanley." Then he introduced Desmond and Collins to the store owner.

Whynman led them toward the back of the store, into an office that was cluttered with boxes of 78s, and mounds of posters and advertising flyers, some of them going all the way back to Robert Johnson and Rudy Vallee.

Whynman cleared some space on a wooden bench, then sat behind his desk. Brennan, who would have taken the bench all by himself, leaned against steel shelves lined with LPs.

"Saul," he said, "you can be honest with these gentlemen. Don't worry about confidentiality. They'll keep your name out of it, whatever it is they're poking into."

Whynman smiled. "What can I do for you?"

"Tell me about bootleg records," Desmond asked.

"What do you want to know?"

"Do you see many of them?"

Whynman laughed. "Come out front for a minute," he said, getting to his feet. He led them back into the store and pointed to the left wall. "Everything on that wall, CD and LP, is bootleg."

"It says 'Imports' on the sign," Desmond said.

Whynman laughed. "A convenient fiction. Some of them are imports, because there's a lot of bootlegging overseas. The Italians and the Germans do a lot of it. They record live concerts without permission and turn out records by the ton, some of them almost studio quality. But there are a lot of domestic things, too, more and more all the time, actually. Some of them are the same damn concerts, cut into pieces and stuck on three or four releases. Sometimes the quality of one is perfect and the other is almost inaudible."

"Where do you get them?"

Whynman stroked his beard and looked at Brennan. The big cop nodded. "Go ahead, Saul, tell him."

"Three or four places, actually. A couple of the places are small outfits, handle nothing but bootlegs. But lately, I've been getting a lot of my stock from Mega Sound."

Desmond looked at Collins, who returned an angelic smile. "See," Collins said. "What did I tell you?"

"Why do you carry the bootlegs, Mr. Whynman?"

"It's good business. You'd be surprised how many collectors there are out there. In rock and roll, it started back in the sixties. There were a couple of Bob Dylan things, a Royal Albert Hall concert with The Band, and a thing called *Great White Wonder*, mostly studio outtakes and some private tapes all jumbled together. More and more stuff started to show up, Dylan concerts, Stones concerts, early Beatles stuff from Hamburg, Germany. At first it was just the best artists. People couldn't get enough, especially with Dylan, because he changed his songs around so much, you never knew when there was going to be a whole new verse or two in 'Desolation Row' or 'Gates of Eden.' Other artists had been taped illicitly before, of course, most notably Charlie Parker. There was a guy followed him everywhere, taped only Bird's solos, but they disappeared, and they were never available commercially. There were rumors all the time, it was like a fucking Indiana Jones plot."

"You get the bootlegs from the same wholesalers now?"

Whynman shook his head. "No. These outfits are like little poetry magazines. It's steady-state theory. One comes and one goes. Sometimes they hang around for a few years, sometimes they only put out one record. There are wholesalers who started to organize the business, of course. That's the capitalist way, after all."

"Spoken like a true son of Trotsky," Brennan said.

Whynman started to paw through the bins, picking several out seemingly at random, then handed them to Desmond. "Look at the differences. Some of these things have high-quality artwork and some of them aren't much more than typewriter and Xerox stuff. The same with the sound quality. And there's no correspondence, either. Some of the best-looking discs sound like shit."

"And you're sure that you get some of these from Mega Sound?"

Whynman nodded. "More all the time. In fact, they put a lot of pressure on me to carry the bootlegs. The rep came around with a big bent-nose type from Mulberry Street. They told me if I didn't take the bootleg stock, I wouldn't get any of the regular stock, either. I asked around, found out some of the other record stores in the area were getting the same kind of pressure. Nobody wanted to take a chance on getting squeezed out. You have a customer come in and wants something new on Griffin, Gargoyle, or Chimera or one of the other associated labels and you don't have it, that customer doesn't come back."

"Did you report the pressure to the police?"

Whynman smiled. "Just to Dan, here. He has the biggest collection of Dylan bootlegs on earth, more than likely. Must be what, three, four hundred items, Danny?"

Brennan gave them a bashful grin. "At least," he said.

"Now, are you sure this stuff comes through Mega, I mean with the regular Griffin stock?"

"I'm not sure I know what you mean. . . ."

"Are the cartons the same? Does the stuff come mixed in with legitimate discs? Are they all on the same order forms, invoices, that sort of thing?"

"It comes on the same truck. But the stock is never mixed, and the paperwork is separate. Why?"

Desmond shrugged. "It could be that Griffin, and even Mega Sound, doesn't know about this. Could be somebody wanted to piggyback their distribution, gave you the impression they were part and parcel."

"I never thought of that, actually."

"Do the same reps sell both legitimate and bootleg stuff, or do you get two separate sales calls?"

"Both."

Desmond looked at the discs in his hand, flipped through a couple of Dylans, a Lou Reed concert from Holland, a Madonna concert, and he stopped at the last one, looking at Whynman incredulously. "Abba?" he asked. "People actually want more Abba?"

Brennan snorted, clapping his hands in delight. But Whynman said, "Listen, last week I had a guy in here wanted to know if I had any Andy Williams bootlegs. Go figure."

Brennan laughed for a moment, then he changed the subject. "I got a strange little situation might tie into what you're looking for, Paul," he said.

"What's that?"

"Found a guy with a couple of bullets in him, up in Orange County. He worked for a custodial company, and guess *where* he worked?"

Desmond shrugged. "I don't have the faintest idea."

"Griffin Records. His name was Ron DeCicco. And nobody can figure out why he was hit. It looked like a pro had taken him out, but DeCicco was just a working stiff. His brother was connected, not in a big way, but enough that they brought us in on it. Let's grab some lunch and I'll fill you in."

Desmond said, "Fine. Let me just check for something a moment." He turned to Whynman. "You have any Brubeck bootlegs?"

Whynman laughed. "You see what I tell you? Sure. I got maybe two dozen on CD, a dozen or so more on vinyl. One Canadian thing has a great version of 'Koto Song.'" He stopped, looked at Desmond quizzically. "You're not related to . . ."

Desmond shook his head. "Nope, I'm not."

– NINE– – –

DESMOND SAT IN THE WAITING ROOM, TRYING TO
decide which was sharper, the spike heels or the
spiked hair of the receptionist. She had a hard edge
to her, and her face looked as if it hadn't smiled in
six months. But her manner was pleasant enough.
Busying himself with the photos of Peter Chandler's
clients on the wall, he spotted half a dozen he knew,
most of them long-faded rock stars. Like Albert
Grossman before him, Peter Chandler had made a
name for himself in the sixties, and like Grossman,
he had moved quickly to corner as much of the bur-
geoning rock market as possible. Where Grossman
had Paul Butterfield, Chandler had his own Chicago

harp player, Dave Simmons, never as well-known as Butterfield or Charlie Musselwhite. Grossman had Peter, Paul and Mary, so Chandler, always one step behind, or so it seemed, had rushed to sign his own folk trio, the Greenwich Buskers.

When San Francisco happened, and Grossman moved in, Chandler must have taken a train, because the Airplane, Santana, the Dead, and Quicksilver had all been gobbled up by the time he got there. Grossman, of course, had his crown jewel in Bob Dylan, and Chandler had done him one better, for once, in Colin Yeats. And Chandler also got marks for staying power. He had kept on signing acts, picking up punkers in the wake of the Sex Pistols and the Clash, and literate songmeisters like Elvis Costello. But again, Chandler was a day late and a dollar short.

If Desmond had to bet, he'd wager a pretty penny that the bottom line of Peter Chandler's Rock Rack, the somewhat pretentiously funky name of the agency, would show plenty of red ink under every name but that of Colin Yeats.

And Peter Chandler just might know exactly what was in the vaults at Griffin, which made him a possible, perhaps even a likely, suspect. Photos of Janis Joplin, Jerry Garcia, John Cippolina, and Carlos Santana, each with a bleary eye on the camera and a limp arm draped over the shoulder of someone Desmond didn't recognize, seemed to be the centerpiece of the photo gallery. And Desmond guessed the vaguely familiar faces in those four pictures would match a name on Chandler's client list. The single exception was a photograph of a pianist, obviously a classical player, sitting alone at the keyboard, his odd posture suggesting the chair had been cut away beneath him. The picture was inscribed, and Desmond got up to read the inky scrawl. *To Peter. Yours, Glenn Gould.*

The receptionist, who had told Desmond her name was Deirdre, saw him looking at the photo. "Classical, ugh! I hate that junk," she said.

Desmond thought about trying to change her mind, at least as far as Glenn Gould was concerned, but another look at the severe purple spikes, which made Deirdre's head resemble an exaggerated violet mace, convinced him not to bother.

A door opened, and a bundle of denim and ginger hair stepped into the reception area, carrying a black leather gig bag hand-painted with a peace eye and half a dozen other symbols from a bygone era. Behind the ghost of hootenannies past, a burly man in jeans and a plain vest over a faded work shirt waved a hand. "So long, Johnny," he said. "Give me a call next time you're in town." The voice was a pleasant baritone that sounded a little like Hoyt Axton.

The vagabond minstrel grunted something unintelligible, then turned to Desmond, shaking his head. "You let this bastard represent you, man, and you might as well bend over and kiss your ass good-bye. You'll be in a fucking black hole by midnight, believe me." The guitarist's voice was even deeper, mellow, with a beery edge that gave it a hint of world-weariness. And there was no hint of whether he was joking or in dead earnest.

He jabbed at the call button, and the elevator door

opened immediately. He stepped in, bumping his gig bag on the doors as they tried to bang closed before he'd cleared them. He cursed without turning around. The doors closed behind him, and he vanished with a pneumatic wheeze.

The burly man stroked his salt-and-pepper beard a moment, then seemed to notice Desmond for the first time. "You my ten o'clock?" he asked.

"If your ten o'clock is Paul Desmond, I am."

The man laughed. "Right. Paul Desmond. And I suppose you want me to hook you up with a piano trio from the Bay Area, do you? Give your alto a good setting?"

Desmond chuckled. "If I could play like *that* Paul Desmond, I'd already have an agent." He stuck out a hand. "Mr. Chandler?"

The agent nodded. "That's me. What can I do you for? Warren just said he'd appreciate it if I'd give you a few minutes."

He draped a heavy arm over Desmond's neck and hugged him toward the door to his office. Passing through the doorway, he called back over his shoulder, "Hold my calls, Deirdre."

As the door started to close Desmond heard the receptionist snicker. "Yeah, right! I'll do that little thang, Mr. Chandler."

Chandler moved behind a cluttered desk, letting himself down heavily into a worn, but comfortable-looking leather chair.

Folding his hands steeple fashion beneath his chin, he said, "So how can I be of help to you?"

Desmond took a seat without being asked, choosing an equally worn leather chair opposite Chandler's desk. "I'm doing research for a book on Colin Yeats. Warren Resnick thought you might be able to help."

Chandler clucked, wagging a scolding finger at Desmond. "You must not have done much research yet, Paul, because if you had, you'd know that Colin Yeats likes publicity about as much as most men like getting their nuts squeezed in a rusty vise. . . . Maybe less."

"I'm well aware that Mr. Yeats doesn't enjoy the limelight. He's not alone in that. Many significant artists have shunned notoriety."

Once more, Chandler shook something in admonition, this time his head. "No, you don't get it, Paul. I said *publicity*. Notoriety is what you get when they write about you in spite of your distaste for the latter. And that's Colin, to a tee."

"I was hoping he might agree to suspend judgment until I had a chance to talk to him."

"Talk to him about what?"

"His life, his music, his career. The usual."

"Paulie, Paulie, Paulie, there are at least a hundred books on Colin Yeats floating around libraries and remainder bins already. What in hell makes you think there's room for another one?"

"This one will be different. I've looked at the others. half of them are fawning fluff, quick takes by quick-buck artists looking to cash in on another man's talent."

"And the other half?"

"The other half are written by imbeciles for imbeciles. They miss the mark by plenty. The authors don't understand the music, they understand the lyrics even less well, and I don't think they understand the man at all."

"And you do? What are you, some kind of fucking genius, is that it? You have a talent equal to Colin's? You're the only man who can do his genius justice? Is that what I'm hearing, Paulie?"

"I don't know what you're hearing, Mr. Chandler, but it sure as hell isn't what I'm saying."

"Then what *are* you saying? Spit it out, Paulie, I'm a busy man, in case you don't know that."

"We're all busy, Mr. Chandler. But Mr. Resnick, who is also busy, thinks it is an excellent idea. He thinks my book would be the perfect complement to the comprehensive retrospective Griffin is planning to release. He thinks that with the boxed set, the documentary film on Yeats that Jarmusch is planning, and my book, we'll have covered all three major media."

"Warren should only know what Colin thinks of him this week. He might want to deep-six the retrospective and expose the film right out of the camera. Colin is pissed at Resnick, at Griffin, and at just about everybody else on the fucking planet."

"Including you, Mr. Chandler?"

"Don't be a wiseass, Paulie."

Desmond had had about enough of Chandler's condescension. "Look, Chandler," he said, "my understanding is that you are about to open negotiations on a new contract for Colin Yeats. It seems to me that a little cooperation with your most significant client's record label would not be that painful a thing for either you or Mr. Yeats. I didn't come here to invade anyone's privacy. But I didn't come here to take your abuse, either."

Chandler seemed taken off guard by the sudden assertiveness. He held up his hands half in defense and half in placation. "Hold on, Mr. Desmond. Let's not get all in a snit now. I'm sorry if I seemed rude. I'm not trying to be. But you know how it is, people pulling you in every damn direction at once, all of 'em wanting a piece of you, and not giving a damn if you get torn apart in the process."

"That's not what I'm trying to do."

"I *know* that. All I'm saying is that sometimes it's hard to remember who you're talking to. I forgot, okay, that's all. I just forgot."

"So, can you arrange for me to see Colin Yeats?"

"I'll see what I can do. I'm not making any promises, mind you. But I'll try. Give me a day or two. Colin is not that easy to find even in the best of times. The mood he's in right now, I don't know whether anyone can do it."

"Why is that?"

Chandler shrugged. "You know, the usual. Temperamental artist, gets a burr under his saddle and won't listen to reason. I been trying to get him together with the *48 Hours* people for more than six months. They want to do a profile of him, you know, follow him around, go into the studio with him, the usual crap. But it's good PR. That was Warren's idea, too, and I'm doing my damnedest to make it happen. But it ain't easy. See, Warren, he bitches all the time about what a pain in the ass Colin can be. And I always tell him that he's lucky, that he has to put up with it every eighteen months, when Colin does an album, and a little tour to support it. But I got to deal with him three hundred and sixty-five days a year."

"You're well paid for the trouble, though, aren't you?" Desmond asked.

"What's that supposed to mean?"

"Just what I said. You're his agent. You get a cut, fifteen, twenty percent or thereabouts, unless you're Colonel Parker, who got half, as I understand it. But twenty percent of a lot is still a lot, when you're talking about the kind of money Colin Yeats generates in a year."

Chandler reached up to wipe a glaze of sweat off his forehead. He shook his fingers as if they were drenched and then licked his lips as if they were dry. That he was nervous was abundantly clear. Why was less readily discernible.

Finally, he shook his head. "Yeah. you're right. But I'll tell you something about being an agent, Mr. Desmond. A lot of people think it's easy, like we're leeches or something, just hook into a cash cow and suck it dry. Like we don't bust our asses, too. We do, I can tell you. And it's no fun, especially when you spend weeks trying to set something up, knocking on doors until your knuckles are raw to get a gig for somebody, then you turn around two days later and call him back, tell him your client changed his mind. Talk about being drawn and quartered . . . hell, I'd take that any day of the fucking week."

"I don't imagine you have to rap too hard to get a door open for Colin Yeats. It seems to me you could write your own ticket. You put out the word he wants to be on the tube, and you'll have camera crews lining up from here to Chicago, I should think."

"You would think so, wouldn't you? But Colin has a reputation as a flake. He's what the Hollywood people like to call 'difficult.' That's the word they use when you make money for them. They have a different vocabulary when you don't."

"Difficult or not, he's never been more in demand."

Chandler groaned. "Yeah. But the thing about Colin Yeats is, he's never less available than when he's in demand. It's like magnets. North and south attract, right, but Colin, he's north, and so is the hype machine. The harder you push them together, the harder they push themselves apart. Anyhow, like I said, I'll get back to you as soon as I hear anything."

"You'll call him this afternoon? I don't mean to be pushy, but . . . Warren Resnick has already tried to reach him, but without success."

"Yeah, yeah, Paulie, yeah. I'll call him this afternoon. And if I'm lucky, he'll even pick up the goddamned phone, instead of sitting there and shooting rubber bands at it, like he usually does when it rings."

"It could be worse," Desmond suggested. "Elvis used to use a pistol on TV sets."

"Unlike Colin," Chandler snorted, "Elvis was not an advocate of gun control."

- T E N - - -

THE PHONE RANG, DRAGGING DESMOND OUT OF A
stuporous sleep. He fumbled for it, hoping it was
Audrey as he glanced at the clock. It was 6:00 A.M.,
and his heart sank. No way she would be calling that
early.

"Hello," he grunted.

"Paulie?" It was Peter Chandler, and Desmond
cursed to himself, but he wasn't going to give Chandler
an excuse to hang up.

"Yeah, this is Desmond."

"Look, I'm sorry to be calling so early, but this is
the story of my life. I spent the night crawling from
club to club, checking out some new acts. I just got

in and thought I'd give you a call before I crashed. That all right?"

"Sure," Desmond lied. "What's on your mind?"

"Look, I been calling Colin for two days now, leaving messages on his machines, but he hasn't called me back. And he probably won't. Don't ask me why."

"Maybe you're on his shit list along with the rest of the world," Desmond suggested.

"That's not funny, Paulie. Look, you got a pencil handy?"

Desmond opened the nightstand drawer, grabbed a pencil and scratch pad before answering. He hated it when people started dictating something before he was ready. It always meant backing up, starting over, saying three times what a little patience could have conveyed in one. "Yeah, I'm ready."

Chandler dictated two phone numbers. "Got 'em?" he asked.

Desmond read them back.

"Good, Paulie. Maybe you can get work as a secretary when your writing career goes belly-up. Which, I hasten to add, it will."

Desmond ignored the gibe. And Chandler carried on. "The first number is Colin's apartment down in the Village. The other is his place in California, the one they all write about, saying it looks like something out of Hearst on acid. I dunno, I kind of like the place, actually."

"Where do you think he is?"

"Don't have a clue. But I got better things to do than sit with a phone stuck in my ear all day long. I figure you can do that much. If you reach him, tell him I gave you the number and I think he ought to talk to you. Tell him Warren thinks it's a good idea, too."

"Do you have the addresses?"

"Jesus, Paulie, you want me to write the god-damned book for you, too?" Desmond laughed in spite of himself, and Chandler gave him both addresses. The agent cleared his throat, then added, "Look, if you do manage to get a hold of him, tell him . . . well, never mind. Listen, Paulie, I got to get some sleep. I'll talk to you, okay?" The phone clicked, and Chandler was gone.

After replacing the phone in its cradle, Desmond lay back and stared at the ceiling. It was too damned early to get up, but it was too late to get back to sleep now. He found himself wondering what Peter Chandler had been going to say. It certainly sounded as if Yeats was hiding, but from whom and why?

The discovery of Ron DeCicco's body could be a coincidence. But Desmond didn't think so. The murder, especially so soon after the realization that the tapes were missing, seemed significant. Stan Collins seemed to agree, although he was anything but garrulous. And Dan Brennan was keeping his thoughts to himself.

Desmond sat up, climbed out of bed, and went through the morning ritual. When he was dressed, he went down to the kitchen, put up coffee, then went to the front porch for the morning paper. Browsing through the *Times* while he listened to the coffee perk, he searched for some mention of the discovery of DeCicco's body. There was none, and Desmond made a mental note to pay a visit to the dead man's employer and to the brother, the only family DeCicco had, according to Brennan.

After a light breakfast, he drove to the city, taking the West Side all the way down to Fourteenth Street, then heading east to Seventh Avenue to work his way through the commercial carnival of the West Village. He found a parking garage, left his car, then walked back a couple of blocks to check out the address Chandler had given him.

From the outside, it was nothing out of the ordinary. It looked like most of the other buildings on Sullivan Street, except for its condition. Where most of the structures needed painting, Colin Yeats seemed to have spent a little of his fortune fixing the place up. The window frames were all neatly painted, the glass fully glazed, bright and shiny behind the black wrought-iron gates that might have been transplanted from the French Quarter of New Orleans.

On a whim, Desmond walked up the recently pointed brick steps and leaned on the bell. He pressed an ear against the heavy wooden door, but heard nothing from inside. When he jabbed the button a second time, he heard chimes, their distant toll almost completely muffled by the heavy oak.

Backing away, Desmond looked up at the windows of the second and third floors, but there was no sign of life, no sudden movement of the curtains, no shadowy figure behind the gleaming glass. He walked back a few blocks, to the corner of Bleecker and Sullivan, where a coffee shop had an old-fashioned pay phone booth in one corner.

Inside, he ordered another coffee and changed a dollar, jingling the quarters as he stepped into the phone booth and pulled the accordion doors closed. The phone itself was more modern than the booth, but not new enough to sport pushbuttons or accept a phone card. He dropped a quarter in, heard the loud clang of the bell, then listened to the dial tone. He fumbled with the rotary dial, trying to keep the notepaper with the number on it smooth enough to read.

When the phone had rung half a dozen times, he expected the click, then the mutter of the canned voice on an answering machine, but the phone just kept on ringing. Either Yeats had disconnected his machine, or its message tape was full. Hanging up, Desmond thought of a third possibility—maybe Peter Chandler had lied to him. Maybe Yeats didn't have a phone machine at all, and the agent was just looking to get out from under an onerous responsibility. Or . . . Desmond stopped, realizing there were a dozen more possible explanations, none of which could be ruled out until he managed to get a hold of Colin Yeats himself. It was too early to try the California number, so he sat down at the counter, drank his coffee, and went back into the cold street.

On a hunch, he turned back, stepped into the luncheonette, and went to the phone booth again, where he found a directory hanging from a chain and flipped through the pages until he found the Ys. Running his finger down the blurry columns, he found, to his surprise, a listing for Colin Yeats. The number was the same one Chandler had given him.

Beneath it was the name Colleen Yeats, with an address right around the corner. With nothing to lose, he picked up the phone again, dropped another quarter, and dialed Colin Yeats's first wife.

To his surprise, she picked up. "Hello."

"Mrs. Yeats?"

"Yes."

"My name is Paul Desmond, I'm a writer, and I was wondering if you could spare me a few minutes of your time."

"I don't know. I—"

"I promise it won't take long."

"What is this about?"

"I'm writing a book about your ex-husband, and—"

"I don't talk about Colin."

"I understand. I won't pry. I just want to—"

"Mr. Desmond . . ." She sounded hesitant. "I really would rather not."

"If you want, you can call Warren Resnick. He'll vouch for me."

"Where are you calling from?"

"A couple of blocks away, the Village Luncheonette."

"Fifteen minutes, Mr. Desmond. No more."

"Where shall I—"

"You stay there. I'll be there in ten minutes."

Dan Brennan stood beside the dusty Buick, his hands in his pockets. Leaning forward to look through the open passenger door, he saw the two bodies, the rusty sheets of congealed blood soaking the white shirts. He knew one of the dead men, Tony Fratangeli, a button man for the Basciano family, but the other was a stranger. One of the uniforms brushed against him to take a look for himself. "Looks like a mob hit, huh, Lieutenant?" he said.

"Were you here when it happened, Officer?" Brennan asked.

"No, of course not, I just, I mean . . ." The young cop stammered to a halt like a pneumatic drill suddenly shut down. He lifted his cap and ran a nervous hand over the shiny blond brush cut. "I just figured that, you know, this is the way the mob gets rid of people." He hesitated for a moment, then added, "Isn't it?"

Brennan shook his head. "No, it isn't."

"Hell, that's Tony the Geek, isn't it?"

"It was, yeah."

"So the other guy must be a soldier of his or something. So it figures."

Brennan started to answer, but the whoop of a siren, truncated as it was shut off, interrupted him. He turned to see the lab van nose through the rickety Cyclone gate and roll to a halt ten yards from the Buick. He turned back to the young officer. "You touch anything?"

"Me? No, hell no. I know better'n that. Soon as I saw the bodies, I got on the horn and called it in. That's all I did."

"How about your partner?"

"She never got out of the car, Lieutenant."

"Don't bullshit me. You're not bullshitting me, Officer, are you?"

"No, honest to God, Lieutenant, I swear. Neither one of us touched a goddamned thing."

Brennan nodded, not so much satisfied as bored with it all. It was always the same, some guy who thought what he did was glamorous, trying to grab a little secondhand glory, tap the front-page photo in the *News* and tell their neighbors how they were there, saw it with their own eyes. Like it was some kind of fucking miracle, Fatima or Lourdes or something, when all it was was homicide, so common in the city that nobody really cared anymore. The tabloids tried to use the Mafia to sell more papers, making heroes of the likes of John Gotti, as if calling him the "Teflon Don" diminished the evil he supervised. And for most of the city, it seemed to work. But not for Dan Brennan.

He stood off to one side, jotting impressions of the scene in his notebook, while the lab techs went to work. The sound of flashbulbs, their light barely noticeable in the midmorning glare, crackled like popping corn as they stabbed their lenses through open doors from every angle. The blinding intrusions struck Brennan as more obscene than the blood-soaked carcasses themselves, stripping the dead men of every last shred of humanity, reducing them to slabs of evidentiary meat, fit only for the cranial saw and the cold stainless steel of the autopsy table in the morgue.

Once the photos had been taken, the ME's office removed the bodies. As Fratangeli's corpse was tugged unceremoniously from the car, something heavy clattered on the running board then landed with a loud metallic crack on the broken asphalt and skittered under the car. Brennan bent to retrieve it. It was an automatic pistol, and he used a pen canted through the trigger guard to pull it toward him, then let a techie bag it.

It was a nine-millimeter Browning, and it set a tiny bell ringing in his skull. Fratangeli's head lolled back, revealing for the first time the full extent of the damage to his throat, severed all the way back to the spinal column. Brennan, inured as he was to the aftermath of slaughter, still nearly lost his breakfast. He'd known Fratangeli, knew him to be a killer, about as cold and ruthless as they come. Almost businesslike in his efficiency, he was still a human being, or had been, and the idea that one man could inflict such butchery on another was appalling.

The minute it isn't, he thought, it's time to quit the business. He saw something on the floor of the car, wedged down in between the seat and the carpet, probably accidentally, he supposed.

Taking a handkerchief, he tugged it free. It was an audio cassette, unmarked except for a strip of tape on the box with a number in runny ink: GR/MLD 49681. He grabbed a plastic bag from the pocket of a techie, bagged the cassette, and stuffed it into his pocket.

- ELEVEN- - -

DESMOND SAW HER THROUGH THE DUSTY GLASS OF the luncheonette window. She crossed the street, her long legs seeming barely to move, and when she tossed her mounds of chestnut hair, it caught the light and seemed to flash. He'd seen pictures of her in a few of the books about her husband, but there wasn't much information about her. She had been born Colleen O'Shea, had been a successful fashion model, came from a wealthy Connecticut family, and had a master's in psychology from Yale. Other than that, history, at least as the authors of pop biographies wrote it, was silent. Colin Yeats had done his best to shield her, and their two children, from the prying lenses of the paparazzi, and the page-six pseudojournalism of the gossip columnists. Judging by the paucity of detail about her, he had been more than passingly successful in his effort.

When she came into the luncheonette, Desmond realized just how tall she was, probably five eight or nine, and the high-heeled boots she wore added another couple of inches. He stood up and started to move toward her, the movement catching her eye, and she stopped in her tracks. She looked him over carefully, more as a way of appraising him than as a measure of her suspicion. She relaxed suddenly and moved toward him again.

"Mr. Desmond, I presume?" Her smile was radiant, and Desmond thought he remembered the face from the cover of *Vogue* or *Harper's Bazaar*. He nodded, just a little too intimidated by her beauty to say a word.

"Cat got your tongue, Mr. Desmond?"

That put him at ease, and he laughed. "You are an extraordinarily beautiful woman, Mrs. Yeats. I guess I wasn't expecting that."

He backed into his booth and nearly fell down, tripping over his own feet. Colleen Yeats slipped gracefully behind the table opposite him, rearranging the long chestnut curls with an unselfconscious flick of her wrist. "Aren't you gallant," she said.

"Not particularly," Desmond said. "But—"

"You didn't call me up to tell me I'm pretty, Mr. Desmond." She cocked her head to one side and examined him quizzically. "Or did you?"

"Actually, no. I wanted to ask you a few questions,

if I might. Nothing intrusive, nothing offensively personal, believe me."

"It's not a question of whether I believe you or not, Mr. Desmond. It's merely a question of what you ask. The first time you offend me, I will get up and leave."

"That makes for a rather daunting circumscription of my field of inquiry, doesn't it? Not knowing, as I do not, what might offend you."

"It's your dime, Mr. Desmond. And nothing within the bounds of good taste will be considered offensive. I might choose not to answer, however, tasteful though the question might be."

"Would you like something to eat?"

She shook her head. "No, thank you. Just a cup of coffee, if you don't mind." Then she laughed. "I suppose I might as well get something out of this, anyway."

Desmond signaled to the waitress, ordered two coffees, then took a deep breath. "I suppose I might as well begin."

She nodded. "The clock is ticking, Mr. Desmond."

"Well, as I told you on the phone, I'm in the process of writing a book about your—"

She raised a finger and wagged it at him. "That's bullshit, and we both know it, Mr. Desmond. I knew the moment I laid eyes on you that you were no rock-and-roll journalist. What are you really after?"

Desmond studied her face, trying to look beyond the dazzling surface. Her green eyes studied him in turn, her lips slightly parted, the tip of her tongue sliding over, almost caressing the upper. He wondered whether he could trust her, thought about

Warren Resnick's obsessive concern with secrecy, and decided that what Warren Resnick wanted and what he needed were not necessarily the same thing.

"Can you keep a confidence, Mrs. Yeats? Or do you prefer Ms. O'Shea?"

"Mrs. Yeats is fine. In some indefinable way, I suppose it's who I am, after all. At least, insofar as you're concerned."

"Fair enough. For starters, you're right, I'm not a journalist. I'm a security consultant."

"And who are you working for, Mr. Desmond, or should I call you by your real name, whatever it may be?"

"That is my real name. Well, now it is. It was originally Pavel Andreczek, but I changed it when I came to this country in the late sixties."

"Andreczek . . . Czech, isn't it?"

Desmond nodded. "Yes, it is. I took my current name as a kind of homage to my favorite saxophonist."

She relaxed completely now, her face lighting up. "I saw his last public appearance with Brubeck, at Avery Fisher Hall, just a few months before he died. Actually, Colin and I went together. Well, we digress, and there is that steady tick, tick, tick to be concerned with."

The waitress brought their coffees, and Desmond watched as she added two sugars, then stirred in a little cream. He sipped his own scalding and black.

"To answer your question, I am working for Griffin Records, Mrs. Yeats."

"What sort of security can concern both Griffin Records and Colin?"

"I'm afraid that's part of the puzzle I've been asked to solve. It seems that several hundred hours of Colin's tapes have been removed from the Griffin vaults. Warren Resnick has hired me to get them back."

Colleen Yeats looked stunned. "You can't be serious, Mr. Desmond. Hundreds of hours?"

Desmond nodded. "Nearly eight hundred, as a matter of fact. Warren Resnick will confirm that, if you ask, although I'd rather you didn't. And please, don't mention it to anyone else. Not even Colin."

"What sort of tapes? What's on them?"

"It is all unreleased material, either alternate versions of songs released in some other form, or songs that have never been released at all, at least by Colin. I'm sure I don't have to tell you that hundreds of his songs have been recorded by other artists, many of them songs Colin had never even intended to release in his own version. Some were recorded as demos for the other artists, and some were discarded because he wasn't satisfied with them, or didn't—but I'm sure you know all this. In any event, they are worth a considerable amount of money, perhaps even an incalculable amount, for any number of reasons."

"Jesus Christ! How in the hell did this happen? Who took them? Why?"

"Those are all questions I've been hired to find out, Mrs. Yeats."

"And how does that concern Colin?"

"I want to talk to him. I can't tell him about the missing tapes, of course, so I'd appreciate it if you wouldn't mention that part of the story, should you speak to him. In any case, Colin's whereabouts are unknown to Mr. Resnick at the moment."

Colleen smiled knowingly. "The contract negotiations. Colin hates that kind of bullshit, and he burrows underground like a sand crab whenever it's time to extend the agreement. I assume you've spoken to Peter Chandler?"

Desmond took a sip of coffee, watching her over the rim of the cup as he answered, "Yes, I have, but somehow I don't think he's going to be very much help."

Colleen Yeats snorted. Taking a sip of her own coffee, she set the cup down and leaned back in the booth. The movement drew the thickly textured heather wool taut over a bosom more ample than Desmond would have thought. "You know," she said, "that's an insight I've been trying to get Colin to achieve for as long as I've known him."

"You don't trust Chandler?"

"Trust is not even in the thesaurus when discussing my attitude toward Peter Chandler. That man is, at best, a complete idiot, and at worst, which I suspect is much closer to the mark, a thief. Colin has made him three fortunes in the last twenty-five years. Two of them he pissed away on drugs and women, and I would imagine that he's well on his way through the third as we speak."

"Why does Colin continue to let Chandler represent him?"

"Because Colin is about the most loyal man on the planet, Mr. Desmond. And he thinks that he owes it to Peter to maintain the relationship, even though

Peter hasn't done a thing for him in at least twenty years. Oh, he negotiates contracts, and arranges tours, but the facts are that Colin could walk into any label in town and write his own ticket. He controls his own publishing, which, you may or may not know, is where an awful lot of rock-and-roll money comes from. He also controls his own catalog, so that if he walks away from Griffin, the entire recorded output of Colin Yeats, released and unreleased, walks with him. As for the tours, Peter was never very good at it. He was all right for knocking on the doors of clubs in the Village in the beginning, but Colin's reputation outgrew that sort of venue very early on. When it comes to the large arenas, the logistics of a major rock tour, Peter Chandler is far out of his depth. Colin does half the work, and he usually brings in a few friends for much of the rest of it, paying them out of his own pocket."

"It sounds as if you're still quite fond of Colin," Desmond observed.

"Of course I am. That he and I can't live under the same roof hasn't changed that. Nobody can live under the same roof with Colin for very long, Mr. Desmond. He's about as intense as any man I've ever met. There is an electricity in the room with him, so much that you can almost smell the ozone. It was too much for me."

"I gather that you are still in touch with him."

Colleen hesitated before answering, almost as if she could anticipate the follow-up question. "Yes, I am."

"Can you arrange for me to see him?"

"I can try, Mr. Desmond, but you'll have to give me some good reason. And short of telling Colin about the missing tapes, I can't think what that might be."

Desmond tapped his palms on the tabletop. He thought about DeCicco and the possible connection of his death to the missing tapes, but it was a slender thread at the moment, and he didn't want to seem like an alarmist.

"I don't suppose he'd do it for you, as a favor?" Desmond asked.

"He might. But I don't want to presume on his good nature. Not unless there's a very good reason."

"Mrs. Yeats, take my word for it, the missing tapes are a very good reason. I know you can't mention them, but if you can see—" Desmond stopped, hearing how lame his argument was, and decided to throw caution to the winds. "Look, let me lay it out for you this way. Unless Colin took the tapes himself, which is a possibility, then there is no legitimate reason for those tapes to be absent from the vaults at Griffin Records. They can be held for ransom, although there has not been a demand as yet. They can be used to make pirate recordings, which could represent a substantial amount of money, made by the pirates and lost by Griffin and, by extension, Colin. Or they could be sold as is on the black market, once again to the detriment of Colin's finances. And I know enough about him to know that he might have artistic reasons for wanting to keep some of the recordings off the market. There is no fourth reason."

Colleen Yeats hung on every word, and when he

was finished, she leaned back in the booth, curling her long fingers around the warmth of her coffee cup, tapping one clear lacquered nail against the china. "There could be another reason, Mr. Desmond. Two, in fact . . ."

"Oh, and what might they be?" Desmond was intrigued now.

"The theft could be intended to sabotage the upcoming negotiations. If someone were interested in getting Colin away from Griffin, then souring the relationship would be very useful."

Desmond nodded in agreement. "All right, I'll accept that. What is the other reason?"

"Suppose you were interested in ruining Griffin Records, or even just Warren Resnick himself? If you destroyed the relationship between Griffin and its most successful artist, particularly under such circumstances, you could precipitate a stampede of other artists away from the label. I'm sure you understand how daunting my husband's—that is, my ex-husband's—reputation is. If he were disaffected, and especially for such a reason, a lot of other artists might choose to bolt the label, feeling that if Griffin couldn't protect Colin's work, then their own would be no safer. If that happens, even if the label survives, Warren Resnick does not, I can assure you of that."

"You're even more devious than you are beautiful, Mrs. Yeats. I have to admit I was looking at the theft from the money angle, not the political angle."

"Politics is money. And if you're trying to flatter me, Mr. Desmond, you're doing a superb job . . . but it will avail you nothing."

Desmond laughed. "All right, let's suppose one of your scenarios is valid, which would it be?"

Colleen shook her head. "I'm sure I don't know."

"Do you have any reason to believe that either might be the case?"

"No, I was simply speculating, Mr. Desmond. It's one way to occupy a restless mind, so I suppose I've gotten quite good at it."

"Let me be candid with you, Mrs. Yeats."

"I'd appreciate it."

"What I'm about to tell you is also speculation, maybe not even that, maybe just remote possibility."

"Go ahead."

"At the moment there is no suspect in the theft of the tapes. But the police have recently discovered the body of a man who had access to the vaults. He worked for a cleaning service, and his company, which was owned by his uncle, had the custodial contract with Griffin. He worked the midnight-to-eight shift, cleaning the offices, and since the vaults were none too secure, just a library, really—"

"I've seen them."

"—it would have been possible for him, with guidance of course, to have pulled off the theft and the substitution."

"Substitution?"

Desmond nodded. "It would appear that the theft took place over some period of time, with blank tapes being substituted for those that were removed. That would have been necessary to get by with piecemeal removal. Anything more comprehensive would have been too risky."

"And this man, you think he was killed as a result of the theft?"

"As I said, it's a possibility."

"Is Colin in danger, Mr. Desmond?"

"He might be. I can't say for sure. But . . ."

She nodded, as if in response to a question. Then, licking her lips, she said, "I'll see what I can do to help, Mr. Desmond. But I can't promise anything."

- TWELVE - - -

DAN BRENNAN LOOKED EXHAUSTED. THE TRASH CAN by the side of his desk was overflowing with crumpled balls of paper and crushed cardboard coffee cups. Another cup full of soggy cigarette butts was at his elbow.

Desmond sat down across from the desk. "What's so important, Dan?" he asked.

Brennan smiled. "I always wish I could answer that kind of question the way Inspector Clouseau used to do, in those Pink Panther movies. 'I suspect everyone and I suspect no one.' In this case, everything is important and nothing is important, Monsieur Desmon. The final *d*, you see, is silent. Or at least I think it is."

"You didn't call me down here to run through your Peter Sellers repertoire."

"No, I didn't. Remember I told you about the homicide they found in a beat-up old Dodge van, way the hell and gone up in the woods?"

"Yeah, DeCicco, wasn't it?"

"That's the one. And you told me he was on your list of people at Griffin, an outside contractor who had access to the tape vaults. Right?"

Desmond nodded. "That's right. You got something on him?"

"On him, no. On the shooters, yeah. The fact of the matter is, we have the shooters themselves . . . or maybe we do. Nothing seems to fit the way it's supposed to."

Desmond knew there was another shoe, and he waited for the thud. Brennan didn't waste any time in letting it fall. "Unfortunately, the shooters can't tell us anything, because somebody pulled the plug on them, too."

"How do you know they did the DeCicco murder?"

"We're not a hundred percent sure, but we're close. We have the pistol that killed DeCicco. Ballistics has a perfect match on Tony's Browning and the slugs the ME dug out of DeCicco's body. The gun was in Tony Fratangeli's pocket. It could have been planted, but I don't think so. The only prints on it belong to Fratangeli."

"You said shooters. How many were there?"

"Well, that's hard to tell. Fratangeli took the last ride with a buddy, but there was only one weapon used in the DeCicco killing, so we don't know whether

Tony's partner was along or not. But we're trying to match some prints from the Dodge van. Now that we know what to look for, maybe we'll get lucky."

"Who was the other man?"

"Some asshole they called Butch Cassidy. His real name was Kieran Cassidy. Used to be with the Westies, the Irish gang in the Hell's Kitchen area. Hooked on with Basciano after the Westies went down. I'm betting a week's pay—no small fortune, I might add—that we can match Butch with some of the UID prints. That's 'unidentified' for the uninitiated, by the way."

"All right, there's got to be some connection between Fratangeli and DeCicco. But where does my problem relate? So far, I haven't been able to connect DeCicco to the missing tapes. I know he had access, and murder is about as suspicious a circumstance as you could want, but unless I can connect DeCicco to the tapes, or the tapes to Fratangeli, anyhow, I'm still paddleless in the frozen north."

Brennan wagged a finger. "You spooks never get it out of your blood, do you?"

"What?"

"That insistence on hard data."

"It doesn't lie," Desmond said, grinning.

"Not often, but I wouldn't say never. Fortunately for you, however, my skeptical friend, I have something hard for you." Brennan opened the belly drawer of his desk and pulled out an envelope. He tossed it to Desmond, who opened it while watching Brennan's smile broaden.

Tilting the open envelope into his lap, he squeezed

his knees together to catch a shower of photographs and a single audio cassette. Desmond spread the photos out on the desktop, examining them one by one. Each of them showed a cassette casing or the clear plastic box in which cassettes were stored. Each of them bore the smears of fingerprint dust and at least one clear impression. Tilting one photo, he read a strip of tape pasted to the side of the cassette. GR/MLD 49681. The same number appeared on the plastic box.

Desmond looked at the tape, then at Brennan, who shoved a small boom box across the desk. "Go ahead," Brennan said, "Pop it in."

Desmond inserted the tape and pushed the play button. The room filled with the buzzsaw shriek of a guitar feeding back, then the solid Texas shuffle rhythm that was the hallmark of so many great blues players. Not until the familiar rasp of the voice fell in over the rhythm section did Desmond recognize Colin Yeats. The searing lyrics, in a staccato delivery, almost declamatory in spots, like some sort of proto-rap, warred with the slashing guitar.

Brennan was grinning from ear to ear when Desmond looked up. "Something, ain't it?"

"Where in the hell did you get this?"

Brennan shrugged. "Hey, a cop has ways of finding things people don't want found, you know what I mean?"

"Is this it, or do you have them all?"

"That's it, Paul. The one and only. It's a solid ninety minutes, though, filled both sides. I assume it is one of the stolen tapes. Am I right?"

"It has to be. I've bought everything I could get my

hands on by Colin Yeats, and I guarantee you I've never heard this, not even on bootlegs, of which there are dozens. I'd have to check with the list Resnick gave me to be certain, but I'd be surprised if it weren't."

"Studio quality, too, ain't it? Sounds to me like that came straight from a master tape. It sure as hell hasn't been watered down as it passed from one hippie pocket to another."

Brennan was still wearing that Cheshire-cat grin, and Desmond looked at him intently. "You *are* going to tell me where you got it, aren't you?"

"Of course I am. You think I dragged you down here to twist your *cojones* a little? I found that little beauty tucked down between the seat and the floorboard of Tony Fratangeli's Buick. Those prints, interestingly enough, belong to three people. One of them is Tony Fratangeli. One of them is Ron DeCicco, and we don't have any idea who the third print belongs to. Maybe Yeats, maybe some engineer. The tape is a copy, so you can keep it. The original is being held in evidence, naturally, but I had the lab dub it for you after they lifted the prints. I'd appreciate it if you'd check with Resnick and get back to me. If that's on the list of stolen tapes, then we have ourselves a pretty fair little melodrama unfolding."

Desmond nodded. "At the very least, it means that DeCicco and Fratangeli were in contact with whoever stole the tapes."

"At the very least. But I hope it's more than that. Otherwise, we're no closer to the bottom of this mess than we were yesterday. And if that UID turns out to be Colin Yeats or some engineer from Griffin, it could be we just have a tantalizing dead end."

"Or it could mean that Guido Basciano is in the mix somewhere. You said DeCicco had connections, although not significant ones. You said Fratangeli worked for Basciano, and so did Cassidy. It could be that DeCicco was blackmailed into lifting the tapes, or maybe paid to do it, then Fratangeli took him out to break the chain."

"I got a feeling we might not know the answer to that one until we find the tapes."

"Why's that?"

"Because I don't think Tony and Butch were taken out by a pro. At least, not by the usual bent noses. Things are usually a lot neater. Either the hit man or, to be politically correct, hit person, was an amateur or it was someone outside the mob. There are too many anomalies."

"Such as?"

"I'd rather not talk about that just yet. I have a couple of ideas, but I want to do a little research before I open my yap."

Desmond popped the tape out of the boom box, stuck it in his pocket, and stood up. "I'll talk to Resnick this afternoon, see if he can identify the tape. He might know it right off, but I don't know how familiar he is with the stolen material. A lot of it was recorded years before he took charge of the label. If that number on the tape doesn't mean anything, he might have to check with a few people. And I'm heading out to Colorado day after tomorrow."

"Skiing?"

"I wish. Actually, I'm following another angle, not so much on the tapes, but on Yeats. The more I think about this mess, the more I think I have to talk to him. I might even have to tell him about the missing tapes, which Resnick doesn't want me to do. That is, if his ex-wife hasn't already told him."

"Colleen Yeats? How does she know about the tapes?"

"I told her. I had to, to buy her trust."

Brennan licked his lips. "You know, it's occurred to me that maybe Yeats himself is behind the theft."

"I considered the possibility, but I can't buy it. Why in hell would he do it? The tapes are his anyway. As soon as his contract with Griffin expires, all rights revert to him in all material, released and unreleased, including physical ownership of the masters."

"Sure, but maybe he thinks he'd have trouble getting them. Maybe he thinks Griffin would copy them all. Maybe there would be some stuff missing. Hell, maybe they'd destroy them, or force him to go to court to get them. That could take years and cost him a bundle. For that matter, maybe he just wants to have an excuse to leave Griffin, and if the tapes are lost while in their possession, he's got all the justification he needs."

"You're too devious for your own good, Dan," Desmond said.

"I come from a long line of devious harps. My grandfather was an IRA man." He held up two fingers side by side. "He was like this with Mick Collins after the Easter 'rising," he said, wiggling the fingers. "So I know from devious. You Eastern European types think you've cornered the market on underground resistance, but the Irish could teach you a thing or two, let me tell you. Speaking of which, do you want to tell me why you're going to Colorado?"

Desmond shrugged. It couldn't hurt, he figured. And Brennan had been decent enough to share his information. A little payback might go a long way toward buying a little more cooperation later on. "Ever hear of Rajah Primasanha?"

Brennan laughed. "Don't tell me you're going to get yourself all dressed up in saffron robes and a turban!"

"I might have to," Desmond said. "But not gladly."

"How's this tie into the Yeats thing?"

"I'm not sure it does. But Yeats used to follow the notorious swami. I'm thinking that maybe he went back. It's a good place to keep out of sight. From what I hear, Primasanha has thousands of acres of woods in the mountains outside Denver—cabins, and all that. What better place to lay low?"

"But you aren't going to ride up to the front door and pull the bell rope, are you?"

Desmond shook his head.

"I didn't think so. They wouldn't tell you squat. But let me tell you something, Paul, and I mean this seriously. Watch your ass. That slick bastard runs a fucking snake pit. And he's the king cobra. I had more than one run-in with some of his muscle. Was a girl, Carmela Guarino. We fished her out of the East River about a year ago. And she didn't jump in, either. She'd been gut-shot and tossed in. Still alive, according to the autopsy. Her old man was a capo in the Gambino family. But she was ashamed of Daddy and ran from pillar to post, looking for some way to make amends. Primasanha was her last stop. Papa Guarino had her kidnapped, and the next thing you know, she's a floater. Prettiest thing you ever saw, too. Big dark eyes, long black hair. Reminded me of Claudia Cardinale, only better looking."

"And you're telling me that Primasanha had her killed?"

"Yeah. I could never prove it, but"—and he thumped his chest—"in here, I know it. So, like I said, watch your ass."

"You think maybe there's some connection between Primasanha and the mob?"

Brennan shook his head. "Not that I know of. Not formal, anyway. The funny thing was, though, that Guarino never did anything about it. I don't know if he wasn't sure Primasanha was behind it, or if somebody called him off. Because you can bet that he would have taken that slick bastard apart with a goddamned chain saw if he got his hands on him."

"Could you do me a favor?"

"Maybe. Depends on what it is."

"Can you check and see if there are any other links? Maybe between Basciano and Primasanha."

"You're not suggesting that they're in bed together, are you?"

"Stranger things have happened."

"I'll look, but don't get your hopes up. And you call me on that goddamned tape, will you?"

Desmond nodded. "One other thing, Dan."

Brennan grinned. "See, like I said, you spooks are all the same. What is it?"

"Whoever took the tapes knew exactly what he was looking for. Now, it's possible that DeCicco got the information on his own, tried to sell the tapes to the mob, and they cut him out. But it's also possible he was working *for* the mob, and somebody else cut them all out."

"And . . . ?"

"And I'd like to know how DeCicco got his information. Maybe he found a memo lying around at Griffin, but maybe he got it from somebody else. Could you check with his employer to get a list of their other clients?"

"Already did. Have it right here." Brennan fished in his desk for a moment, found a folder, and slapped it down, then thumbed through the contents. "Here it is . . . here it is . . . right . . . here!"

He flipped it across to Desmond, who proceeded to scan it, running down the list with a fingertip. Halfway down, he whistled. "Jesus H.!"

"What? Whaddya got?"

"Rock Rack."

"Which is?"

"Peter Chandler's talent agency."

"And he is, don't tell me, Colin Yeats's agent, right?"

Desmond nodded, already going on down the list. He found another name and Brennan leaned forward. "Come on, what now?"

"You haven't looked at this list yet, have you?"

Brennan shook his head. "Just got it."

"Mega Sound."

"That's Basciano's outfit!"

- THIRTEEN- - -

TIMMY CORMAN WAS ONE OF A KIND. DESMOND KNEW him only slightly, and then only through Audrey. When she was doing album covers more regularly, she had worked the music-industry circuit, lunching with art directors, photographers, and agents, pushing for the freelance jobs only a high profile would get her access to.

Corman had been making a name for himself long before that, touring with Dylan, palling around with Mick Jagger, and when he started to happen, with the Boss. He was almost a legend, in his own mind, if not to the world at large, patterning himself after the original Gonzo, Hunter S. Thompson. But Timmy was less disciplined than the good Dr. Thompson, more volatile, at least in public, and his constitution was far less rugged.

For a while it hadn't made a difference. Timmy had, after all, been there at the table that immortal night John Lennon got himself and Harry Nilsson thrown out of a Hollywood club for drinking too much, being too loud, and mostly, for wearing a Tampax on his head.

Corman had written that episode up for *Rolling Stone*, and done such a fine job of it that even Lennon forgave him. But that was a long time ago, and Timmy had taken to the bottle, and the coke he shoveled like snow had caused him to wear out his nose—and, as a consequence, his welcome.

Timmy's books were out of print, his articles now few and far between, and mostly in obscure periodicals. He was no longer happening, no longer well-known, and sadly, no longer well-heeled. But even minor legends have a way of hanging on, and Timmy Corman's had done that. He still knew what was happening in music, both above- and under-ground. He had pipelines into most of the major corporations and most of the significant agencies. His improvisational prose had earned the admiration, even the respect, of some of the better singers and musicians, and they still invited him to parties. Because Timmy Corman still was what he had always been—good company.

That he was willing to meet with Desmond was no small stroke of luck. Whether anything of value would come of it, Desmond wasn't sure. Corman was staying at the Hotel Chelsea, where Dali used to hang when he was in town, and where Sid Vicious breathed his last breath and became a legend the only way he could. Desmond entered the tatty lobby. Like the man Desmond had come to see, the place had seen better days. The lobby had the musty smell of decay staved off with Lysol and elbow grease. The narrow hallways seemed to soak up light, leaving very little for the eye.

The elevator to the third floor wheezed like an asthmatic old man, and Desmond was reminded of far too many ancient hotels on the Continent, where he had led a dozen secret lives, meeting strangers in the crumbling vestiges of nineteenth-century opulence the communists had tried, but failed, to preserve in Belgrade and Bucharest, Berlin and Budapest. It gave him the creeps, wavering there on the end of a creaky cable, wondering whether it would snap before he got safely out of the car.

Corman answered the raspy bell, barely audible over the thunder of Cream pounding in a room down the hall, Jack Bruce doing his best to push out the walls to make room for Ginger Baker's flailing arms and sizzling cymbals. When the door opened, Corman bopped into the hall, did a three-sixty and boogied down the corridor, his air guitar clearly set on 11.

Desmond shook his head, leaned against the wall, and waited for Corman to finish miming Clapton's solo on "Crossroads."

When the thunder died, Desmond said, "You planning an encore, Timmy?"

Corman laughed, a phlegmy gurgle choking it off as he fished a crumpled pack of Camels out of his shirt pocket. He was barefoot, a fact that served only to accentuate his diminutive size, and his spindly arms looked emaciated in the red-and-yellow-striped polo shirt that brought back the look of the Lovin' Spoonful with indifferent success.

Corman bobbed his head and popped his fingers as the unseen stereo, now at a lower volume, started up again, this time with J. J. Cale's "Lies." He ducked into his room, reached back with spidery fingers, and grabbed Desmond by the sleeve and dragged him into the room.

"Good to see you, Paul," he said. "How's Audrey?"

Desmond smiled. "Good, Timmy. Very good."

"Haven't seen her in three, maybe four years. She out of it, or what?"

Desmond shrugged. "She still does an occasional cover, mostly classical, though. She's spending most of her time at the easel working for herself."

"That's the only way, man. The only fucking way. Do it for your own self, 'cause there ain't nobody gonna do it for you."

Corman jabbed a bent cigarette into his thin lips and lit it with a Bic. "What brings you through the looking glass, Paul? Don't tell me you want to become a folksinger or a guitar hero."

"Nothing like that, Timmy. I'm working on something I thought you might be able to help me with."

Corman laughed. "I don't think I'd be too welcome in the rarefied atmosphere you frequent these days, Paul. I read about you and that museum thing. Places like that see me coming, they usually raise the draw-bridge and set the moat on fire."

"This one's right up your alley, Timmy. Music. Your kind of music."

"They stopped making my kind of music, Paul. It's all synthesizers and drum machines, sampling and special effects. Ain't nobody around plays guitar like Jimi did. Dylan's gone bonkers, Lennon's dead. Hell, they're *all* either fat, rich, and useless or they're dead."

"Even Colin Yeats?"

Corman sucked on the cigarette, held the smoke in so long Desmond was starting to wonder whether it was tobacco, then exhaled in a long, thin plume. "What about him?"

"Can't tell you much yet, but I was hoping you could tell me a few things."

"I can try."

"I'm willing to pay you, Timmy."

"I don't need charity, Paul. What I need is a clean slate. I can still write, only nobody will let me." He held his hands two feet apart. "I got a stack of script this fucking thick, good stuff, too, but I can't get arrested anymore."

"It's not charity, Timmy. I'm getting well paid for this job, and I need the kind of help you can give me."

"How do you know I can?"

"I don't, not for sure. But I know one thing—if you can't, then nobody can."

"All right. You pay what you want, Paul. I don't need the money. What I need is self-respect. If you can help me find that, *I'll* pay *you*. What do you want to know?"

"For starters, what can you tell me about Peter Chandler?"

Timmy fairly spat. "That bloodsucker. If I told Colin once I told him a thousand times to get rid of that slimy bastard. He's about as crooked as a hairpin, or Barbra's nose, you know what I'm saying? Why Colin puts up with him is beyond me."

"Colleen Yeats says her ex-husband is very loyal."

"Loyal to a fault. And how the hell did you get Colleen to talk to you? I thought I was the only one she trusted." Corman laughed, leaned forward to stub out the cigarette, and leaned back in his chair. "Anyhow, the deal on Chandler is that he's got bad habits. The kind of habits a man shouldn't have if he's responsible for managing people's lives, careers, and especially, their money."

"What kind of habits?"

"You want the whole smorgasbord?" He started ticking items off on his splayed fingers. "Women, especially blondes, the younger the better, especially if they're top-heavy. Chandler is a tit man. Drugs. It used to be smack, then it was coke. Whatever was in. He'd sniff glue, drop acid, chew peyote and eat a bushel of sacred mushrooms, then read a contract for a client. I don't know about you, but if I'm signing on the dotted line, I don't want some druggie giving me advice. Gambling. Vegas style, corner store style. Crap games, floating and otherwise. Horses, football. Hell, he'd bet on whether the sun will come up tomorrow, and not even ask for odds. How he managed to keep his kneecaps is one of the modern miracles, if you ask me."

"Organized crime? He gamble with the mob, did he?" Desmond was looking for a connection between Chandler and Basciano, but he didn't want to mention names, hoping Timmy would volunteer them on his own. He wasn't disappointed.

"Used to lay his bets with Vinnie Glazewski, a Polish guy who handled book for Guido Basciano. Vinnie was a nice guy, used to let him float awhile. Chandler was usually good for it, with a little vig of course, but I always wondered where he got the money. I mean, he was handling a lot of big names, but he was spending pretty much everything he made. Yachts, houses, a fucking Ferrari must have cost two hundred grand."

"Who's Guido Basciano?"

Corman didn't answer right away. Instead, he reached for a package of tissues on the table by his chair, yanked two out, and stuffed them in his cheeks. "Guido's the kind of man makes offers you can't refuse, Paulie." His Brando was more than passable. "What I could tell you about Guido and the rock scene would make your teeth hurt."

"You know Yeats pretty well, don't you?"

"I used to. I still see him from time to time, but not lately. The fact is, he seems to have gone to ground."

"Any idea why?"

"Hell, Colin is kind of weird, you know. Mystical. Weird enough to make Van Morrison look normal, if you want to know the truth. But if he's missing in action, he probably has his reasons. Maybe he's finally had it with Chandler. Hell, maybe he's hiding from Chandler."

"Why do you say that?"

"Just a hunch. Chandler's got some heavy friends. I know Colin's contract with Griffin is up soon. Fact is, his contract with Chandler's up at almost the same time, maybe a month or so later. And if I were Colin, I know what I'd do. . . ."

"What's that?"

"I'd hide out until the Griffin deal expired, stay hid until the Chandler contract expired, too, then get myself another agent and let him sell me to the highest bidder. Colin can name his price, too. Not just for the record deal, but for the agent. He could get a cut-rate deal, because just having him in your stable is worth millions, and the prestige and clout it gives you is worth millions more. And I mean yearly, too. Then I'd get a good auditor and microscan Chandler's books."

"What about Warren Resnick?"

"What about him?"

"Is he somebody Yeats would hide from?"

"Resnick's all right. A little too straitlaced for my taste. For Colin's, too, I'm sure. But he seems like a pretty decent sort. He doesn't know a whole hell of a lot about Colin's kind of music, but then who does? Anyhow, Resnick's no problem. But Colin's got another reason to hide out, too. That goofy Indian, or pseudo-quasi, semi-hemi-demi-Indian bloodsucker. What a fucking ghoul that one is."

"Rajah Primasanha, is that who you're talking about?"

"The very same."

"Can you find Yeats for me?"

"You're working for Resnick, right?"

"Right, and he doesn't know where Yeats is. Neither does Chandler, or so he says."

"Word is Colin's out west someplace, holed up with his new band. That comes from Chandler's office, but it just might be true. Colin is liable to tell Chandler something like that, and just not tell him where."

"Can you find him, Timmy? It's important."

"Life and death important?"

Desmond nodded. "Possibly, yes."

Corman shrugged. He stood up, started to shuffle across the floor, looking for all the world like Ratso Rizzo, the Herlihy character whose name he used on occasion, supposedly after Yeats saw *Midnight Cowboy* and told Timmy how much Dustin Hoffman's portrayal called him to mind.

"Look, maybe I can. I can't promise you, Paul. I mean, I wouldn't want to promise and not deliver. But even if I can't find him, I can probably get word to him. Do I tell him you want to talk to him, or what?"

"Yeah."

"Mind if I ask why?"

"I'd rather not say, Timmy. Not yet, anyway."

"That won't be too convincing to Colin."

"All he has to do is call me. If he doesn't like what I tell him, he can hang up."

"This is on the up-and-up, Paul? I mean, look, I don't want to ask this, but I have to . . . I consider Colin a friend, and I don't want to see him get hurt."

"Neither do I, Timmy. Neither does Warren Resnick, hard as that may be for you to believe."

"All right. I'll try."

"You know, Timmy, you look more like Larry Sloman every year."

Timmy affected a hurt look. "I thought you were my friend, Paul."

- FOURTEEN- - -

THE AIRPLANES SEEMED AS IF THEY WERE CLOSE
enough for Desmond to reach out and touch them.
Every time one went over, the thunder threatened to
crush him, and it was all he could do to keep from
hitting the ground with his hands pressed against his
ears. Stan Collins seemed unfazed by the racket.

Collins noticed his discomfort and grinned. "Gives
a whole new meaning to the term *fear of flying*,
doesn't it, Paul?"

"It amazes me that anyone would chose to locate
an operation like this so close to an airport, especially
one as busy as Newark."

"That's the beauty of it, don't you see? There is

traffic in and out of here day and night, seven days a week. One more truck is not going raise an eyebrow."

"But recording—"

"Soundproofing. I'll bet you that once we're inside, you won't even hear a murmur. Hell, the Concorde could break the sound barrier right over the roof and you wouldn't hear a thing."

"It's beginning to look like we'll never get inside anyway, Stan."

Collins laughed. "You're too damned impatient, Paul. I don't know how you got as far as you did in the Company, always ready to jump like you are."

"You remind me of somebody," Desmond said. "I used to hear that all the time."

"Good to know nothing much has changed. Gives an old man like me hope. Maybe the eternal verities will last longer than I used to think."

Desmond shook his head. "If you're looking to me for confirmation, don't!" He raised binoculars and trained them on the front door of the long, low building on the other side of a Cyclone fence. The place was the headquarters of Mega Sound, the mob-owned recording studios, manufacturing plant, and warehouse complex. As near as Collins had been able to figure it out, after years of study, Mega was the nerve center of the mob's infiltration system into the music business. Whatever angle they were playing, they could play right here, within a stone's throw of the runways of Newark Airport.

Desmond looked around, and had to admit that the setting was the perfect cover. The place was so exposed, and at the same time so perfectly isolated in its exposure, that nobody would think twice about what went on behind the Cyclone fence. Security was, of course, essential, and Mega had plenty. But it didn't look at all out of place, because everywhere you looked, there were similar buildings behind similar fences, sporting endless miles of similar razor wire.

Mega Sound was just one more company nobody had ever heard of, clinging precariously to the margin between swamp and tarmac. Off in the distance, the sound of a freighter's horn suddenly bellowed. The Port of Elizabeth was not that far away, just one more layer of hurly-burly to hide the comings and goings at Mega Sound. On reflection, Desmond had to admit the location made perfect sense for a business, legitimate or otherwise. Access to road, rail, sea, and air transportation meant you could send anything anywhere without leaving your backyard. It also meant you could receive anything from anywhere without attracting unwanted attention. And, if you had a sideline like that of the powers behind the throne of Mega Sound, you also had the bogs and meadows to dispose of the occasional nuisance. After all, it wasn't only Jimmy Hoffa who waltzed off into the night never to be seen again.

"Your guy is sure this is where the tapes would be, Stan?" Desmond asked.

"According to Louie the Lip, if the mob has the tapes, this is where they'll be. He says he's heard some rumors about a big score, but nothing he can pin down, and he doesn't know if it's the same thing you're looking for. But like he says, if it has anything to do with music, this is the best and, not coincidentally, the only place that makes sense. If they're gonna make bootlegs, this is the only place they can do it. And according to Louie, if the mob got their hands on a significant stash like the one we're talking about, it would be for that one reason. Any other way they turn it into cash, they get chicken feed. Bootlegs, they can milk for years, instead of a one-time payment like ransom or peddling them on the collectors' market."

"I'm not sure they're here, but I have to think there's a fifty-fifty chance. I know that one tape doesn't make a case, but that one tape suggests that Fratangeli either had the others, or knew somebody who did. I checked the number on the cassette Danny Brennan found, and it was on the master list. It may not be the whole chain, but at least it's a link. I have to know, and I can't afford to wait. I may never get this close again."

Collins chuckled. "Seems kind of funny, being on the other end of a blackbag job. I kind of miss the old days. I could stay here all night."

"Well, I'm getting a little anxious. I wish to hell whoever was inside would go home already. It's nearly one A.M."

"Relax, Paul. We might have to come back tomorrow, or the next night, or the night after that. The only other alternative is a search warrant, which you don't want because of the confidentiality. You want to blackbag it, you got to be patient."

"I know, I know, Stan. But—"

"No buts, Paul. Relax, have a cup of coffee, thaw out a little."

Desmond shook his head. "No way I'm walking through that muck again. Bad enough I got to worry about these goddamned waders. I feel like I'm already wearing cement shoes."

"You fuck this up, and they'll fit you for a real pair, Paul," Collins warned. "Then you'll see what they *really* feel like."

A door banged, and Desmond gripped the fence like an anxious prisoner. He reached for the binoculars, trained them on the front of the building, and saw two men, barely more than shadows, moving across the parking lot to the only remaining car. The lights were out in the building now, and it looked like the moment he had been waiting for was finally here.

He tracked the shadows to the car, watched as the dome light went on and the men climbed into the late-model Cadillac, but never got a clear look at either of their faces. The sound of an engine drifted across the chilly expanse and was almost immediately drowned out by the roar of another airliner. Desmond glanced toward the runway as a 737 wound up and thundered down the runway, then lifted off, banking almost immediately. When he turned back to the car, it was already at the main gate, and he watched as the passenger got out to work the electronic lock to open it. The Cadillac rolled through, and the gate closed as the passenger climbed back into the Caddy and the car was gone.

He and Collins worked their way along the fence, rounded the corner, and reached the electronic gate.

Desmond yanked a tool kit from his pocket, removed the cover from the electronic panel, and bypassed the keypad. The gate slid open and Collins clapped him on the back. "Glad you were never one of the bad guys, Paul. You made that look easy."

"I hope I have as much luck bypassing the alarm, Stan."

"Unless I miss my guess, the Langley boys taught you pretty well. The alarm should be a piece of cake. The thing about the mob is, they're arrogant. They always assume nobody would have the balls to hit them, so they tend to cut corners on security, except for muscle."

Desmond closed the gate again, leaving the cover panel and mounting screws on the ground beside it. At the front door, Desmond sized up the alarm. "It's just a simple burglar alarm," he said, surprised, despite what Collins had told him.

Collins was too much of a gentleman to say, "I told you so."

It took five minutes to bypass the alarm. Another sixty seconds to pick the front lock. But when Desmond held his breath and turned the knob, the door swung open easily.

They slipped inside as another jetliner passed overhead, so low that the glass rattled in the door and the rush of air past the flaps was audible. With the door closed, Collins turned on a flashlight. "We better get moving. This is a big place, and we want to be out of here in under an hour, if we can manage it."

Desmond nodded. "I just want to know if the tapes are here. If they are, I can get a warrant and have the place tossed. If not, I'm all the way back up the creek."

They moved through the front office suite and into a corridor. On the left, a maze of desks separated by partitions took up what looked like an acre. "Order processing," Desmond guessed, noting the computer terminals on every desk. "They must do legitimate shipping from here."

"Like I said, it's their primary facility. They have branch offices in Philly, L.A., Memphis, and San Francisco, but this is the nerve center."

At the far end of the corridor, they came to a glass-paneled door, and Desmond yanked it open. Collins played his light inside and stepped into the next passage. When Desmond followed him, closing the door behind him, all sound seemed to disappear. "Must be the studio area," Collins said. Several doors were set in one wall, and he tried the first, found himself staring at a control board and, beyond it, a glass panel. Stepping into the room, he aimed his light through the glass panel. The floor was littered with cables, and baffles divided the large studio into several discrete sections. Amplifiers, a drum kit, and a Hammond B-3 dominated the spaces. Turning away from the panel, Desmond played the light over an array of tape containers on steel shelving against the wall. But there was no sign of the missing Colin Yeats recordings.

As they moved back into the corridor Desmond said, "There must be some central storage area. If the tapes are here, I'm betting that's where they'd be."

"You're probably right, Paul," Collins responded.

"But you have to keep in mind one thing. If they *are* here, they may not be out in plain sight where anybody and everybody could see them. There has to be a secure area where they can be safe from prying eyes."

Desmond nodded in agreement. "You're probably right, but it would still be in the general storage area, more than likely. Maybe a locked cabinet, or a separate room, kept under lock and key."

"If you want to find it, you better get moving."

They checked each of the doors on the way down the hall and found that each was another studio, five in all, each obviously in the middle of being used for something. One even had instruments set up, and the standby lights on the amps were glowing. "Looks like somebody'll be here pretty soon," Desmond guessed.

"Yeah, unless it's a typical snotty bunch of kids. They figure they ain't paying for the juice, so who cares. Of course, when they find out they're paying for everything, including overhead, they'll change their tune, but by then, they'll be locked up tighter than they thought possible. Clarence Darrow couldn't bust them out of the contract."

Desmond laughed. "Let's move on into the next wing," he suggested. Without waiting for an answer, he moved toward a steel door blocking the far end of the corridor. It was open, and when he stepped through and tossed the light around, he knew he was getting close. Several signs, sporting arrows pointing in three different directions, were screwed to the cinderblock wall. One read WAREHOUSE, a second said, PLANT and a third pointed the way toward ARCHIVES.

The fourth steered them back toward the studios and the fifth and last read ORDER PROCESSING.

"I'm betting on Archives, Stan," Desmond muttered. "What do you think?"

"Lead the way, Paul."

Desmond turned his flashlight beam in the direction the arrow pointed, and moved off at a brisk pace. His footsteps echoed off the cinder blocks, and when he reached the far end, another arrow instructed him to turn left.

The archives were fifty feet down a narrow hall. The door was closed, and when Desmond tried it, he found it locked. He was getting anxious now, and as he knelt to work the picklocks, he hoped he would find what he was looking for on the other side of the door. When the lock clicked open, he jerked the door back as he got up, pulling it so fast it banged against his knee.

"Steady, big fella," Collins joked.

Desmond reached inside, slapped the wall until he found a light switch, and clicked it on. The archives were vast, stretching off in every direction, row upon row of steel shelving lined with every manner of tape storage container. He trained the light on the end of one shelf and breathed a sigh of relief. It was labeled: JAZZ, C–F. "We're in luck, Stanley," he said. "No wonder it's called organized crime! Find the rock section."

"I should be able to hear it right from here," Collins said, but Desmond gave him a withering glance, and Collins apologized. "Not too good, huh?"

They followed the alphabet. The next section was

classical, and rock followed it. When they found the section with artists whose names started with *W* through *Z*, Desmond fairly skipped down the aisle. "Yeats," he mumbled, "Yeats, where the hell are you, Colin? Whitesnake, whatever that is, XTC, Yeats— here it is." He tapped a tape canister, and another, right next to it. And his heart sank. That was it, that was all the Colin Yeats on the shelves. He pulled the two canisters off the shelf and knew immediately that all he'd managed to find was the master tape for the two Colin Yeats bootlegs already on the market, one a live concert from Sydney, Australia, and one from the Hammersmith Odeon.

"Damn!"

"Nothing, Paul?" Collins's voice drifted through the shelving from a distant corner. "There's a cabinet over here, maybe it's in here."

Desmond shoved the two canisters back in place and walked off to find Collins. "Look," he said, "while I try to get this damn thing open, look and see if you can find any more rock. Maybe this is the section where stuff already on the market is stored. maybe there's another section with stuff they haven't released yet."

"Do my best, Paul."

Desmond had no trouble with the cabinet, and when it swung open he knew immediately that it had been a waste of time. Boxes of paperwork, labeled by year, and a single carton of Bob Dylan concerts on cassette were all he found. He closed the cabinet in disgust.

"Find anything, Stan?" he called.

"Nada!"

Desmond made a quick pass through the shelving, hoping against hope that he might stumble on something useful, but he came up empty.

"Maybe it's in the plant, Paul. Maybe they're getting ready to manufacture."

"I don't know much about the CD-manufacturing process, but somehow I doubt it. We'll take a look, but I'm not expecting much."

And a half hour later, with three minutes remaining of their allotted sixty, it was no longer possible to hope. It was a dry well, and Desmond was crushed. If the mob had the tapes, they had decided to keep them someplace other than Mega Sound. But where?

And where the hell was Colin Yeats?

- FIFTEEN- - -

THOMAS GRIFFITH MUST HAVE BEEN DOING ALL
right. His offices were in the Trump Tower. As he
waited for the elevator Desmond looked at the lobby.
He'd heard about the atrium but never been inside,
and it looked to him now like something more appropriate for an aviary at the Bronx Zoo or, as it liked to
style itself, the New York Zoological Society. The lush
greenery glistened from the cascading waters, and the
soft lighting made a pleasant impression, alien to anyone who had seen the impossibly garish Taj Mahal in
Atlantic City, a structure Desmond had always
assumed to be emblematic of the master builder's
extravagant personality—it had flash, but not taste.

On the twentieth floor, he found Griffith's office without trouble. The receptionist looked like a paragon of civilization after Peter Chandler's purple-spiked Cerberus. A plump, pleasant woman with white hair and rhinestone glasses on a chain, she wore an angora sweater draped over her shoulders and held in place with golden clasps.

"May I help you?" she asked.

"I have an appointment with Mr. Griffith."

She glanced at her calendar, then smiled. "You must be Mr. Desmond."

When he nodded that he was, she buzzed, and Griffith's voice crackled back. "Mr. Desmond is here," the receptionist informed him.

"Send him in, please, Grace."

Grace came out from behind her desk and opened the door to Griffith's office, and Desmond thanked her before stepping in. The parquetry of the floor glistened with a diamond-like polyurethane sheen. A single Berber rug, the largest Desmond had ever seen, occupied about half of the floor. Griffith himself sat behind a desk that was all chrome and plate-glass. The walls sported several paintings, good ones, abstracts in the styles of Mark Rothko and Frank Stella.

Griffith was in shirtsleeves, his rep tie tugged down to allow the unbuttoned collar of his blue shirt to be opened. Under the desk, his penny loafers and argyle socks gave him the feet of a collegian, or given the shock of snowy hair that framed his round Irish face, those of an Ivy League poetry instructor. On the chair behind him, a brown Harris-tweed jacket, elbow patches right out of Dartmouth, sprawled as if it had been abandoned.

Griffith leaned forward to shake hands, getting halfway out of his chair. "Pleased to meet you, Mr. Desmond," he said. "What can I do for you?"

"I need some information on a cult, and from what I have been given to understand, nobody knows more about the subject than you do."

Griffith smiled, the corners of his eyes crinkling. "I think that's a bit of a stretch, Mr. Desmond. But I'll do my best to live up to such a grand reputation. Any cult in particular?"

Desmond nodded. "Yes, but why don't you fill me in a little on the generalities. I know about as much as the next guy who reads the newspapers, and not a hell of a lot more."

"There are so many, it's hard to know where to begin. But in general, I suppose you can say that the determining factor in deciding whether a group is a cult or not is the degree to which its focal point is a single individual, rather than an ideology. I'm a sociologist by training. Like most sociologists, I learned about the various religious groups—the ecclesia, the sect, and so on. So I knew cults in a kind of textbook way, but never paid much attention until my own son came to me for help. His girlfriend had belonged to one for some time, and she disappeared without warning, and without a trace."

"So you started researching the specific group, is that it?"

Griffith nodded. "The more I researched, the more fascinated, and frightened, I became. It was clear to

POWER TRIO ~ 143

me that the group Rosalie—that was my son's girl-friend—belonged to, was well advanced in the cycle that seems to govern the life and death of cults."

"Cycle?"

Griffith nodded. "Yes. It's not quite ironclad, not as hard and fast as the laws of physical science. Of course, nothing that involves a human dimension can be. But most cults follow a pattern. It's pretty clear-cut, and happens often enough that you could almost say the development is inexorable and irreversible. A lot of them form, just loose accretions of similarly disaffected souls. They tend to coalesce around one or more strong figures, usually male, although not always. This central figure tends to gain prominence rather slowly at first. Sometimes the group breaks up before it can even be properly called a cult. In that case, the reason is usually that the central figure was not strong enough to dominate and hold the group together by the force of his personality."

"We're not talking about the cult of personality in the totalitarian sense, are we, Mr. Griffith?"

"Not quite, although they are much alike in many respects. In fact, once a primary leader emerges, the first thing he or she does is try to consolidate power. That is what Hitler, Stalin, Mao, and other dictators did, only the ostensible justification was political rather than religious. Some political scientists even talk about them as if they were the same."

"But surely people see through that kind of thing. I mean, a naked grab for power is obvious by defi-nition."

"True, but you have to understand that the world

is full of people who want nothing more than to relinquish responsibility for their own actions. Some of the original members are ordinary seekers, people looking for something to believe in, something to make sense of the world. But they usually don't last very long. They tend to be spiritual vagabonds, moving from place to place, group to group. One week it's Scientology, the next it's astrology. They tiptoe through the ologies, make side trips into Zen and Confucianism. They read Ouspensky and Blavatsky and Gurdjieff. But they seldom stay."

"And those who do?"

"They're the accidents waiting to happen. They tend to be weak-willed, only too willing to submerge themselves in some nebulous notion of the common purpose. They're ripe for the picking. Perfect victims of exploitation. And they generally become the true believers, the heart of the cult. They tend to surround the leader like the layers of an onion. He keeps them close because he knows he can control them. They buffer him from the more transient membership, and they insulate him from the outside world. Think about it. Jim Jones had his apologists. Even after the mass suicide at Jonestown, some of the few who survived tried to portray Jones as an innocent victim. Some of them said they wished they had died with the others."

"Is that the way they all end?" Desmond asked.

Griffith smiled. "No. Sometimes the apocalyptic impulse gets short-circuited. The leaders tend to be older than the followers. If they're paranoid, it can end like Jonestown. But if the leader dies before the curve flattens out, the group dissolves. Some followers try for a while to keep it going, but without that charismatic center, their efforts are rather short-lived. You have to understand that cults are a lot like modern American corporations."

"How so?"

Griffith laughed. "Obviously you've never worked in one, or you wouldn't have to ask that question. But it's quite simple, and the parallel is extremely striking. Many times, a strong leader builds a corporation from scratch, often slowly, swallowing up smaller companies on the edge of extinction. He melds them into a larger and increasingly aggressive entity. At a certain point, he can no longer realistically pretend to manage the ongoing affairs of the conglomerate, but he refuses to surrender his absolute authority. Generally what he does then is to surround himself with nonentities, sycophants who treat his every word as holy writ, divine revelation. They have power, but it is only a reflection of his. They are there, maybe as a multipersoned advisory board, maybe as some sort of ruling body under the CEO. But they are there precisely because they can go no higher, they are not capable. That is why the leader has chosen them. He cannot tolerate a threat to his own authority, so he puts puppets in place. When he dies or is otherwise incapacitated, they are quickly eliminated because they are not able to defend themselves or think for themselves. All their thinking was done for them. The only originality that was acceptable was that of the central authority, and with that removed, as Yeats says, 'the center cannot hold.'"

"Funny you should mention Yeats," Desmond said. "The reason I'm here concerns, at least indirectly, another Yeats—Colin."

Griffith smiled knowingly. "We'll get to him and the Swami Rajah shortly. I just want to finish describing the archetypal curve. In cults, as opposed to corporations, where there are at least some protections, the cult leader has absolute authority. He tends to be paranoid by nature, and as his power increases he sees more and more threats to it. He begins to be abusive, and surrounded by a flock that is only too willing to cater to his every whim, he begins to abuse his authority. Most often, it starts with money, with members being asked to liquefy their assets and donate them to the 'church'—and I use that in quotations, because most often these are churches in name only."

"That's why so many rich kids end up getting into trouble, isn't it," Desmond suggested. "They must be sought out precisely because they can be induced to surrender some of the family wealth."

"That's one of the primary reasons, yes. It's also why so many of these groups use the veneer of religion, to take advantage of the tax-exempt status of churches in this country. For that matter, it may be one reason why America seems to have so many more of these groups than any other country on the planet. But soon it is not money, but sex that matters most. The leader insists on sexual property rights over the membership. Refusal is met with ostracism or the threat of expulsion. The members are usually too weak-willed to resist. They capitulate because they don't know how not to. That's what happened, in all likelihood, with David Koresh. The stories seem to suggest that he was having sexual relations with most of the younger women, sometimes girls little more than children. According to some accounts I read, he even forbade wives to sleep with their husbands, asserting his right even over the marital relationship."

"I still don't see why people put up with it."

"You know the expression *in for a penny, in for a pound,* Mr. Desmond?"

Desmond nodded.

"Well," Griffith went on, "that's usually what happens here. Once they are hooked, the members feel like they have to go as far as the leader wants them to go. They are afraid to say no, afraid to leave because they will seem like fools to those on the outside, and of course, the cult hierarchy has done its best to alienate them from any possible assistance from family and friends. Then, increasingly, there is the threat of violence to keep them under control. Some groups, although not all, have even been implicated in the murder of defectors. Like any totalitarian system, the cult cannot tolerate independence. If one person is allowed to leave without punishment, then all have that right. Such a notion is antithetical to the very idea of the cult. Power is absolute, membership is irrevocable or, at best, terminable only at incalculable cost. Which brings me to Rajah Primasanha."

"You're not telling me that he is another Jim Jones, are you?"

"Not yet, he isn't. But he does have the potential.

He is very far along on the typical pattern of development. What I have described is not, as I indicated before, an immutable law, but it is a highly reliable predictor of behavior. Primasanha has been suffering some defections. The stories that are circulating are not unlike those we heard about Jones and Koresh and many other, similar groups at a similar, late phase of their development. I don't know whether there is any truth to the rumors or not, although I suspect there is. But I would be willing to make a sizable bet that if there has not yet been violence, there soon will be."

"How can somebody as obviously intelligent as Colin Yeats get himself into a situation like that? I mean, I understand that he no longer follows Primasanha, but still . . ."

"You'd have to ask him that question. More often than not, cult leaders are on the lookout for celebrities. It gives them cachet. They tend to be more flexible in dealing with someone like Colin Yeats, at least until they have the hook secured. When that happens, of course, all bets are off."

"Have you had any dealings with Primasanha?"

Griffith shook his head. "I interviewed him twice, four or five years ago. But none of my clients has been a member of his cult."

"Can you deprogram anybody at all?"

"I don't know. So far, I've been successful most of the time, but not one hundred percent. I don't know whether that is because the deprogramming techniques are imperfect, or if some forms of indoctrination are more effective than others. And it just may be that these groups have some slight differences, like viral mutants, so that adjustments might be necessary, some sort of fine-tuning. Or it could be that abusive cult leaders, like other sorts of social miscreants, stay one step ahead of the sheriff. It may be that as our deprogramming gets more sophisticated they adjust their own techniques to keep pace."

"Would you be willing to help me with Colin Yeats, if it proves to be necessary?"

"I'm not sure what I can do. He is an adult. All of my work has been with minors, conducted with the explicit authorization of their parents. And even in such cases, the courts are making it more and more difficult. It is a First Amendment question, in part. And other primary concerns of the Bill of Rights come into play as well. And I can see the point. If someone can authorize me to deprogram a follower of Jim Jones, then why can't someone else give me the same charge vis-à-vis a follower of Buddha or Jesus Christ? And since so many of the cults have a veneer of Christian fundamentalism, they have a rather forceful array of allies concerned about their own security. The difference between Jesus and Jim Jones is negligible, according to some people. And they may not be far wrong, as far as that goes."

"Would you at least be willing to talk to him, if I can arrange it?"

"Of course. But I think you'll find there's no need. From what I understand, Mr. Yeats is free of the cult, has been for a while."

"I have reason to suspect he may not be as free as he thought. As I told you on the telephone, I'm going to Holy Sanctuary in Colorado, tomorrow. I don't know whether Yeats is there, but—"

"If he is, you will have a difficult time getting him away, perhaps even if he wants to leave."

"Why?"

Instead of answering, Griffith picked up a pen and jotted something on a sheet of notepaper. He tore the sheet off the pad, folded it, and leaned across the desk to hand it to Desmond.

Desmond unfolded the paper to find two phone numbers. "What's this?"

"These are the telephone numbers of two people who have more direct and more recent experience of Master Primasanha and his Holy Sanctuary. You might want to talk to them before you go to Colorado."

"Will they talk to me?"

"If you tell them I gave you the number, they will."

– SIXTEEN– – –

AS HE LEANED BACK IN THE PLANE AND CLOSED HIS eyes, Desmond felt uneasy. Timmy Corman had called as he'd been on the way out to the car, and Corman's words kept echoing. "It's weird, Paul. Nobody knows where the fuck he is. It's like he's flat gone, like aliens took him away. If I didn't know better, I'd think maybe he was dead."

"What about Colleen, has she heard from him?" Desmond asked.

And Corman had said no. No one had heard from Yeats—not Peter Chandler's office, not Warren Resnick, nobody. Desmond called Colleen, told her to leave a message on his machine if she heard from

Colin, but she didn't sound hopeful. And it was evident that she was getting worried now. Desmond felt more than a little responsible for that. All she wanted to do was live her own life, but the world wasn't willing to cooperate. He'd promised to call her as soon as he got back to town, but now he was wondering if maybe the best thing he could do for her was to leave her alone.

The flight to Denver left him plenty of time to think, but all thinking did was make him dizzy. Once on the ground again, he expected to feel better, but it didn't happen. Even the hectic scurrying to the baggage carousel and the car-rental counter couldn't get his mind off Colin Yeats.

And the more he thought about him, the more suspicious it seemed that Yeats had chosen to disappear. Why now, of all times? Desmond kept asking himself the same question, over and over again, from a dozen different angles. But no answer seemed to make sense.

As he pulled out of the Hertz garage it was beginning to snow. The mountains all around Denver were already blanketed, and he should have expected it. After all, it was nearly December and those were not the Shawangunks, they were the Rockies. They were serious mountains. He'd opted for a Cherokee, and had it in four-wheel drive, so the thickening slop on the roads was no problem.

As he left the clutter of the Mile-High City behind, heading out I-6 toward Idaho Springs, he lit a cigarette. He'd been trying to quit off and on for years, but no matter how hard he tried, at the first sign of stress, he reached for the Marlboros. And there was never a better time to abandon his current attempt to renounce the nasty habit. As the car filled with smoke he listened to the hypnotic clatter of the wipers. The snow was heavy now, covering the windshield between strokes, and he flicked on the Cherokee's headlights. In the twin beams, he could see the heavy flakes swirling like befuddled moths, then whipping along the fenders as the slipstream sucked them in.

He was looking for the junction with Route 119, where he would head north. Ordinarily it was a half-hour away, but in this weather, his journey was going to take twice as long. He crossed his fingers and hoped the roads weren't closed altogether. He kept thinking about plane crashes in the mountains, the Donner party, Italian villages swept away by avalanches, and wondered why anyone would want to spend entire winters at the mercy of the snow.

He had a road map open beside him. The recruiter had given him precise directions, but he wasn't comfortable without a more concrete reference. The road signs seemed to leap out at him as the sky darkened. Now he was surrounded by swirling white so thick he wondered if he was crazy to try to keep on going.

To begin with, he wasn't sure that either Colin Yeats or the missing tapes were at Holy Sanctuary. But he was coming to believe that to find the tapes he needed to find the man. That the man did not want to *be* found was doing little for Desmond's humor. Doing still less was the information he had gotten from Griffith's two sources. They had given him, as the man who identified himself only as "Gordon" called it, with more than a little tongue in cheek, "chapter and verse." It wasn't a pretty picture, and according to Gordon, it was getting worse by the week. Visions of Jonestown danced in Desmond's head, as if in time to the beating of the Cherokee's wipers.

The more he thought about it, the more uncertain he was about whether he should continue. But finally, the green-and-white interstate sign for Route 119 loomed up overhead and he slowed to make sure he didn't misread it. To be sure, he glanced at the rearview mirror to make certain there was no one behind him, then at the map. As he swung into the lane for the off-ramp, he realized that 119 was not going to be nearly as easy going as I-6 had been. The road ahead was deserted, not a single pair of head-lights visible. And in the mirror, all he could see was a white so thick it looked like whipped cream. When he braked, the snow took on a ruby cast, and he fumbled with a switch for the rear wipers, breathing eas-ier when he spotted headlights in the gray distance through the semicircle of snowless glass.

This was his turnoff, and he slowed again, letting the Cherokee's momentum carry him through the turn and into the ramp. He watched the rearview, hoping the car behind him would make the same turn, but when it kept on straight ahead, he shrugged and gave the Cherokee a little gas. It was almost five o'clock in the afternoon, and the pale gray sky was darkening, not so much turning black—the cloud cover was too heavy for that—as thickening into a charcoal gravy.

According to the map, he still had twenty miles or so before reaching Pinecliffe. The road ahead was ridged on either side, testimony to the passage of a plow, but the snow was accumulating so quickly now that even those ridges were smooth, pristine, and softly rounded. He kept running over in his mind everything Griffith had told him about cults in general, and about Primasanha in particular, factoring in Gordon's information to add a little spice.

When Griffith had hooked him up with a couple of refugees from Primasanha's cult, Desmond hadn't expected much. He figured they'd be reluctant to tell him very much at all, and at first they had been. They seemed not to trust him, as if they suspected he might be an emissary from the guru himself, testing them to see whether they knew how to keep their mouths shut. But once they realized they had nothing to fear from Desmond, they told him more than enough to let him know he was heading into a very volatile situation.

He groped in his pocket for the spare set of keys for the Cherokee. And he ran over a mental checklist of everything he had to do when he arrived. Griffith had advised him against going, but Desmond was running out of time, and he couldn't shake the feeling that somehow Primasanha held the key to the puzzle. The apparent links between Yeats and the cult leader were few, and subject to any number of interpretations, but Desmond didn't believe in coincidences, and they were too many to be ignored. Yeats and Primasanha seemed inextricably connected, like the two men at the bottom of a missile silo, each with his own key, neither one of whom can launch the missile without the other. So, Desmond figured, he might need them both.

Up ahead, he saw the winking orange lights of a huge truck stopped at a side road. He slowed, let the truck pull out, and was relieved when he saw the gigantic plow on the truck's front end. The truck turned in the same direction he was headed, and Desmond fell in behind it, watching the road, thinking, and trying to avoid being hypnotized by the blinking of the orange lights.

When Desmond reached the next, and thankfully last, turnoff to Primasanha's compound, the truck continued on, and the going got rough again. A single set of tire tracks broke the pristine snow, already seven or eight inches deep. The tracks went right down the center of the road, so he couldn't tell whether the vehicle that had left them was headed up toward the Holy Sanctuary compound or away from it. But for the moment it didn't much matter. He steered the Cherokee into the ruts and let them ease his passage a little.

He was moving slowly now, no more than ten or fifteen miles an hour. He saw the green sign he had been told to look for, the gold lettering almost obliterated by snow. Stopping the Cherokee, he got out, walked to the sign, and brushed off the snow. In the glare of the headlights, the lettering looked cheap, the gold paint already beginning to craze, but at last he was there. The sign read TEMPLE OF THE HOLY SANCTUARY, the name by which Primasanha identified all of his enclaves around the country.

Before getting back into the Cherokee, Desmond slipped the spare set of keys into a magnetized box and secured it under the body of the Cherokee, clearing snow from it first to make certain the magnet would hold under the constant battering of clumps of snow tossed off by the rough-treaded tires. He had already secured an automatic pistol and two clips in a canvas bag, wiring it to the undercarriage. He had another weapon, one he hoped to smuggle into the compound, but Gordon had warned him that he would be asked to leave his possessions in a storage room on entering, except for some toilet articles and underclothing, so he wasn't sure he'd be able to get the gun through. He was hoping that he wouldn't need it in any event, but having it would be a definite plus.

As he headed up the winding road, steep even for the Cherokee in the driving snow, he noticed that the tire tracks he'd been following went right on up the hill ahead of him. But he still couldn't tell whether they were coming or going.

The snow was too heavy for him to see much beyond the tall pines that lined the approach on either side. He knew there was a gate somewhere ahead and, nearly a quarter mile beyond it, the main building and its stylized array of outbuildings, which he'd seen in an aerial photograph *Time* had used to illustrate a cover story on Primasanha. In typical *Time* fashion, the story had been titled "Gurus or Goons?" He also had a rough map Gordon had supplied, with the warning that he had not been privy to all of the temple's secrets.

Primasanha was only one of a half dozen of the new breed of cult leaders, specializing in rehashed Eastern mysticism leavened with PR savvy, financial acumen, and a hint of militarism. But Primasanha was accorded the most column inches, partly because he was apparently the wealthiest, and partly because he seemed to be more explosive than the others. Lately, *Time* never a missed a chance to spice up its covers and feature stories with a touch of tabloid sensationalism.

Griffith had said that the volatility *Time* had commented on was attributable to the fact that Primasanha was farthest along on the growth curve. Whatever the reason, Desmond had determined that he was not entering the compound unarmed, if it could be helped.

He saw a light then, dim but definite, momentarily obscured by the snow, then reappearing. He clicked the headlights on high, saw the heavy iron gate across the road, and then the guardhouse, where the light was located, beyond it. He rolled to a halt a few yards from the gate and climbed out. He saw shadows moving in the guardhouse, then a door swung open and a man in a heavy parka stepped out, walked along a footpath to a narrow gate for pedestrian use only, and opened it.

He had a holster on his hip, and even in the short walk, snow had accumulated on the leather flap, which Desmond noticed was unbuttoned. The guard shone a flashlight into Desmond's face for a moment through the open window. "You lost, partner?" he asked.

"I don't think so. This is Holy Sanctuary, isn't it?"

"That's right. You expected, or just curious?" The guard's tone had softened, but not much.

"Expected." Desmond saw a second man standing in the open doorway of the guardhouse. "The name's Desmond, Paul Desmond," he added.

The guard turned to his companion. "Lou, check the list. See if there's a Desmond on it."

"I got a late start, and the snow wasn't any help," Desmond explained. "I was supposed to be here an hour and a half ago."

The second guard interrupted him with a shout. "Yeah, we got a Desmond on the list. First name Paul. That him?"

"Maybe." The guard looked at Desmond. "May I see some identification?"

Desmond reached into his pocket for his wallet, noticing the man's sudden tension, the way his hand drifted toward the holster on his hip. Whoever this man was, he was no ordinary religious zealot, that much was certain. The reflexes were too pure, and too subtle, for that.

Handing the wallet through the window, Desmond watched as the guard compared his license ID photo to the original, narrowing his eyes and using the flashlight again, just to be sure, then handed the wallet back. "All right, thank you." Turning to the other guard, he shouted. "It's him. Open up."

The man in the doorway disappeared, and the whine of servos announced the opening of the gate. The guard said, "Follow me up to the parking lot. There, we'll switch your bags to the Jeep and you'll give me the keys. We keep them at the blockhouse."

"Why's that?"

"Security."

Desmond nodded that he understood. The guard trudged through the open gateway, and Desmond waited for him to get a few yards ahead before putting the Cherokee in gear and whining through in first, the snow crunching under the tires. The gate started to close almost immediately, and Desmond pulled alongside the guard. "Hop in," he said. "No point in walking."

"It ain't far," the guard said, in declining the offered ride. Trees pressed in on both sides, thick spruces, bending under the snow, making an impenetrable blue-green-and-white wall. With the thick clouds overhead, it was like driving through a tunnel. The trees broke on the left suddenly at the crest of a small hill, and Desmond saw a large, flat area, probably paved, in which more than three dozen vehicles of all kinds were parked. A white Jeep, with the logo of Holy Sanctuary on its doors, sat at the front, and Desmond pulled into an empty space in the nearest row of cars, grabbed his suitcase, and jumped out.

The guard was standing there, palm out, waiting for the keys, which he jingled once before dropping them into his pocket. Nodding to the Jeep, he said, "It's open."

Desmond opened the vehicle's door, tossed his bag in the back, and climbed in. The guard slid in behind the wheel, giving the impression of a man putting on an old suit, so snug was the fit. He started the Jeep, threw it in gear, and they lurched out of the lot and back into the evergreen tunnel, still heading uphill.

"The main house is about a quarter mile from here, too far to walk in the snow with your bag," he said.

The road leveled out eventually, and Desmond had the sensation that he had rolled onto the very top of the world. He knew from the photo that the walled compound was on the crest of a mountain, and the terrain fell away on all sides.

"Some place!" Desmond said as the wall came into view. The guard ignored the comment, reached up to the visor, and pressed a button, opening a heavy iron gate dead ahead. He drove through, reaching up again to press the button, and Desmond turned to see the gate closing. He was starting again to wonder whether he had made a mistake, decided that he hadn't, but that he sure as hell couldn't afford to make one now.

Not here.

— SEVENTEEN — — —

DESMOND FELT STRANGE IN THE ROBES. THE DARK brown cloth, rough as a sack, held at the waist by the thick rope, made him aware of how vulnerable he was, and it was a feeling he didn't like. The first general meeting was scheduled in fifteen minutes, and he wanted to make sure that the gun was where it was supposed to be. He opened his travel kit, pulled out the can of shaving cream, and twisted the bottom. It came open reluctantly, as it was supposed to do, and he had to shake the can to get the cylinder of Styrofoam to come free.

The plug of plastic foam came apart in halves and inside was a .25-caliber automatic, one clip in place, the spare tucked into another niche in the foam. Just seeing the weapon made him feel a little more secure. Reassembling the canister, a carryover from the old Company days, he tucked it back into the travel kit. In case anyone tried it, it would ooze shaving cream, just like it was supposed to, but only enough for three or four shaves.

He turned off the light and headed out into the hallway. He left the door open, because there was no point in closing it. It didn't lock. None of the cell doors did. Each had a small bathroom, the only nod toward modernity, while the main chamber was furnished with a rude cot and a single chair, designed with no concern whatever for comfort.

Already, the hallway was filled with people, all dressed in the same austere garments. Their sandals scraped on the tile floor and there was something almost monastic about the silence, as if people were forbidden to speak rather than simply stunned into silence.

No one seemed interested in looking at anyone else, and Desmond felt like some sort of misfit as he examined the new recruits shuffling along in single file. He wondered whether any of them had come as couples, and guessed that some must have, because the numbers of men and women were almost equal, although it looked as if there were three or four more women.

At the end of the hall, a huge man in a saffron robe, one that looked far less monklike than Desmond's own, stood with folded arms, scrutinizing the recruits as they turned the corner and headed toward the main hall. Alcoves on either side of the hall held windows, and Desmond glanced through the first, seeing the snow still coming thick and heavy, swirling in the glow of security floods. It made him cold just to look at it.

The main hall was huge. Its high ceilings were beamed, its walls stuccoed. It looked vaguely Nordic, as if designed by some sort of refined Viking, and he wondered whether Grendel was going to burst in and tear a few of the recruits into bite-size morsels.

So far, he hadn't seen the man himself, and Primasanha seemed more like a rumor than a reality, haunting the place like the ghost of some dead king. More saffroned minions directed the recruits to three rows of rude wooden benches arranged across the hall directly in front of the massive fireplace that took up the entire wall. The hearth was broad, and raised a good eighteen inches above the floor. Desmond suspected that it served a dual purpose, possibly as a podium. He sat on the rear bench, next to an attractive blonde in her early twenties, who looked as if she'd rather be anyplace on earth but this room at this time.

Desmond leaned toward her, but before he could open his mouth, one of the yellow-robed sentries clapped a pair of hands like slabs of steak, and the report echoed off the walls while he shook an admonishing finger. "Quiet!" he said, his voice like a pistol shot in the huge space.

Suddenly the sound of a sitar welled up, and Desmond found himself looking for the speakers, which he hadn't noticed on the way in. He still hadn't spotted them when a door opened at the rear of the hall, banging against the rear wall like a thunderclap.

Four men, looking for all the world like the front line of the Pittsburgh Steelers on a Zen retreat, walked through, side by side, their beef filling the enormous doorway from jamb to jamb. The saffron phalanx moved with the precision of a drill team, splitting down the middle and folding into wings of two, their backs turned now to the doorway. A much smaller man seemed to materialize out of the darkness, and he strode through with a certain majestic grace as the phalanx closed behind him, then he strolled toward the front of the hall, his footmen right behind him, their eyes on the recruits in the benches as if they expected them to mutiny at any moment.

It was the guru, Desmond was sure of that. He'd seen enough photos to leave no doubt. So that's Rajah Primasanha, né Roy Mitchell, he thought, and tried hard to keep his mouth from twisting into a derisive smile. But he had to watch himself. The last thing he needed to do was to attract attention to himself, get his ass booted out before he learned anything.

He bit the inside of his cheeks to keep control and watched Primasanha climb two steps to the gigantic hearth, then turn to look at his audience. He raised his hands high and wide, as if in supplication. "Welcome!" he said. The voice was deeper, more resonant than Desmond would have thought. It was the voice of a much larger man.

"I suppose you're wondering why I've called you here," Primasanha said. Then he smiled broadly. "A joke, of course. But that, I promise, is the last one you will hear for the next three days. We are not here for amusement. We are not here for fun and games. We are not here to schmooze and party. We are here for a very serious purpose, one you know as well as I do. We are here to pursue enlightenment!" He clapped his hands together, and the fireplace seemed to erupt in a cascade of red and blue sparks. Most of the audience hissed in surprise, the sound rippling through the recruits in waves.

Nice trick, Desmond thought, trying to identify the chemicals just dumped into the flames, something with strontium, for sure, and maybe cobalt for the blue. Kind of medicine-showy, but it seemed to work.

Primasanha brought his hands down and turned his back, kneeling before the fireplace as the sound of the sitar swelled to fill the room. The guru bowed his head gracefully, until his forehead brushed the stone. For the first time, Desmond could see the gargantuan bronze Buddha nestled in the back of the fireplace, curiously free of soot and discoloration, gleaming in the firelight.

Once more, the fireplace erupted, this time in brilliant white sparks Desmond took to be a magnesium compound, or maybe phosphorus. The sitar died away, and Primasanha got to his feet without using his hands and once more turned to face his novices.

"Enlightenment is not easy. It is not a joke. It is not a trick. It is, most of all, not for everyone. You have to be ready, you have to be open to it, you have to be purified, all the poison of your lives burned away. You are all full of poison. Your past lives have soiled you, steeped you in corruption, and before we can show you the light, we have to cauterize the dark. Over the next few days you will hear a lot of things from me, and from my disciples, that will sound strange to you, perhaps contradictory, perhaps even offensive. Don't worry and don't resist. Let the truth percolate through you, let it leach away the poison, and leave behind the purity you were born with, the purity you need to receive the light."

He clapped his hands, and the sitar returned. With practiced ease, he stepped down to floor level and glided back the way he'd come. The muscular footmen closed the door and all five were gone.

Desmond looked at the blond woman next to him. She stared at her lap, her hands trembling where they lay on her thighs. Desmond leaned over to her again. "Are you all right?" he asked.

She nodded, chewing on her lip, but said nothing. He was about to slide closer when one of the berobed guards appeared at the end of the bench, rested a hand on her back, and glared at Desmond. Another guard ascended to the hearth to announce that they should all return to their rooms for one hour. "That time is yours, and it is the last free time you will have for the next seventy-two hours."

The blond woman got to her feet, and Desmond tried to follow her, but the guard blocked his way, and she disappeared into the hall before Desmond could get out of the bench. The guard grabbed him by the shoulder, leaned close, and hissed, "Don't be a troublemaker. I'm watching you."

"She seemed upset. I wanted to see if there was anything wrong."

"She's not upset."

"But—"

"She's not upset," the guard reiterated, this time with an edge. "Go to your room."

Timmy Corman stood in the doorway. The band was in the middle of a number, and he had enough respect for the music to wait until it was finished before moving to his table. The Snake Pit was not his favorite club, but it was a good place to plug into what was happening, because so many people moved through it on a given night that he was bound to run into half a dozen people he knew.

The band was a new group, but there was no mistaking their influences, because snatches of Dylan and Yeats peppered the lyrics. The guitarist wasn't bad, but he was no Stevie Ray or Colin Yeats, either, just a solid player with decent chops and some imagination. If the band was just beginning to develop, they might have a future, but too often, by the time a band made the stage at the Snake Pit, they were as good as they were ever going to get.

When the song was almost finished, he was finally able to recognize it as an updating of "Subterranean Homesick Blues." The original was one of the Dylan pieces Timmy had once argued in print to be the unacknowledged wellspring of rap's staccato lyrical approach.

When the guitarist closed with a sharp solo that sounded more than a little like Mark Knopfler, replete with quotes from "Sultans of Swing" and

"Once Upon a Time in the West," Timmy threaded his way through the chairs and tables until he found an open one in a corner, just off the bandstand.

Anna, the Swedish waitress, whose husband was a folksinger of some talent and not much success, waved a menu at him, but he waved it off. She came over anyway, to say hello, and he decided to order one of the club's tall drinks full of sherbet. As Anna moved off he hollered after her, "Make it green, Annie."

He pulled out a pad and opened it to the first blank page, then uncapped his Rolling Writer and dated the top of the page. A shadow fell across the table and he looked up to see Pete Costello, a bass player he knew, one who had played on an early Colin Yeats tour.

"Pete, how's it hangin', buddy?"

Costello laughed. "As usual. Stepped on it this morning, as a matter of fact. Still hurts." He pulled up a chair and sat down. He didn't ask, because he knew he didn't have to. "Where you been keepin' yourself, Ratso?"

Corman shrugged. "Here and there."

"Working on a book, are you?"

Corman grinned. "Thinkin' about it is as close as I get these days, Pete."

"At least you still think about it."

"Seen Colin lately?"

Costello shook his head. "Nope. Not in six, eight months. I played on a couple of songs on the last album. But I haven't heard from him since."

Corman nodded. "Yeah, that reggae-flavored thing was you, wasn't it?"

Costello grinned. "Yup. Nice line. Right out of Robbie Shakespeare's trick bag. Colin was happy with it, so . . ."

"What's he up to these days?"

"Search me. I been hearing rumors, but that's about all."

"There are more rumors about Colin Yeats than there are about Lee Harvey Oswald, Petey, you know that."

"This wasn't the usual stuff, though. I don't know if there's anything to any of it, but with Colin, you never do know."

"What sort of rumors?"

"That he wants to drop Chandler, you know. 'Course, I been telling him that for fifteen years. Chandler's nothing but a bloodsucker. And he ain't done shit for Colin, either. What I hear, Chandler's in trouble. He's been bouncing checks all over town. Colin ought to get an audit, you ask me."

"Chandler is a dirtbag, everybody knows that. But Colin's about as loyal as they come. Too loyal, probably. But I don't think he'll ever change."

"Probably not. But I also hear that that asshole pseudoguru is looking for him. Supposed to be pissed that Colin bailed out on him."

"That was years ago."

Costello laughed. "Yeah, but them spiritual types got long memories, Ratso. You know that. Hell, you still duck around the corner when you see a priest coming."

"That was different. Besides, I was drunk, and the woman wasn't really a nun."

"Maybe not, but she was talkin' to God like she knew him pretty well. I'm surprised at you, Ratso. In a church . . . ?"

"It seemed like a good idea at the time."

The drink arrived, and Anna set it down, nodded to Pete, and said, "One Green Monster, just like you ordered. So, Mr. Corman. Where have you been keeping yourself?"

"Around. You know how it is."

Costello got up. "Listen, Ratso, I'll be seeing you, all right?"

"Take care, Pete. Give me a call, you hear anything about Colin."

When Costello was gone, Anna leaned across the table. "Were you talking about Colin Yeats?"

"Yeah, why?"

"Some men were in here last week looking for him. I didn't much like the look of them."

"What men?"

Anna shrugged. "I don't know who they were. They didn't say and I didn't want to ask. I didn't want anything to do with them. They looked like gangsters look, you know? In the movies? What do you call it . . . *The Godfather*. One of them looked like the one who slept with the fishes. Luca something."

"Luca Brazzi . . . Jesus. You sure, Annie?"

Corman sipped the Green Monster through a pair of straws, watching her nod, and not wanting to think about what it might mean. But he knew he had to get ahold of Desmond.

- EIGHTEEN- - -

DESMOND LAY IN HIS ROOM, STARING AT THE CEILING.
It was 1:00 A.M., and so far he felt as if he had been
wasting his time. His temper was near the boiling
point, and once it blew, there would be nothing at all
to be gained by staying. And the thought that he was
living something akin to the rule of Saint Benedict
did not amuse him in the least.

Primasanha had made one more appearance, about
as brief as the first, and all he'd done was babble
about enlightenment, no more convincingly than the
first time. Most of the training was being done by
"disciples" who seemed to have spent some time as
drill instructors in the marine corps, judging by the

ease with which they dispensed insult and abuse. So far, there had been no physical punishment, but the threat of it seemed to hang in the air like a bad smell.

It seemed impossible to imagine Colin Yeats in such an environment. If the lyrics, and the testimony of everyone who knew him, were any indication, then Yeats had a very low threshold of tolerance for bullshit, and none at all for pointless regimentation. And that seemed to be the stock-in-trade of Rajah Primasanha, and the only instructional technique employed at the Temple of the Holy Sanctuary. There was a jumbled helping of neo-Zen laced with Hinduism served up at every training session, but as theology, it was about as persuasive as the Warren Commission Report.

Although there had not been much time for private conversation, Desmond had taken every opportunity to make contact with other trainees, on the off chance that one of them might have seen Colin Yeats or heard something useful. The instructors were not communicative at all, and the trainees had either been cowed into submission or were taking the gobbledygook seriously, and thus were ill disposed to breaching the rules.

Only the blond woman Desmond had seen at the first session seemed resistant to the training, and Desmond hadn't seen her again. That troubled him, because she had seemed upset, and he was beginning to suspect that she might be in trouble. But he couldn't afford to raise the issue with the trainers, because it might get her in still deeper trouble. All Desmond could do was keep a weather eye out for her.

Getting up off the cot, he went to the tiny bathroom and retrieved the small automatic. There were no pockets in his robe, and he didn't want to trust the weapon to the knotted sash, so he'd have to carry it in his hand. It was small, but not so small that he could conceal it completely. He also retrieved Gordon's map and a small set of picklocks from his gear, concealed in the lining of the travel kit.

It was time to have a look around. At the door, he listened for a few moments, but the hallway seemed deserted. He opened the door as quietly as he could, listened again for several seconds, and when he was certain there was no one about, he slipped out into the dim light. He had no idea where to start, but knew that all the buildings in the compound were connected by underground tunnels, whether as a concession to the brutal winters of the Rockies or as a further expression of the guru's penchant for secrecy, he didn't know.

When he reached the corridor leading to the main hall, he stopped again, heard nothing, and pushed on. This might be easier than he'd feared. It just could be that Primasanha and his minions were so cocksure of their influence over the trainees that they worried less about internal security than about guarding their perimeter. At least he could hope so.

The main hall was gloomy, the rafters high overhead barely discernible in the murk, but at least Grendel hadn't shown. Yet. He found the doors through which Primasanha had entered, and pressed his ear against the cold wood. Behind him, embers crackled in the fireplace, but their soft pops were the only noise he could hear. He tried the latch, the handle gave, and he started to pull the heavy door toward him, pressing against it with one hand to keep it under control.

Dim light appeared in the gap between the doors, and he peered through the crack into another long hall, this one with floors of polished wood divided down the center by a long runner of dark green wool. He slipped through and pulled the door to after him. It was already obvious that this corridor did not branch off into another series of spartan cells. The doors were more ornate, more widely spaced, and the walls, instead of being plain beige, were papered with linen. Several paintings hung on each, the display running the length of the corridor.

So far, so good, he thought. He'd committed the hand-drawn map to memory, and the stairwell to the underground chambers of the compound was supposed to be at the last door on the left. He moved quickly now, because there was no place to hide. If anybody opened one of the doors, or entered the corridor from the far end, he'd be a dead duck.

He reached the door, tried the knob, and as he feared, found it locked. He dropped to one knee and started on the lock with the picks. He was more than a little rusty at lock picking, but this one was fairly simple, and in thirty seconds—not record time but not bad—he was able to turn the knob and pull the door open.

He stepped onto a landing, pulled the door closed, and reached for the light switch. It clicked on with a loud snap, and he turned the thumb latch to lock the door from inside. A random check would not give him away now. He started down the stairs, wishing he'd worn sneakers instead of his sandals, but that would have attracted too much attention if he were seen. As long as he was wearing prescribed clothing, he might be able to talk his way out of trouble if anyone stumbled on him.

At the bottom of the stairs, he found a long corridor that looked more like a bunker than anything else. He started along it, stopped at the first of several doors, all on the left, and opened it. Inside, he found a light switch, and when it went on, he realized that it was a pantry. Steel shelving lined with large boxes of dried foods filled the room from floor to ceiling. But he had a bit of luck, too, because a long flashlight, the kind that took four batteries, was lying on a shelf near the door. It was a hell of a lot better than the tiny Black Max he'd brought with him. He tried it, found that it worked, and left it on. A quick survey of the room showed him nothing but food. Leaving the room, he walked back to the foot of the stairs, where a two-way switch allowed him to turn off the corridor lighting. It would be better to rely on the flashlight, because anyone entering from above would turn on the lights and warn him.

The next room was a duplicate of the first. Sacks of beans and flour filled half the shelving, while large containers of condiments made up the rest of the inventory. If the Colin Yeats tapes were here, it was going to take forever to find them. The next room, and the one after that, were jammed with more foodstuffs. He gave them a cursory look, backed out, and closed the door, moving on to the next.

This one was locked. Crossing his fingers, he knelt again, picklocks in hand. The door came open easily, and he aimed the flashlight inside, trying not to get his hopes up. And once more, he was disappointed. This room was filled with racks of clothing, robes in every size and all three colors he'd seen. It was a kind of wardrobe. Why it was locked, he couldn't guess, and on a hunch, he moved inside, playing the light around in darting probes from one corner to another. But when he reached the back wall, all he found was a set of shelves jammed full of sandals.

Frustrated now, he followed the circle of light back into the corridor, pulled the door closed, and made sure it was locked. So far, he hadn't found a damned thing that suggested, or even remotely hinted, that Holy Sanctuary was anything other than its master wanted the world to believe it was—an indoctrination facility for just one more fringe religion.

Out in the corridor, he trained the light along the remaining length of the hall. There were just two more doors to be checked. He barely had the heart to continue the search, but told himself he had come this far and might as well finish the job. Like the last door, the next was locked. Once more, the picklocks were inserted, but this lock was tougher than the other. It took him nearly two minutes, and when he finally felt the last pin move aside, he held his breath as he reached for the knob and tugged.

The door swung open, and the sharp tang of oil flared into his nostrils. He aimed the light inside, and this time what he found was neither cuisine nor couture—it was armaments. Racks of automatic rifles, pistols, cases of ammunition, even some LAWS rockets and RPG launchers and shells. The gun oil swirled around him as he moved into the darkness, the light glinting off metal in every direction. Against the back wall, he found nearly two dozen suits of body armor, the latest in chemical and biological warfare protective gear, and a variety of other defensive paraphernalia. It looked as if the good swami were expecting some sort of war—or thinking about starting one.

A door in the rear right-hand corner was open, and he aimed the light through its frame. It looked as if the next chamber were simply an extension of the armory. He stepped in, shone the light around, and shook his head. Cases of ammunition for all the weapons he'd seen, and some he hadn't, were stacked nearly to the ceiling, the aisles between them just wide enough to let a man maneuver a crate from one of the stacks and lug it out.

He wondered if the police were aware of the munitions stockpile. Desmond had seen enough stories about wacky cults with a millenarian bent, white supremacist groups, neo-Nazi commando battalions, and a seemingly endless series of permutations of each to know that such ammo dumps and weapons caches were a lot more common than anyone wanted to believe. In some cases, they were known to the government, but there was no way of telling how many of them were not. In all his research on Primasanha, he had seen no hint that the Temple of the Holy

Sanctuary had a paramilitary inclination or apocalyptic bent. But there was no other way to explain the mountain of munitions towering over his head.

He was about to move back to the corridor when he spotted a metal hatch set in one corner of the concrete floor. He bent down, grabbed the handle, and pulled. The heavy hatch ground in its seat, but didn't open. It wasn't locked, it was just heavy, and he was at a bad angle. Dropping to his knees, he grabbed the handle a second time and lifted. This time the hatch swung back and thumped against the concrete wall.

A stab of the flashlight showed him a steel ladder descending into pitch blackness so deep the flashlight beam petered out before it reached the bottom. Desmond wondered whether or not to turn back. He had no idea where the tunnel led, because it hadn't been mentioned, and it wasn't on the map. But if he ignored it, he might be turning his back on the one thing he needed to know—the whereabouts of the stolen tapes. In for a penny, he thought, shrugged, and turned to lower his sandals into the yawning abyss. He held the flashlight in one hand and worked his way down carefully, the slick soles of the sandals finding only precarious purchase on the rounded metal rungs.

By the time he reached the bottom, the light no longer reached the ceiling of the room above him, and he could not see the metal seat of the hatch. He couldn't even tell whether it was open or closed, it was so far above him.

The floor was gritty beneath his feet, and he shone the light on the cement work, roughly finished with a single pass of the mason's float. The passage ahead of him was narrow, and not more than six and a half feet high. It smelled musty, and here and there as he moved along, trickles of water seeped down the walls and collected in pools on the floor. Lichen, pale as the sides of a battleship, grew in crevices in the walls, and the rasp of his sandals echoed from way in the distance, faint little hissing slaps that might have come from the moon.

Every fifty feet or so, Desmond clicked off the light and listened. All he could hear was the drip of the seepage. There was no glimmer of light, and for all he knew, he could walk all the way back to Denver without finding a door or seeing another soul. Fifteen minutes later he clicked the light off for what seemed like the fiftieth time, and this time he saw a small slash of light. It seemed to be waist-high, but he couldn't tell for certain, because the darkness skewed his perspective. He left the light off now and groped along the wall, keeping his eye on the glowing strip of illumination.

He still couldn't hear anything but his own feet and the now labored hiss of his breath. He was getting tense, and remembering the outlandish costume he wore didn't help to calm his nerves. The strip of light he was nearing went out suddenly, and he felt a wave of disappointment. But he was reluctant to turn on the flashlight too soon, in case someone opened a door ahead of him. When nothing happened after more than a minute, he clicked the flashlight on again. Faintly outlined at the end of the beam, a heavy metal door blocked his way.

He sprinted toward it, throwing caution to the winds. He hugged the cold slab of metal like a long-lost relative until his breathing slowed. He hadn't realized how claustrophobic the interminable passage had made him. He could hear his heart hammering in his chest and worried that it might be echoing beyond the bulkhead like a tom-tom.

When he regained his composure, he found the door's levered handle, clicked off the light, and worked the lever. The door swung open easily, on well-lubricated hinges, and heat swirled into the tunnel, making him aware of just how chilly the cement confines of the passage had been. He pulled the door closed, listened to be certain he was alone, and clicked on the flashlight once more.

Ahead, he saw another corridor, this one carpeted like those in the main hall. Apparently, he had gone from one building to another, but without a map to guide him, he now had no idea where in hell he was.

He moved down the passage, using the flashlight. He'd taken no more than five steps when he heard a voice, faintly familiar, but too distant for him to be sure. He tiptoed now, finding the wall with his hand and sliding the light off once more.

Another voice, deeper, sounding angry, muttered in the darkness. Then the first voice, this time clearer but still unrecognizable. The words, though, were intelligible. It was a woman, and she was repeating over and over, "I will not. I will not. I just won't. I will not."

Again the deeper mutter. And the woman answered, raising her voice in anger.

Then the baritone rumble, this time comprehensible. "You have no choice, Miss Alexander."

"Screw you," she snapped. "I will not, no matter what."

"Get her the fuck out of my sight," the baritone ordered.

Desmond froze, knowing that in a moment a door was going to open, and he didn't have the faintest idea which one or where. He started to backpedal until he bumped into the metal door and shoved it open with a hip, ducking through and starting to pull it closed just as the hallway flooded with light.

Desmond left the door open a crack and watched as the young blond woman was dragged into the hall by one of Primasanha's bodyguards. She struggled to break free, but the man was too big and too powerful for her. He twisted her arm into a hammerlock and shoved her ahead of him, moving away from the metal door, then disappearing around a corner.

Desmond realized that they were probably going back to her room, and he wanted to be back at the cells before they arrived. He shoved the door closed all the way, making sure the levered latch was set, clicked on the flashlight, and sprinted down the concrete passage, wishing his sandals were winged like Mercury's.

- NINETEEN- - -

DESMOND JUST MANAGED TO GET THROUGH THE
door to his cell when he heard a snarl of hushed
voices moving his way. He closed the door and flat-
tened himself against the wall. He wanted to be able
to hear and at the same time be ready to move, if it
seemed warranted. He was conscious of the pistol,
thought about cocking it, but decided against it. He
had seen too much violence in his lifetime to doubt
that those who were most prepared to employ it most
often did so. He didn't want to burst through the
door with a cocked pistol in his hand, because he still
hoped to learn more about Rajah Primasanha.

He no longer held out much hope that the tapes

183

were anywhere in the building, but his underground tour convinced him that in all likelihood only the guru himself and a handful of trusted lieutenants were aware of the compound's every nook and cranny. That meant if the tapes were here, Desmond would have to be lucky to find them without help. And help wasn't at all likely.

From what he had seen of the atmosphere of the Holy Sanctuary, he knew that if Colin Yeats were here, he would be here as a prisoner, and no other way. Like the tapes, then, he might as well not be here at all, for all the good it did Desmond and his quest.

That left getting a little insight into the presiding genius of the temple as the only reason to stay. Desmond was already wondering whether it was reason enough when he heard the sound of flesh on flesh. It was clearly a slap, probably to the face, but it could have been a pistol shot, so loud did it sound in the monastic quiet of the corridor outside his door.

A guttural snarl and the word "Bitch!" was followed by another slap. This time he heard a whimper in response, and with that, he had had enough. It wasn't his business why the woman they called Miss Alexander was here. But it was now inarguably clear that whether she had come of her own free will or not—and that was anything but certain—she hadn't come to be slapped around by a goon three times her size.

Desmond reached for the knob, the pistol in his right hand. As he started to open the door he heard the young woman's voice, curiously hushed, as if she were concerned about disturbing the silence. "Take your fucking hands off me!"

Another slap now, this one the loudest yet, as the door came open. Desmond moved into the hall in two steps. The guard had the young woman by one arm in a modified hammerlock. He was using the pressure on her shoulder socket to control her, and Desmond knew how painful the grip could be. When you factored in the relative size and strength of the captive and the captor, well, it didn't warrant consideration.

Desmond moved swiftly in behind the guard, jabbed the pistol into the small of his back, and hissed, "Let her go!"

"What the fuck . . . ?" The guard started to turn until Desmond rapped the pistol against his spine.

"Now!" Desmond snapped. The guard gave the blonde a shove and started to swing around, and Desmond closed his fist around the pistol and swung from the heels, catching the man on the side of the jaw. The added mass of the small pistol in Desmond's fist was just enough to coldcock the beefy guard, who sank to his knees, then slumped over onto his side.

The blonde lay sprawled on the floor, sobbing. Desmond went to her, knelt, and whispered, "It's all right, it's all right. Stay here and be quiet."

Then he grabbed the guard and tugged him out of the corridor and into his room, using his sash to tie the unconscious man's hands, then tearing a strip from the robe's sleeve and knotting it around the man's mouth.

Back in the corridor again, he found the blonde exactly where he had left her. She was still sobbing, but more softly now. So far, no one had opened a door to peer out into the hall, but Desmond was worried that this could change at any moment. He helped the young woman to her feet and whispered, "Where's your room?"

She chewed on her lip like a frightened child, and Desmond took her by both shoulders and shook her slightly. "Where's your room?" he repeated.

She gestured with her head, her lower lip now pinned by her teeth. Desmond started pulling her in the direction she indicated. When they reached the fourth door on the left, she reached for the knob. Desmond pushed the door open and shoved her in after it. Following her in, he pulled the door closed and whispered, "Listen, Miss Alexander, I—"

"How'd you know my name? I don't know who you are. How do you know who I am?"

"There's no time to explain. Get dressed and grab anything you want to take with you."

"Take with me, where?"

"Out of here."

The light clicked on suddenly, and she stood there with her hand on the wall switch, her mouth agape as if she had just heard the most astonishing thing imaginable. "You must be out of your mind," she said. "There's a blizzard out there. We wouldn't get a mile from here. Maybe they'd find us in the spring, if the wolves and the bears don't find us before then."

Desmond shook his head. "I have a car."

"But they have the keys." She smirked at him, proud

of herself, the way an impertinent student preens after catching the teacher in a mistake.

"There is another set at the car."

"But why should I go with you, even if you do have a car? I don't who or what you are." She was shaking now, her voice quavering as if she were on the verge of crumbling. All traces of impertinence had vanished. She was just a scared little girl now.

Desmond moved toward her, and she cringed. "I'm not going to hurt you, Miss Alexander. But we have to move quickly if we're going to make it. They will be rousing us for the next session in less than half an hour. I want to be at the car by then."

She shook her head. "No, I won't. I won't do it."

"That's what you were telling *them* not fifteen minutes ago. What was it that you wouldn't do?"

She looked at him with suspicion almost paranoid in its intensity, her eyes suddenly narrow slits.

"I overheard you talking," he explained.

"That was in another building. How did you get back here before we did? Why didn't I see you there?"

"It's a long story."

"If you want me to go with you, make it short, and make it convincing."

"There's a tunnel from the basement of this building to another building. I don't know which one, because I just followed the tunnel, and I'm not certain of its layout. While I was in the other building, I overheard them threatening you, and you were refusing to do something. I don't know what, because the conversation had already started by the time I got there. I heard one of them say to take you back to your room, so I hotfooted it back here. I wanted to be here before you and that goon arrived."

"Why? What difference does it make to you what happens to me?"

Desmond was out of patience. He had no obligation to the young woman, and decided to tell her so. "Look, I'm leaving in ten minutes. You can come with me if you want, or not. Whatever. I don't give a damn. But I want to know now."

She hesitated, again narrowing her eyes. She started to open her mouth, but Desmond had had it. He was already turning toward the door. As he put his hand on the knob the light clicked off and she whispered, "I'll be ready. Don't leave me here. Please don't leave me here. . . ."

Desmond reached out for her hand and patted it gently. "Don't worry, I won't. I'll be back as soon as I can." He pulled the door open a crack and, when he was sure the hall was deserted, slipped out, closing the door softly behind him. He rushed to his room and ripped off the bulky robe, then dropped to the edge of the bed to remove the sandals.

He dressed quickly, threw the rest of his belongings into the canvas overnight bag, and pulled on his parka, tucking the flashlight and pistol into his pocket before he slipped into the hall, this time leaving the door open behind him, and sprinted to Miss Alexander's room.

True to her word, she was ready, dressed in ski pants and jacket, her bag packed and waiting by the door. He wanted to leave the building at the point closest to the road leading back to the parking lot, but it took him a moment to get his bearings.

He assumed the building was wired with a security alarm, but that couldn't be helped. "Ready?" he asked.

She nodded. "I guess. But at least tell me who you are."

Desmond shook his head in annoyance. "My name is Paul Desmond. The rest will have to wait until we get the hell out of here."

Incongruously, she extended a hand, which he took without thinking. "Pleased to meet you, Mr. Desmond. I'm Samantha Alexander."

"Samantha," he blurted, not bothering to conceal his impatience. "Let's go."

He pulled the door to her room open, his bag thumping against the jamb as he moved into the hall. Samantha was right behind him, her bag slung over her shoulder by a leather strap. He started toward the main hall, but she grabbed him by the arm.

"We should go the other way," she whispered. "There's a service entrance with an interrupt on the alarm, if we can find it. It will take us outside the wall."

Desmond nodded. "I'll find it." He changed direction, reaching into his pocket for the pistol. This time he was going to have to shoot, because there was no turning back. They reached the far end of the hall and Samantha directed him to the right, through a wooden door and into a dark and narrow corridor.

He still had the big flashlight, and as the wooden door reclosed he clicked it on and stabbed it into the darkness. As far as the beam reached, he saw no door on either wall, and he could not see the end. As they started to jog he realized the floor had begun to slope downward, but he didn't want to waste his breath asking where the exit was. He'd find out soon enough.

Soon the beam picked out a metal door with a waist-high press bar across it. "That's the door," Samantha whispered. As soon as they reached it, Desmond traced its perimeter with the beam, searching for the alarm bypass.

"I know it's here, I just don't know where," Samantha said.

Desmond traced the edge of the frame with his fingertips, found a small slide panel, and pulled it loose. Beneath it, a black button was recessed in the metal-encased frame. "Gotcha!" he whispered. Then, turning to Samantha, he said, "We want to go straight for the parking lot. Do you know which direction to go from here?"

She nodded. "Yes."

"Ready?"

Again, she shook her head in the affirmative and swallowed with an audible gulp. Desmond leaned over to kiss her on the forehead. "We'll be fine, just stay right behind me, Samantha."

Before she could answer, he pushed the interrupt. The bypass would have a timer built in, probably no more than sixty seconds, just long enough to allow someone to go through the door and reclose it. He shoved the door open, but it wouldn't go all the way.

Desmond was too large to get through, and he

grabbed Samantha's bag. "There's snow blocking the door. Squeeze through and scrape it away so I can shove it open a little wider."

She slipped off her bag and into the crack with a confidence that surprised him. He could hear her scraping away at the snow and he leaned on the door until it suddenly popped open another six inches. Tossing the two bags through, he squirmed after them and slammed the door, breathing heavily.

So far, so good, he thought. They were in a cement stairwell partially canopied by an awning of metal slats, without which the stairwell would have been completely buried and the door would not have opened. They were now, Desmond realized, running on luck. It was good to have it, but luck always ran out.

They grabbed their bags and started up the steps, struggling in the snow that was deeper on every step. When they reached ground level, the wind slammed into them, and the swirling snow hissed against their clothing.

"The road to the parking lot is to the left, about a forty-five-degree angle."

"How far?"

"Fifty or sixty yards, I guess. Something like that. When we find the road, we go to the right. The parking lot is close to a quarter mile."

Desmond plunged up the last step and into the howling storm, turning to make sure Samantha was behind him. When he'd gone no more than forty or fifty feet, he turned to look back at the buildings. They were barely visible beyond the top of the wall.

The security lights, all but blotted out by the snow, were so pale they looked as if they were about to be extinguished altogether.

He sighted back along the holes their feet had left in the snow, making sure they were heading in a straight line, then plunged on. It seemed to take an eternity to find the road, but just when he was starting to doubt that Samantha had known what she was talking about, he stumbled over a curb buried in the snow.

He sprawled headlong, and broke his fall with both hands. Beneath his palms he could feel the imprint of tire treads under a couple of inches of new loose snow. This was it.

Samantha nearly tripped over him and stood aside as he got to his feet. "We're on the road," he said. "Now all we have to do is get past the guards. You stay right behind me, and if somebody spots us, you go on to the car. It's a black Cherokee. The keys are in a magnetic box under the left rear fender. Get the car started, and I'll catch up to you."

It sounded easy, anyway.

- TWENTY- - -

COLLEEN YEATS SAT FACING THE DOOR, HER HANDS in her lap. The lights were out, but she could still see the gleaming metal of the heavy weight pressing against her thighs. She never thought she'd see the day she was glad she owned a gun, but then she never thought she'd see the day when Richard Nixon would be an elder statesman. It just proved what Hamlet had told Horatio about the limits of philosophy.

It was snowing outside, and the street was preternaturally silent. It seemed to glow with an unearthly light that seeped through the drawn drapes. She heard a car, moving slowly, its tires crunching on the four inches of white fluff already covering the litter-filled asphalt of Sullivan Street. The car seemed to be looking for something, or at least that's what her frazzled nerves told her was happening, and she got to her feet, almost forgetting the heavy pistol in her lap and catching it just before it slipped to the floor.

At the drapes, she felt her hand shaking as with cold as she reached for the drapes and pulled them apart just enough to peer through the lace curtains beyond. With the film of white lace between her eye and the glass, it was difficult to see clearly, even the flood of reflected light, and she leaned closer, separating the gauzy lace with the tips of her fingers.

A cab sat in front of the house, its rear door just beginning to swing open. When the passenger slid toward the door, she couldn't see his face, because he was leaning over the front seat to pay the driver. When he finally turned, and his features were bathed in light from the street lamp, she almost shouted. It had never occurred to her that Timmy Corman would be so welcome a sight.

She watched as Corman straightened up, closed the door with a typical flourish, and turned to look up at the house. She stuck a hand through the drapes and waved. Corman saw the disembodied limb and waved back, then bounced up onto the curb and climbed the stairs. He didn't bother to ring the bell, and he smiled as the door swung open. Colleen stepped aside and fairly dragged him inside, slamming the door.

"It's kind of dark in here, Colleen," he said, his voice a mixture of amusement and confusion. "Is this some sort of surprise party?"

When the light went on, he saw the automatic in her white-knuckled fist and threw up his hands in mock surrender. "I'm not resisting arrest. I'm not resisting arrest."

The joke broke the tension, and Colleen nearly collapsed as Corman reached out and took the gun from her trembling hand. "You know who said that, Colleen?"

She shook her head, only half-aware of the question.

"Lee Harvey Oswald, when they were taking him from the Texas Theater. He already knew they needed him dead for any of it to work, and was trying to make sure the police didn't ice him right there on a flimsy pretext."

She started to sob and he tucked the gun into the huge pockets of his overcoat. He stepped closer and wrapped his arms around her, standing on tiptoe to kiss the tip of her nose. "It's all right, hon, I'm here now. It's all right."

"I didn't know who else to call," she said, blubbering, and shaking her head in embarrassment at the same time.

"Don't apologize, I owe you and Colin more than I can ever repay. You both know that. Now, tell me what the hell happened. I could only understand half of what you were saying on the phone, and only half of that made any sense."

She led him into the next room, one without windows, turning off the light with a two-way switch, then clicking on a small hurricane lamp. She closed the sliding doors, sealing the room off from the front, and sat on a sofa. Only then did she seem ready to answer the question. "These calls, they've been driving me crazy."

"What calls? From whom?"

"I don't know who. They keep calling and calling. I stopped answering, letting the machine pick up, but I couldn't turn the sound down because I'm waiting to hear from Colin."

"What do the callers say?"

"They keep telling me that Colin is dead. They said he was hit by a truck. That he was killed in a plane crash, that he was shot to death, and I don't know what all. But always it's the same. Always they talk about Colin dying. They describe his mangled body and—" She broke off in a storm of sobbing, and Corman crossed the room to kneel in front of her.

He took her hands from her lap and folded them in his long fingers. "I feel like I ought to propose or something, Coll."

She laughed in spite of herself.

"Should I take that as a no?"

She laughed again, and looked at him then. "What does it mean, Timothy? Why are they doing this to me?"

"They're not doing it to you, Coll, not really. They're trying to get to Colin. They're using you to get at him. When did they start?"

"Last night, almost midnight. At first I thought it was some stupid joke, or maybe one of those sicko friends of Colin's, trying to be funny. But then another one came an hour later, and another hour brought a third. Then they started to get closer together. I haven't slept since the night before last. I'm exhausted and I'm terrified."

"I wish to Christ Paul was back."

She looked up sharply. "That man Desmond, is that who you mean?"

Corman nodded. "Yeah."

"You know him?"

"He's a friend, Colleen. He told me he'd spoken to you. I guess you know what he's doing."

"He told me some story about missing tapes, but I didn't know whether to believe him or not. I mean, he seemed to be telling the truth, but it was so strange, and . . ." She shook her head, unable to accept it yet. "And when he told me that a man had been killed and that there might be some connection to Colin's tapes, I . . . it all seemed crazy. I thought he must have gotten something mixed up." She searched Corman's face for a moment, the penetrating eyes seeming to be almost bright enough to pierce the skin and bone and see right into his skull. Then she asked, "Is that what this is about? Those tapes?"

"Probably. It's true, Colleen, all of it. And two more men have been killed. And there's no doubt that they were connected somehow to the missing tapes. Paul knows how, but he wouldn't tell me. He said he'd explain when he got back."

"Where is he?"

"Colorado."

Her head jerked as if she'd been slapped. "Where in Colorado. Not . . . ?"

Corman nodded. "Holy Sanctuary. He thought that maybe the tapes, or Colin, or maybe even both, might be there."

"I knew that man would come back to haunt us."

"What man, Coll?"

"Rajah Primasanha . . ."

Desmond stopped just long enough for Samantha to fall in beside him. He took her bag and draped it over his shoulder, providing a nice counterweight to his own gear, but leaving both hands free. The wind was whipping across the open space, driving the snow ahead of it, the flakes moving almost horizontally. The steady tattoo of the pellets against the stiff cloth of the parka made it sound like he was being scoured by a sandblaster.

The snow was nearly a foot deep and in places the drifts were nearly twice that. It wasn't hard to keep to the road, because the faint depressions left by the passing of the Jeep were discernible even in the faint light. Suddenly the wind seemed to die down, and Desmond realized they had entered the tree-lined portion of the approach road. Without the press of the wind, it was easier to walk, and he picked up his pace. Samantha slogged along in his wake, placing her booted feet in the holes left by Desmond's sneakers.

His ankles were cold, starting to grow numb, and he could feel the snow packed in around the edges of his sneakers, even hear it squeak when he flexed a foot at an angle sharper than normal. He wore one glove, but kept his right hand bare, in case he needed the pistol.

The walk seemed to take forever, but when the wind suddenly slapped him again, he realized they had reached the opening where the parking lot lay off to the right. He broke into an awkward sprint, kicking high to get his feet above the snow, and plunging in nearly to his knees on every stride. He felt like he was floundering in the surf, and the thought suddenly made him miss Audrey and the kids. Florida seemed so perfect a place to be now.

He reached the first row of cars and moved among them until he found the Cherokee. He had left it open, and he moved to the passenger door to get Samantha inside, but when he tried the door, he found it locked. He cursed, and Samantha whispered, "What's wrong?'

"They've locked it. I'll have to get the key before you can get inside." He dropped the bags and moved around to the rear of the Cherokee, then knelt in the snow. He could feel the meltwater soak through the knees of his jeans as he groped up under the fender with his bare hand, clawing at clotted snow until he found the small metal box and pried it loose with fingers numb as sticks.

He shook it, and smiled when he heard the rattle of the keys. It took him a few seconds to slide the halves of the case apart because the seams had been clogged with ice, but they finally came loose and he tilted the keys into his hand, tossing the key case into the snow.

Moving to the door, he opened it and tossed the

bags into the back, then helped Samantha inside, handing her the ignition key. He went back to the side of the Cherokee and lay down in the snow again to retrieve the wrapped pistol. It took some doing groping in the dark, but he didn't want to risk using the flashlight. As soon as he had the canvas bag free, he unzipped it and removed the Browning with two spare clips then got to his feet.

Moving toward the passenger door again, he motioned for Samantha to roll the window down. "Listen," he said, handing her the .25-caliber automatic and extra clip, "do you know how to use this thing?"

She held it up to see it better, worked the safety a couple of times, then nodded. "I target-shoot. How many rounds?" she asked.

"Eight. Now listen, what time do you have?"

She checked her watch. "Two twenty-five."

Desmond nodded, checking his own watch. "In five minutes, they'll know we're missing, if they don't already. The first thing they'll do is call the block-house on the main gate. I'm going to try to get there before that happens. At two-thirty, on the button, you start the car and head on down to the gate. If it's open, that'll mean everything's all right and I'll meet you on the other side, so just drive on through and stop once you're past the gate."

"And if it's closed?"

"Get a running start and drive like hell. You shoulu be able to take out the gate if you hit it hard enough, then just go as far as you can. Get to the nearest town, if possible, whatever that might be."

"Eldorado Springs."

"All right, go there. If you have to abandon the car, well . . . let's hope you don't."

"Be careful," she whispered.

Desmond waved over his shoulder and started back toward the road. It was easier going once he reached the second tree-lined stretch. Two minutes later he could see the blockhouse, dimly outlined under a light on its roof. The wind still howled, and the snow swirled all around him as he moved off the road and in among the dense rows of spruces.

At the bottom of the tree line, he was within fifty feet of the blockhouse. Through a small window, he could make out the silhouette of one man sitting at a small table, hunched over a magazine. If there was a second guard on the night shift, he wasn't visible. Desmond slipped the Browning nine-millimeter from his pocket, took off the safety, and worked the slide to chamber a round.

As he moved toward the wall of the blockhouse, he whispered a silent prayer that the door was unlocked. If not, he was in something a lot deeper than the snow dogging his every stride.

He nearly stumbled as he reached the blockhouse, and checked his watch: 2:29. And counting. He moved around the rear of the blockhouse, along a windowless wall, and reached the front corner. He had to duck to get past the larger front window, almost crawling on hands and knees, but careful of the pistol. On the single step, he balanced himself, raised the pistol, and reached for the knob. Its metal felt cold to his numbed fingers, but when he twisted, he felt the knob turn, and he burst in, just as the phone on the wall rang.

The simultaneous assault seemed to confuse the man at the table. There was a second guard, and he was frozen halfway out of his chair, staring at Desmond as the phone continued to buzz.

Leveling the Browning, Desmond moved like a cat, somewhat awkward with the cold, but still more quickly than the confused guards were prepared for. Slamming the butt of the pistol into the temple of the nearer guard and knocking him to the floor, Desmond gestured toward the door with his free hand. "Open the gate."

"Fuck you," the guard snapped.

Desmond smiled, waved the Browning in a vicious arc, and squeezed the trigger, blowing out the front window. "I can find the controls if I have to, buddy," he said.

The man nodded, certain that the next shot would not be aimed at anything so inanimate as plateglass. He moved gingerly, his hands over his head, until he reached a small control panel on the wall beside the door.

He pressed a sequence of three buttons, and Desmond snapped a glance at the gate in time to see it shudder and start to draw back. A moment later the twin spears of approaching headlights slashed at the swirling snow, and Desmond grabbed the guard with one hand, moving so suddenly the man offered no resistance, and slammed his head into the door frame hard enough to put out his lights.

Desmond snatched at an Ingram Mac-10 hanging

on a hook over the control panel and dashed out the door just as the Cherokee came even with the gate pillars. The 4X4 braked as it slid through, spilling ruby fireflies in the snow, and Desmond raced to the passenger door and yanked it open.

"Get us out of here," he snapped, jerking the door closed.

- TWENTY-ONE---

THE MOTEL WAS COLD. DESMOND STOOD AT THE window, watching the snow. Samantha Alexander sat in a chair, her hands folded in her lap. She was still trembling, and Desmond was worried that she might be losing her grip on reality.

"You know what I think?" he said. "I think we need to get something to eat. You'll feel better, Samantha. Why don't we go out and find a restaurant?"

She shook her head vehemently.

"You can't hide the rest of your life. Don't worry about Primasanha's people. They can't hurt you now."

"You don't understand. You don't know anything about it."

"Sure I do. I know a lot more than you think."

"You can't. If you did, you'd know. They'll never let me get away."

Desmond walked to the chair and knelt beside it. He took her hands in his. He could feel them trembling like small, frightened animals. "Why don't you talk about it? You'll feel better if you get it out, share it with somebody."

"You're starting to sound just like them," she said.

"If you're trying to offend me, you're doing a good job of it." He laughed, but she looked at him as if she weren't sure whether or not to believe him.

"Why were you there?" she asked. "You're not like the usual acolytes."

"I was looking for someone," he said, patting her hands.

"Are you one of these deprogramming people? Is that it?"

He shook his head. "No. Nothing that clear-cut. Let's just say I had a job to do, and let it go at that."

"Who were you looking for?"

For a moment he didn't answer. But he knew that she might be able to help him. If she trusted him, she might be able to throw some light on an increasingly murky situation. But if he didn't trust her, she wouldn't trust him. He took a deep breath, patted her hands again, and asked, "Can you keep a secret?"

She nodded, almost eagerly, like a child playing at being an adult, suddenly about to become privy to adult secrets. "Yes, I can keep a secret."

"I mean really. You can't tell a soul."

"I promise."

"All right, then. I was looking for Colin Yeats."

Her eyes lit up. "I met him here once, several years ago. It was my first time. I had just joined. He was one of the reasons I considered joining in the first place. I figured that if it worked for him, it should work for me, too. Boy, was I ever wrong."

"Did you see him while you were here this time?"

She shook her head. "No. He doesn't belong to Holy Sanctuary anymore. In fact, he's on their blacklist."

"Why is that?"

"Because he and Rajah Primasanha had some sort of falling-out. I don't know the details, but I know that Rajah was really pissed about it. For months there were attacks on Colin in the newsletter. Every single issue. I guess I should have realized that if Colin Yeats was reason to join, then he was reason to leave, too. If it didn't work for him, then—"

"What did the articles in the newsletter say?"

"I always read the articles, but I couldn't follow what it was about. All I know is that Rajah accused Colin of refusing to submerge his ego for the common good. They always called him a—what was it?—an apostate. But the party line didn't kill the stories. Some people I knew who knew more than I did said that supposedly Colin didn't like the way people were being treated, and he said something about it."

"Is that what got you in trouble, Samantha?" Desmond asked.

"No. I . . ." She looked at him then, suddenly uncertain again, her eyes brimming with tears. "I . . ."

"It's all right. You don't have to talk about it if you

don't want to. If it's too painful . . . but I think you'll feel better if you do. An old friend of mine used to say you can't conquer your fears in the darkness. He meant the darkness in your own mind. You had to force them into the light, where you could see them. Sunlight is antiseptic, he used to tell me."

"No, it's all right," she sniffed. "I want to. You're right. It will be better for me. I know that. I just . . . it's so hard."

"How about if we go get some dinner? We can talk at the restaurant."

She nodded, reluctantly at first, and then more animatedly. "I am kind of hungry."

Desmond stood up. He retrieved his coat from the closet and slipped it on, then got Samantha's parka and helped her into it.

Desmond asked, "What do you feel like having?"

"I like Chinese. If we can find a place."

"I'm sure we can."

"Especially Szechuan."

"General Tso's chicken?"

"Is that the same as General Tang's chicken?"

"Sure is."

"Sounds perfect."

Desmond rifled the drawer of the night table, found a directory of local bars and restaurants, and stabbed a finger at an ad. "Here we are," he said. "Jade Palace, specializing in Szechuan and Hunan cuisine."

Desmond patted his hip to make sure he still had the Browning, then opened the door. Samantha led the way down the hall, and when they moved out into the parking lot, the snow swirling in sheets, she suddenly seemed very small. She turned toward him, waiting for him to catch up, and when he did, she hooked her arm through his and squeezed. "I don't know why you were there," she said, "but I'm sure glad you were. I don't know what would have happened if . . ."

"Forget about it, Samantha, it's over. Just worry about getting on with your life. They can't hurt you anymore. Tomorrow we'll get you on a plane, and before you know it, this will all seem like a bad dream."

Desmond unlocked the Cherokee on the passenger side, helped Samantha in, then moved around to the driver's-side door. When he was inside, she said, "I can't believe I was so stupid. I never should have come back here. When I left the last time, I told myself I'd never come again. But . . . it's like a habit, more like a drug habit, maybe, an addiction. As soon as I take off my clothes and put on that robe, it's like I can't think for myself anymore. I can feel it happening, feel my will slipping away. But I guess that's not quite what happens, or I wouldn't feel the need to come back in the first place."

"Don't feel bad about it, Samantha. These people are experts, they know how to capitalize on your vulnerabilities, to exploit them. They're like some sort of predator. Just thank your lucky stars you managed to get out without any real harm."

"I still think they'll come after me. They've done that before. I know that. I heard a lot of stories. More and more all the time. People are always trying to leave, and it's always the same thing. We're told not to have anything to do with them, that they're trying to undermine the temple, that . . . I don't know what all."

As she spoke Desmond rolled out onto the highway. With the snow still falling heavily, traffic was light. "What kind of stories have you heard?" he asked.

"I . . ." She hesitated, turning her head to look over her shoulder, as if afraid she might be overheard.

Desmond asked again, "What kind of stories?"

"You know, revenge, that sort of thing. They don't like it when somebody says no. Especially if they haven't managed to sink their hooks into a person's bank account. That's what they were trying to do with me, trying to pressure me to sign over my trust fund."

"But what about people who do manage to resist them. What happens to them?"

"I . . . I've heard stories, but . . ."

Desmond asked again. "What kind of stories, Samantha?"

"I'm sure they're just exaggerations. I mean, you know how it is—you fall out of line, it doesn't matter whether it's a person or an organization, there's always an ax to grind. So people say things that aren't true. You know what I mean . . . just rumors."

The sign for the restaurant glowed blurrily through the swirling snow, and Desmond slowed. Pulling into the parking lot, he found a place close to the front door and parked before responding. "Actually, no, I don't know what you mean, Samantha. Tell me."

He let the engine idle, and for a long time there was no sound in the Cherokee but the rush of air from the heater, going full blast.

"I don't think I should say anything more."

Desmond turned to her. "Samantha, I told you why I was at Holy Sanctuary. It's very important that I find Colin Yeats."

"You mean he's really missing? You're not just one of those tabloid types trying to get some juicy gossip?"

Desmond laughed. "Nothing could be further from the truth. But I don't know if he's really missing; at least I don't have any concrete proof of that. But no one has heard from him in quite a while. He hasn't returned phone calls from me, from his agent, from the president of Griffin Records. Even his ex-wife says she hasn't head from him in weeks."

"Colleen? You met her?"

"Yes."

"She's great, isn't she? I mean so warm, so natural. She's so . . . genuine."

"You know Colleen Yeats?"

"Sure. I met her at the sanctuary. Some people say it was she who got Colin to join. I don't know if it's true. I mean, that's not the sort of thing you ask somebody, you know. The master frowns on that sort of thing. He says that what's important is that you find the way, not who sold you the map. But anyway, I heard from more than one person that it was the Holy Sanctuary that ruined their marriage. I don't know if it's true, but that's what I heard. But the master said that—"

Desmond clucked. "Samantha. You don't have to call him that. He's not your master anymore."

"Sorry. I keep forgetting."

"Don't apologize. Especially not to me. That's what they've done to you. They've made you afraid of thinking for yourself. It'll take a while for you to get over it, but you have to. And you have to start now." He opened the door, killed the engine, and jumped down to the snow. "Come on, let's get some dinner. We can talk inside."

He closed the door, walked around the Cherokee, and helped Samantha down, then led the way into the Jade Palace. They knew what they wanted, so the hostess sent a waiter immediately, and as soon as they had ordered, Desmond said, "Tell me everything you know. It's very important, Samantha. I can't tell you how important. Already, three people are dead. I can't tell you why, and I can't tell you how Colin Yeats fits into this, partly because I don't know and partly because I'm not at liberty to. But I *can* tell you that it's very important. More important than you can guess. When did you first start to think the Holy Sanctuary was trying to exploit you?"

"Is that what's going on, are they trying to do something to Colin Yeats? Destroy his reputation or something?"

"I'm not sure, Samantha. I'm really not."

"Well, they have this man; he's on the staff, I guess. I met him in New York. He's kind of creepy, in a funny way. I don't know how to describe it, but he's different, at least from the kind of people I grew up with, you know. Waspy Connecticut didn't prepare me for somebody like him. I don't know where to start, really."

"Start with his name."

"Bobby. That's what they call him. I guess it's Robert. Robert Basciano. He's—"

"Did you say Basciano?"

Samantha nodded. "Yeah. He's, you know, kind of like an accountant or something. I mean he knows all about finance, trusts, stocks. They had him interview me pretty early on. I guess I should have realized they were interested in the money, but . . . God, I feel so *stupid*." She shrugged, and Desmond reached out to pat her hand.

"It's all right," he said. "They were manipulating you. You weren't stupid, you were trusting, and they took advantage of that trust. That's all."

She nodded uncertainly, looking at him with wide eyes, trying to find some reason to believe him.

To get her mind off it, Desmond prompted, "So Robert Basciano is affiliated with Holy Sanctuary?"

"Yeah. I mean, they pick on him all the time. I think it's to make him humble or something, strip away his ego or whatever. Anyway, they make him dress like the novices, but it's obvious that he's pretty high up."

"Maybe," Desmond suggested, "they have him dress like the novices to put the other novices at ease. It's another way of gaining their trust. If he's just like you, what harm can he cause?"

"You know, Mr. Desmond, I think I'm already starting to see things a whole lot better than I ever have. I guess I'm lucky you got me out of there when you did."

"Did they ever threaten you, Samantha?"

"Not me, no. But they threatened other people. I heard it myself, too, this is not hearsay. I mean I was there." She stopped then and looked at him, her eyes welling up once more. "You think they did something to Colin, don't you? You think they kidnapped him, or—"

"I don't know, Samantha," he said. And he didn't dare tell her what he feared. "Tell me more about Basciano."

"There's not much to tell, really. He's supposed to be from some crime family. His father and his grandfather are—what do they call it?—dons, or something. Or at least his grandfather is. I don't know much about that sort of thing, so it all sounded like Mario Puzo stuff to me. You know, *The Godfather*."

"Believe it or not, you're not far off the mark, Samantha. It *is* Mario Puzo stuff. Tell me everything you can remember about him."

- T W E N T Y - T W O - - -

DESMOND MADE THE LAST TURN HEADING TOWARD
home, bone weary and frustrated. He was looking
forward to collapsing into his own bed, sleeping
until Morpheus himself grew tired of listening to
him snore, then doing the same thing all over
again. He was starting to think that he would never
find the tapes, and beginning to wonder whether he
ever should have taken the assignment in the first
place.

The moon was out, just above the horizon, and the
snow that had fallen since he left for Colorado,
although paltry by Rocky Mountain standards,
looked magnificent. He watched a pair of deer pick

their way across a ridge, their movements almost dainty, and when they disappeared, he felt a wave of profound sadness sweep over him.

Turning into the driveway, he pictured the answering machine, its green light blinking once for each call, pausing, and starting over again, the flashes too many to count, the prospect of listening to them all daunting and probably pointless, except on the off chance that there might be a message from Audrey and the kids. For that reason alone, he would play them back. At the moment he didn't care if he ever heard the voice of Warren Resnick or Timmy Corman again.

When he pulled up the driveway, the tires slipping a little on the unshoveled asphalt, he decided to stop and walk to the mailbox before going all the way up the hill and having to slog back down for a stack of catalogs full of stuff he didn't want from merchants he'd never heard of.

He opened the door and stepped out, the snow coming to his ankles, deep enough to spill into his sneakers. He slipped as he turned for the mailbox, caught himself on the open door, and hung on until he'd regained his balance.

Down at the mailbox, he pulled down the front door and reached in to grab three days' worth of mail. As he was closing the mailbox door he heard something in the shrubbery to his left and turned as a man emerged, holding a gun leveled at his waist.

"Careful, Mr. Desmond," the man said.

Desmond thought about the Browning, realized it was in his suitcase, and raised his hands slowly, trying not to alarm the gunman. The man stepped close, gesturing with his head for Desmond to walk up the driveway toward the car.

When he turned to do as he was instructed, he saw a second man standing beside the open car door. "What's this all about?" Desmond asked.

"Get in the car, Mr. Desmond."

Desmond walked to the Cutlass carefully, not wanting to slip and get himself shot by an overanxious triggerman. He tossed the mail into the backseat as the other man walked around to the passenger side and gestured for him to open the door.

"It's open," Desmond said.

The man tried the handle, yanked the door open, and got into the passenger seat. "Get in," he said, then smiled. "You should be more security conscious, I think."

Desmond did as he was told, noticing a small automatic in the man's right hand as he did so. The first gunman reached into the back, unlocked the rear door, and closed Desmond's door before climbing into the backseat.

Acutely aware of the two guns aimed at him, Desmond patted the steering wheel once, then again, harder, and asked, "Well, gentlemen, where to?"

"The thruway."

"Far? Because I need gas."

The man in the front glanced at the fuel gauge and said, "You have enough."

"Do you want to tell me what this is all about?"

There was no answer. Desmond threw the car into reverse and backed out of the driveway, then headed back the way he'd come. It was ten minutes to the thruway entrance, and neither of the gunmen said a word the whole time. As Desmond rolled up to the tollbooth for his ticket, he looked at the man beside him. "North or south?" he asked.

"North."

Desmond nodded as if it made perfect sense. In a way it did, or at least made no less sense than any other aspect of his current situation. Once they were on the thruway, the men seemed to relax, as if the worst were over.

The gunman in the back said, "Take Exit Nineteen, and once you're through the gate, look for Twenty-eight."

"Do you mind if I ask where we're going?" Desmond asked.

"Not at all." But there was no amplification.

"All right," Desmond said, "I'll bite. Where are we heading?"

"Shut up and drive," the gunman said.

Since Exit 19 was the next thruway interchange, it was a short hop. Desmond fished a dollar bill from his pocket and handed it to the gate attendant. He was relaxed, and more than a little curious. Whoever the men were, they seemed somehow harmless, as if they were not so much abducting him at gunpoint as riding shotgun on a trip he hadn't realized he wanted to take and hadn't known might be dangerous.

Once on 28, he was directed to pick up 375 and head north.

"Woodstock, is that where we're going?" Desmond asked.

There was no answer. But the silence did nothing to shake the sudden certainty. He was beginning to get an inkling of what was happening, but he couldn't put his finger on an explanation that made any sense. Three seventy-five was tortuous in its serpentine wriggling up the side of a mountain, and the road was embroidered with spiderwebs of glittering ice that caught his headlights and seemed to glow.

If the men were familiar with the road's twists and turns, they gave no hint, and did not caution him even for the more sinuous stretches. Just before reaching the town line, he was ordered to turn left, into a narrow road that had seen just a single pass of the plow since the last snow. The pavement was crusted with packed snow stained brown by the passage of tires, and Desmond slowed for the snaking turns and unpredictable swells and dips of the road. Woods, bleak but not barren, lined both sides of the road, unbroken except for an occasional house, built far too close to the shoulder for Desmond's taste.

After three miles worthy of a ski route, he was told to slow, the man in the rear leaning over the seat back, more like a friend giving directions than a kidnapper. "Slow up a little, it's just ahead, on the right. There, by those trees."

Desmond negotiated the turn into a winding lane bordered by the black skeletons of apple trees. Two ruts in the snow were the only indication that anyone had been in or out since the snow. They were still climbing, and in the dark it wasn't possible to gauge how high they might be or how far they might yet have to go.

The lane turned to the left, and as Desmond swung into it he saw the glimmer of lights through the interlaced branches of a thick stand of trees, the gray ghost of a large house faint against the moonlit sky beyond.

"Stop in front," the man in back said, and Desmond did as he was told. The man then said, "I'll get out first, then you. Turn off the engine and give me the keys."

Once more, Desmond followed orders, killed the lights and the engine, and jerked the keys from the ignition, dropping them into the gunman's extended palm. He knew they weren't intending to kill him, at least not just yet, because there would have been no need to take him all this way just to put a bullet in his head. But he still wasn't sure who they were or why he was here.

The rear door opened, and the man got out, then opened the door for Desmond, more like a doorman than a gunman. Desmond climbed out, looking longingly at his bag, and the oh-so-distant security of the nine-millimeter Browning buried in its heart.

The other gunman climbed out of the car, put his gun in his pocket, and to Desmond's surprise, the first man tapped him on the shoulder and, when Desmond turned, flipped him the car keys. "Come on," he said, "let's go on inside. It's too damn cold out here. I need some coffee."

More confused than ever now, Desmond followed him up the front steps leading to a full-length gallery across the front of the house. At the top of the steps, he turned to look back and saw the twinkle of lights scattered across the blackness of the forest and, a little farther, the cluster of lights he knew to be the town of Woodstock.

The gunman opened the front door, and the sound of an acoustic guitar spilled into the night, the sound rich and resonant, perhaps made a little warmer by the heated air that wafted through into the cold.

The gunman gestured for Desmond to precede him in, and when they were all inside, the door closed, and Desmond could smell the sweet tang of burning cherry wood. They were in a hallway separated from the rest of the house by an oak door in which was set an etched glass panel. The door was open, and in the next room, only dimly lit, he could see one corner of a fireplace, and guessed it to be the source of the smoky aroma.

Desmond moved into the house without being ordered, half expecting to be told to stop, but no one said anything, and he entered a large room, three walls of which were book-lined, the fourth taken up almost entirely by the fireplace.

In one corner of the room, a battered Guild Dreadnought braced on one knee, Colin Yeats looked up, finished a run, and spun the guitar around to the side of the chair and got to his feet.

"What the hell are you doing in my life, Mr. Desmond?" he asked. There was no trace of a smile, but the voice was not unfriendly.

"Well, I wanted your autograph, and when you didn't return my calls, I figured the best thing to do was to get myself kidnapped at gunpoint and brought to you for a personal explanation."

Yeats cracked up. "You are one nervy son of a bitch, aren't you?"

"Nervy, no. Just a hardworking man who likes to see through to the end any job he agrees to accept. In this case, though, I'm beginning to wonder why."

Wordlessly, Yeats nodded toward a sofa, and Desmond sat down, after taking off his parka and draping it over one arm of the couch. "Who are you working for?"

"I'll answer that if you agree to answer a few of my questions."

"This is not some sort of information barter, Mr. Desmond. I just wanted to see who the hell you were and why I keep tripping over your shoes every time I turn around."

"Do you want the truth, plain and unvarnished?"

"That depends. . . ."

"On what?"

"On how painful it is. I am not well-disposed toward any more truth than I need at the moment."

"I can't tell whether this will hurt or not. But if I had to guess, I'd say yeah. A lot."

"Then just tell me what you have to say."

"Have you spoken to your ex-wife lately?"

Yeats tensed noticeably, and Desmond tried to decide whether it was due to some feeling about Colleen, or some resentment that Desmond would mention her at all. "No," the singer said, "I haven't. Why?"

"Because I have, and I told her what I was doing, why I wanted to get in touch with you. I've had half the population of North America leave a message on one or more of your answering machines, but you have been uncommunicative, to say the least."

"I have nothing to say at the moment, Mr. Desmond. Unlike a lot of people, when I have nothing to say, I have sense enough to say nothing. From what I have been told, you are working on a book about me. Is that right?"

"Yes and no. Yes, that's what you've been told. But no, it isn't so."

"I didn't think so."

"That was for public consumption, not by my choice but at the behest of Warren Resnick."

Yeats nodded as if that meant something to him, but he didn't respond, so Desmond went on. "I'm working for Mr. Resnick, actually."

"Doing what?"

"Looking for something that belongs to you."

"If you're working for Warren, why are you looking for something that belongs to me? Or, let me put that another way. If you're looking for something that belongs to me, why are you working for Warren? You see the slight difference? The English language is amazingly subtle, isn't it?"

"Do you want my answer or would you rather play Noam Chomsky to my Ludwig Wittgenstein?"

"Your nickel, Mr. Desmond."

It was time to fish or cut bait, and Desmond decided that he wanted to fish. "Nearly eight hundred hours of your tapes have been stolen from the vaults at Griffin Records. I've been hired to find them." Desmond steeled himself for a volcanic upheaval that would dwarf the destruction of Krakatoa.

Colin Yeats, though, threw him a curveball. "Why?" he asked.

"Because Warren Resnick wants them back. For a variety of reasons, each of which is compelling and none of which I need spell out for you. In fact, you may be aware of several that have occurred to neither Mr. Resnick nor myself."

"Actually not. I don't give a sh:t. Please, leave me alone." He reached for his guitar and nodded to the two gunmen. "See that Mr. Desmond gets home, would you, Jerry?"

Desmond was nonplussed. "That's it? That's all you have to say?"

Yeats looked at him with a slight smile on his face. "What do you expect me to say?"

"Those tapes, they're worth a fortune, from what Resnick told me."

"Probably."

"And you don't care?"

"Not really."

"You know that other people do, don't you?"

"That's their prerogative."

"Is it also their prerogative to die for those tapes?"

Yeats seemed puzzled now. "Die for them? I don't understand."

"I'm sure you don't. But there have been three deaths connected, certainly but how directly I am not sure, with those tapes. Apparently, the man who actually removed them from the Griffin vaults was shot to death for his trouble. There is now reason to believe that the men who killed him were also killed, probably to shut them up and possibly to obtain the tapes."

"Who were these people?"

"Does it matter?"

"It might."

"All of them had connections to organized crime."

Curiously, the news seemed to calm Yeats down somewhat. "I see," he said.

"You expected someone else, did you?"

"No, of course not. I didn't know the tapes were gone. Why would I have expectations concerning those responsible for their disappearance?"

"I thought you might have a guess, once you did learn they were missing."

"No, no guess."

"No? Not even Rajah Primasanha?"

"Jerry," Yeats snapped. "Take him home. Now!"

- TWENTY-THREE - - -

DESMOND HEARD THE POUNDING BEFORE HE WAS
fully awake. He reached for the clock, saw that it was
just past seven, and groaned. He got to his feet, aware
now that someone was pounding on the front door.
Knowing that he wasn't expecting anyone, he threw
on a pair of jeans and a sweatshirt and raked crooked
fingers through his hair on the way down the steps.

When he opened the front door, he didn't know
whether to laugh or seek medical assistance. Timmy
Corman, his disheveled hair jutting out like an imita-
tion Irwin Corey, his baggy overcoat serving only to
heighten the impression, tapped him in the chest
with a rolled-up newspaper.

Without waiting for an invitation, Corman barged into the house, and over the smaller man's shoulder Desmond saw a car, curls of exhaust floating in the air behind it, idling behind his Cutlass. He could barely make out the shadowy figure behind the wheel and squinted to try to sharpen his focus. "Who's that?" he asked, turning to face Corman and feeling now that he was the visitor, since Corman was deeper in the house than he was.

"Colleen."

"Well, don't leave her there, Timmy. Have her come in."

"No time. We have to go."

"Go? Go where? Why?"

Corman waved the paper under Desmond's nose, brandishing it as if it were a club. "This is why," he said, slapping it once more against Desmond's chest. "Here, look. . . ." Corman unrolled the paper, sorted frantically through the pages until he found Section D, opened it to the third page, and stabbed a slender finger at an article circled with red marker. "Read this."

The headline was enough. ROCK STAR'S HOME DESTROYED BY FIRE. COLIN YEATS PRESUMED DEAD. BODY OF UNIDENTIFIED WOMAN FOUND IN RUINS.

"Yeats?" Desmond asked.

Corman nodded. "You don't have to read it. I'll tell you what it says. It says that Colin's house in California was burned to the ground, that the police suspect arson, and that two bodies, one male and one female, were found in the ashes. Neither one has been identified, but the man is presumed to be Colin."

"It's not Colin," Desmond said, knitting his brows.

"What? How the hell do you know that?"

"I know because I saw him just last night."

"Get out of town," Corman spluttered. "You must be losing your mind."

"No, I'm telling you, I saw him. He had two gun-men escort me, for all he or they knew or cared against my wishes, to a house in Woodstock last night."

"But—"

"Get Colleen in here. I don't want to have to tell the same story twice."

Corman dashed out the door and down the steps, waving frantically and shouting something that only he could possibly understand. Desmond saw Colleen roll down the window of the car, Corman bending toward her, looking, in his baggy coat, as if he were trying to convince her to let him wash her wind-shield. Then the sound of the idling engine died away, and the door swung open so quickly that it took Timmy by surprise.

Once the visitors were inside, Desmond closed the front door and led them to the living room. "You want coffee, either one of you?"

Neither did, and Desmond sat down on a chair, indicating that they should share the sofa. As soon as they were seated, he described his abduction and the meeting with Yeats in detail, watching the two of them try to absorb the meaning of his nar-ration, watched their faces reflect the war between early-morning certainty of death and this unex-pected resurrection.

When he was finished, Colleen was the first to speak. "You're sure it was Colin? I mean, you'd never met him. How could you be sure?"

"Colleen," Desmond said, as gently as he could, "I've seen more pictures of Colin Yeats than I have of myself. There's no doubt in mind that it was he."

"But . . . I don't understand . . . how . . . ? Why?"

The what of those questions was left to waft in the air, but Desmond thought he understood. "I think he genuinely wants to be left alone. He didn't say why, but maybe that's something he doesn't expect anyone to understand. I think maybe he's tired of his celebrity and he wishes it would just go away. Like Garbo, maybe. But he knows it won't, so he's decided to take a more aggressive approach."

"But the fire, the two victims. Who were they? The paper speculated that the woman was probably Joan Hunter, the woman he lived with when he lived with anybody, which has not been often of late."

"Perhaps that's who it is," Desmond said.

"But that speculation was based on the assumption that the male victim was Colin. Since it isn't, who is it?"

Desmond had no answer for that. "The medical examiner will no doubt make that determination in two or three days."

"Maybe not, the bodies were so badly burned . . . there's no way that—"

"Do we have to talk about this?" Colleen interrupted.

"It could be important, Colleen," Corman argued.

"You don't think that Colin had anything to do

with this, do you? My God, you don't think maybe he was faking his own death? Is that what you're thinking?"

"I don't know what to think, Colleen. But it could be connected to the phone calls you've been getting."

"What phone calls?" Desmond asked.

Corman answered for her. "She's been getting these weird calls, people claiming that Colin is dead. They keep calling and calling. They never identify themselves, and they stay on the line just long enough to make their point, which is to describe Colin's death in one gruesome manner or another, then they just hang up."

"Have you called the police?"

Colleen shook her head. "No. I . . . I didn't want to. I mean, I didn't know where Colin was, and I was so frightened and so confused. I wanted to talk to you before I did anything, but you were out of town."

"You know what I think is the strangest thing of all?" Corman asked, almost shouting in his agitation. "I don't understand why Colin said he didn't care about the missing tapes."

"Maybe he *doesn't* care," Desmond offered. "Maybe it's just that simple."

"But all those calls, then someone turning up dead, somebody that people think is Colin, maybe because they're supposed to think that very thing. It's all too complicated for me. And then when you add that people are getting killed over those damn tapes, and now the man they rightfully belong to says he doesn't even give a good God damn . . . it doesn't sound right to me."

"Maybe you're trying too hard to read into events, Timmy," Desmond said. "Maybe you should start at the surface and look deeper only if the surface can't be explained in any rational way."

"Don't give me that Occam's-razor garbage, Paul. This is some weird shit, and we both know it."

"No, wait," Colleen said. "Let him explain what he means." She hunched forward as if to get closer to Desmond's words, her eyes fixed on his face while she waited for him to speak.

"If it's arson, maybe it was done to cover up murder. Maybe Colin was supposed to be the victim, and the killers either thought they got him and killed the wrong man without realizing it, or had no choice but to kill whoever was there in the house."

"But why? Why would they have no choice?"

"I don't know. Maybe someone recognized them. Maybe they were getting paid to do it, and figured they'd collect no matter what. Hell, there could be a dozen explanations."

"Maybe it was some sort of lovers' quarrel. Maybe it's Joan and she was double-dealing. Maybe there's a drug angle. Joanie liked her crack, from what I hear."

"I still think it all comes back to the tapes in some way," Desmond insisted. "It can't be a random series of unrelated events. They all dovetail too perfectly, seemingly in some sort of causal relationship—the tapes disappear, Colin disappears around the same time, Ron DeCicco turns up dead, the men who probably killed him turn up dead, one of the missing tapes is found in the same car with their bodies, Colleen gets threatening calls talking about Colin's death, Colin's house is burned to the ground, and two people die either before the fire or in it, one of them believed to be Colin, although we know it is not. To me, that constitutes a pattern, currently unexplained, but logical nonetheless."

"So, the tapes weren't in Colorado, then?" Corman asked.

Desmond shook his head. "No, not as far as I was able to determine. But I saw enough in the Holy Sanctuary compound to give Janet Reno déjà vu . . . and a month of nightmares. They had enough munitions in underground storage to equip a third-world army."

"Jesus . . ."

Desmond looked at Colleen. "You were there. Did you ever suspect, or hear rumors, anything at all, that might lead you to believe the cult was heavily armed?"

She shook her head. "No, nothing. I mean, when Colin and I were there, the people around Primasanha were brusque, military types, all spit and polish and no bullshit, but that was the only thing that seemed at all unusual. And the novices were all unreconstructed flower people, just like we were."

"Were they armed?"

"The supervisors, you mean?" When Desmond nodded, she shook her head. "No. They were big and they talked tough, but that was all."

"I learned one other interesting fact when I was out there," Desmond said. "There is a link between Primasanha and the mob's music-business presence."

"What kind of link?" Corman demanded, his journalistic antennae beginning to twitch.

"One of the higher-ups in the Holy Sanctuary is a man named Bobby Basciano. He's some sort of financial type. Mega Sound, the mob's quasi-legitimate music enterprise, is owned by the Basciano family. The three men who were killed in New York all have some sort of connection to the Basciano family. What makes it all stick together, for me, is not the Basciano angle, though, but the Holy Sanctuary angle. The mob has no real need to eliminate Colin, or anyone else, over the tapes. If they have the tapes, they have everything they need. But Primasanha has it in for Colin. He wouldn't mind seeing Colin dead. In fact, he'd probably be more than happy to make it happen."

Desmond looked at Colleen, half expecting an argument from her, but there was no hint of disagreement.

"But how does it work? I don't see how you make it go. The cart needs wheels, Paul."

Desmond shrugged. "I don't know. All I can do is guess. The ice is thin here, I admit it, but it makes a kind of sense, even so. What I think happened is that Primasanha prevailed on Bobby Basciano to make use of his family resources to get the tapes, possibly to make money, but possibly to buy Colin's silence, or even to force some sort of cosmetic reconciliation, stage it for PR purposes. Then, whether Basciano knew about it or not, the temple's people took out the mob's legmen, which will really piss off old man Basciano, if he gets wind of it."

"But why would Primasanha go to such lengths to get at Colin?" Corman demanded.

Desmond shrugged. "This is just a guess, but an educated one. I met a young woman in Colorado who told me that Colin was on the temple's blacklist, which clearly is Primasanha's blacklist, since he's the presiding genius of the organization. They were attacking Colin at every opportunity, all the proof anybody would need that Colin's defection stung them, maybe even triggered mass defections by others. Maybe it was just a personal thing, an ego thing with Mitchell—"

"Who?" Corman asked.

"Rajah Primasanha . . . his real name is Roy Mitchell. And my guess is that it galled him unbearably that Colin walked away from him. Maybe he even thinks he can have it both ways—make money off the tapes *and* force Colin to submit or to recant somehow."

"That will never happen," Colleen said. "I know Colin. I know he would never submit or recant. He's too stubborn for that, even when he's wrong. And in this case, he's not wrong."

"Why did Colin ever hook up with that charlatan in the first place?" Corman asked. "He would never tell me."

Colleen looked away. "It was because of me. I wanted to see what it was like. Oh, I guess for a while I was even a believer. Colin went along because he always went along with whatever whim I might be indulging at the moment. It was the way he was. Still is, I suppose. He hated it from the first meeting. When we went to Colorado, he grew to despise it utterly, but he kept up a facade for a while. I don't know whether he was hoping I would change my mind, because he never tried to do my thinking for me. Or maybe he was just willing to be patient for my sake. But as soon as I realized what a fraud the whole business was, he couldn't sever the connection soon enough. By that point, Primasanha was already trying to exploit the relationship, sending out brochures that prominently featured Colin's name and photograph. Colin asked him to stop, but he kept it up for nearly three years."

"What happened then?" Desmond asked.

"Colin sued him. That was the only reason he stopped. There was a settlement. The temple would cease and desist using Colin in any way, and Colin would refrain from attacking the temple."

"No wonder Primasanha wants to get even," Corman said. "Hell, forget PR, just look at it in terms of money. Using Colin's endorsement was worth a bundle, maybe millions—that kind of shit increases geometrically, too. Hell, if Colin had stayed in the fold, so to speak, who knows who else might have wound up in the flock? Primasanha must have had blood in his eye."

"The real question," Desmond reminded them both, "is whether he has blood on his hands."

– T W E N T Y - F O U R – – –

"WHAT ARE WE GOING TO DO?" COLLEEN ASKED.
"Shouldn't we call the police and tell them that Colin
is alive?"

Desmond shook his head. "No. Someone clearly
wants him dead. If whoever that person is—and you
both know who I think it is—thinks he *is* dead, then
Colin will be safe. As long as he stays out of sight,
and I don't think there's any question that that's
exactly what he intends to do."

"But you saw him last night, not by accident,"
Timmy pointed out, "but by choice. *His* choice. That
must mean that he doesn't care whether anybody
knows where he is now, or not. Hell, according to

Audrey, you used to find your way around Beirut blindfolded in the dark. How hard can it be to find a farmhouse on top of a mountain in Woodstock?"

"He's not there anymore."

"How do you know?"

"Because he made no attempt to keep the location secret. He had no way of knowing what I would do once I knew where he was. He sent his men back with me not just to get their car, but to make sure he had at least an hour to get away."

"Get away where?" Colleen asked.

"You probably have a better idea than I do. Think about it, you know him best. Where would he go next?"

"To know that, I'd have to know what he's thinking, and I don't have a clue."

"Does he own any place other than the houses in California and Woodstock and the apartment in the Village?"

"Not that I know of. But he could have a dozen that I don't know about. You have to remember that money means nothing to him, so he doesn't spend it on flash the way so many rock stars do. Most of it is put to work in community charities, and the rest of it is invested."

"I don't suppose you have a joint bank account, by any chance . . . ?"

"No, we don't. I mean we do have one, but it's not the main account."

"What about his accountant? Do you have access to him or her? To the books?"

Colleen shook her head. "No, I'm sorry."

"We could subpoena the accountant," Corman suggested. "Force him to open the books. But what would be the point? Why look at the books?"

"They'd reveal the location of other properties. They would all be listed as assets, and that means addresses would be available. But it could take days to get a subpoena. And the accountant would check with Colin as soon as it was received, asking what to do. If Colin said to fight it, to have the subpoena quashed, which he almost certainly would, then it almost certainly would be quashed. Colin is not a suspect in a crime, and there is no reason why the court ought to grant third parties access to such information."

"What about a warrant. Could we get a warrant? I mean your cop friend, what's his name, Brennan?"

"Same situation," Desmond argued. "Colin's not a suspect. The court is under no obligation to help someone find an innocent man who does not want to be found, even if it's arguably for his own good, even if it might save his life. Besides, it would put Dan Brennan in a very awkward situation, because he'd be obligated to inform the Los Angeles authorities that Colin is alive, and that's the one thing we want to keep secret as long as we can."

"So what do we do, sit and watch the tube until Colin turns up dead again, or *ET* starts covering stories about Colin sightings? Hell, he's not the King, for Christ's sake. Or maybe you'd like to see *Current Affair* do a feature on 'Rock Star's Fatal Tryst.'"

"Of course not," Desmond snapped. He was in no mood to hear Corman vent his cultural spleen. But he tried to keep the edge off his voice when he continued. "No, the only choice we have is, unfortunately, the most difficult—we have to find him ourselves."

"What good will that do? You said yourself, he doesn't want to be found. And if we do find him, he'll just go to ground again, unless you're prepared to bring him in at gunpoint like some upper-crust bounty hunter." Corman peered at him closely. "You're not, are you?"

"No. But Colin is an intelligent man, and he's a decent man. Once the situation is laid out for him in full, I think he'll do what he can to help. If for no other reason than that it's in his own best interest. But I think there are other reasons as well. I think he would not want to see Warren Resnick in trouble. I think he would not want to participate in the ruin of the only record label he's ever had. But he sure as hell would not want to see Rajah Primasanha have the last laugh, and make millions of dollars into the bargain. Especially if that bargain cost several human lives."

Desmond looked hopefully at Colleen.

To his relief, she nodded in agreement. "You're right. That's the last thing he'd want to see happen. I believe him when he says he doesn't care about the tapes one way or another. Which means that he doesn't care if they're released or not. But I know that he wouldn't want Rajah to make a penny off them. But there is just one problem, and it's a major one."

"Which is?"

"You can't prove that Primasanha has the tapes.

You said yourself not ten minutes ago that it was nothing more than an educated guess."

"I did. But consider this—if, as I suspect, Primasanha was behind the attack on the house in California, then he thinks Colin is dead. But if we can convince Colin to come forward, then Primasanha will almost certainly attempt to contact him, either to make a deal, or to try again to kill him. Either way, we tempt him and he bites. I'd bet on it."

"You mean you want Colin to be the bait?"

Desmond nodded. "It's not a pleasant prospect, I know. And I wouldn't blame him if he refused to go along with the idea, but if he does refuse, then I am fresh out of options."

"And Primasanha wins, is that what you're saying, Paul?" Corman asked.

Again, Desmond nodded, tugging on his lower lip with thumb and index finger.

"But if Colin doesn't care about the money, why should he care who makes it? What difference would it make to him if Primasanha makes millions?"

"Colin has nothing but contempt for him, and the way he exploits people," Colleen answered. "If he thought he had a chance to stop that, I know he'd jump at it."

"And if we can't convince him, then I know someone who can," Desmond added.

"Who?"

"I'll tell you when and if it's necessary. Otherwise, I'd just as soon leave her out of it."

"That girl in Colorado," Corman said. It was a guess, but a damn good one, and Corman knew it.

"All right then, genius, where do we start looking for him?"

"That's your end, Timmy," Desmond reminded him.

Rajah Primasanha paced back and forth, his hands folded behind his back. Dressed in jeans and a flannel shirt, his feet encased in thick-soled boots, he looked more like a lumberjack or a fashion-conscious construction worker that a spiritual leader. His newly shaved head gleamed in the orange light from the fire, the oil on his pate catching every flicker and reflecting it in dancing surges of oily flame.

He stopped suddenly and stared at Bobby Basciano. "Are you sure," he asked, "that it was Colin Yeats?"

Basciano forced a grin. "Sure I'm sure. Who the fuck else would it be? It was his house. It was his broad. He's history, I'm telling you. You can take it to the bank."

Primasanha was not convinced. "The *Times* this morning said that two unidentified bodies were found in the ruins, and that the man's body was presumed to be that of Colin Yeats. Notice the verb, Bobby, *presumed*. I don't like presumption. I deal in facts. In truth. In reality, Bobby, not hypotheses or presumptions."

"The fuck you want me to do, call the coroner and ask for the fucking dental X rays? Look, in a couple of days, the papers will carry the results of the autopsy. Will that satisfy you, or are you like one of these nuts who wants to know who's buried in Grant's tomb?"

"Don't smart-mouth me, Bobby." Primasanha turned suddenly, moving toward him with clenched fists. "Don't push me and don't smart-mouth me."

Basciano took a step back. He knew the guru had a short fuse, and it kept him on edge. It was like walking on eggs just being around him. You never knew when one of them would break, and if one went, you lost your balance and had to wade through a fucking omelette to get out of the room and out of his sight. It was that or stand there and go toe-to-toe with him. But only a fool would try that. Primasanha had all the muscle on his side, freaks like Gandar. It was better to just drop anchor and ride out the storm.

Trying to placate Primasanha, Basciano said, "Look, Rajah, I'll make a couple of calls, see what I can find out. My grandfather has his hooks into L.A. through the music business. Maybe I can see if he's got somebody on the inside of the LAPD."

"Don't talk about it, Bobby, do it! You know, I still think there's some connection to that incident in Denver. I don't like that one bit. I don't know what happened there, but I know that whatever it was, it shouldn't have happened." He held up two fingers a quarter of an inch apart. "We were this close to getting Samantha Alexander to sign on the dotted line. And we blew it."

"We didn't blow it. That asshole—what's his name?—Desmond, blew it for us. I'd like to know who the fuck he is."

"So would I," Primasanha said. "Something doesn't

smell right. This guy walks in off the street and signs up. He's there a day, and he pulls a prime prospect out the door with him. That was no accident."

"Probably her parents again, just like last time. They probably hired some deprogrammer and he figured the direct approach was the best."

"Why doesn't anyone know who he is? If he's a deprogrammer, he should be in our files."

"You're assuming he gave his real name. It was probably an alias."

"There you go again, speculating, hypothesizing—let's call a spade a spade—*guessing.* I told you before, I don't like guessing. It's quick and it's dirty, and it gets you in trouble more often than not. This is delicate business, we are not riding through the country on a goddamned back hoe, plucking people off the streets. We are choosing our recruits carefully. Too much work goes into cultivation to let something like this slide by so easily."

Basciano shrugged his shoulders, the movement inadequate to the circumstances, and he knew it. So he added, "Look, it happens. There are variables, we always understood that. Psychological profiles, financial profiles, they're all well and good, but when push comes to shove, most people fall over. But once in a while somebody pushes back. That's all that happened here. Don't go reading any cosmic significance into it. She got away. But she got away before, spat out the hook. For all you know, she didn't even leave of her own free will. Desmond might have kidnapped her."

"The evidence does not support that, and you

know it. Sure, her escort was surprised by Desmond's assault. But the footprints in the snow show no signs of anyone being dragged kicking and screaming. And the men on the gate say that she drove the vehicle down *after* he disarmed them. She was cooperating with him, not resisting him."

Basciano bobbed his head. "And you want to know more about Desmond, am I right?"

Primasanha glared at him. "You're damn right I do. Thank God all he did was abduct the Alexander girl. If he had prowled around, who knows what he would have found, what would have happened?"

"Sometimes I think you worry too much. Look, you got what you wanted. Yeats is dead. You have the tapes, and they're worth a fortune. In the scheme of things, the few hundred grand you might have gotten from Samantha Alexander is chicken feed, a drop in the fucking bucket."

"Make the calls, Bobby. I don't want to be in limbo. I want to *know!* And I want to know now, not tomorrow, not next week. Now!"

— T W E N T Y - F I V E — — —

I'M ONE MOODY BASTARD, COLIN YEATS THOUGHT, staring at the fire. He watched the logs shift, the coals spurt into cherry red from their dull orange, the smoke coiling in fitful strands. It was like watching a colorless vine grow, maybe grapes on the moon, or some filamentary liana spiral toward the sky, waiting for a diminutive Tarzan to swing out of the burning trees, beating his chest and calling to Simba or Cheetah.

At first, reading the headlines in the paper, he had gone numb, felt every nerve in his body tingle for an instant, go into overload, and then shut down under the influence of some hitherto unsuspected circuit breaker. He didn't mind the loss of the house. It had become a millstone of gargantuan proportions, weighing him down a little more every day. He felt bad for Joan, though, although it was only an assumption that the woman found in the charred wreckage was indeed Joan Hunter. But the part of him that had cared about Joan had long since shriveled away. She had used him, and he knew that, had known it, in fact, long before she had admitted it to him in one of the endless series of tearful confrontations that had become their life together. The house was hers now, really, anyway.

He had built it, never knowing quite why, never really caring, just sitting back, letting Joan add room after room, filling each with the garish assortment of mismatched curios and overpriced antiques that passed in her judgment for exotic taste. Her choices weren't exotic so much as quixotic, and they surely had nothing to do with taste. There were times toward the end when he wondered whether she was simply pushing him, trying to see how much he would let her spend before putting his foot down.

But he hadn't cared, so he hadn't bothered to stop her. Now, perhaps as the final demonstration of her commitment to excess, she was lying in a morgue, a once vibrant woman, charming, bright, even warm at times, reduced by the penultimate warmth to human charcoal. There remained only the remote possibility of the ultimate warmth, and if it existed anyplace but in Dante's imagination, Joan Hunter was surely there, its latest star resident.

He looked at his hands, at the veins that bulged on

their backs as if he were some steroidal iron pumper from the elbows down. His forearms were thick with muscle, his wrists those of a linebacker, and his fingers strong enough to poke holes in sheet metal. It was all those hours he spent welded to the guitar until it throbbed against his rib cage like another organ, pulsing more subtly than his heart, refining his essence like a rosewood liver, purifying his blood the way no kidney ever could.

And what did it all amount to? The dedication had made him the best guitarist of his generation and certainly among the richest. But the money had failed, as he knew it would, to buy him happiness. Unfortunately, the consummate artistry he had attained had bought him nothing close to this state. He was miserable, could barely stand to look at himself in the mirror, and then only when he was capable of enduring the self-loathing that invariably resulted from even a passing, sidelong glance.

What nobody seemed to understand was that his lyrics were not about the world at all, they were about himself. His indictments were of the world refracted a thousandfold through the complex prism of his brain. He saw nothing that did not contain him. He contained nothing but what he saw. He was one of Eliot's hollow men, a scarecrow without a brain, a tin man without a heart—empty as the purest vacuum that existed only in the dreams of theoretical science, the perfect void.

He thought about all the idiots in the world still teasing their hair into hives fit only for killer bees, plastering muttonchops to jowly cheeks, seeing Elvis on every corner instead of heaven in a grain of sand. The tabloid loonies were out there, and they were taking over, spreading like triffids. You couldn't turn on the tube anymore without seeing one more Geraldo clone talking to trailer-park white trash about having sex with vacuum cleaners or the neighbor's dog. To watch television was to peer through a one-way mirror into a world where incest and child abuse had replaced baseball as the national pastime, and talking about such things for money on television had replaced the lottery as the ultimate manifestation of the American Dream.

He remembered when he was young how passionate he had been about changing things, making them better. Bob Dylan had told him that the times were a-changin', and he by God did not want to stand in the doorway or block up the hall. He wanted to lend a hand, make things better. By the time Dylan had seen through his own hope into the black pit of despair beyond it, it was of no use to Colin, because he had seen his own.

Idealism had come to nothing. Hope had been frustrated, the desire for change transmuted to desire for cash in larger denominations. Hell, Jerry Rubin had gone from Haight Street to Wall Street in a New York minute. The insistence on the sacredness of the individual had become justification for self-indulgence of the basest kind, "artists" spending most of their time and energy trying to figure out how to make the most money for the least effort, cranking out shit by the hundred-pound sack, then playing with it like Freudian theory in the flesh.

Colin lifted the glass of whiskey, swirled it around, admiring how the rye caught the light and seemed like liquid amber for a moment, and staring back at him from its heart, he saw his own eye, the eye of a suddenly and perhaps irreversibly morbid cyclops who saw things as they are and did not bother to ask why. He knew that no one, least of all himself, wanted to know the answer to that question. Better to ignore reality, turn that solitary eye inward, count his ribs from the inside, track through his circulatory system millimeter by millimeter, explore every single artery, vein, and capillary in the quintessentially pointless self-examination. Learn nothing, just look, see, and forget.

He tossed off the fiery amber, half expecting it to burn on the way down, forgetting that he was already so numbed by anomie and anesthetized by his earlier consumption of alcohol that he could outdo any fakir on the planet—walk on coals, sleep on a bed of nails, stick foot-long pins through his cheeks—it didn't matter. He was devoid of feeling now and, he hoped, forever.

He thought about suicide, as he often did when he went over the Niagara of his depression without a barrel, but suicide was no answer. He knew that. It was more like a temptation. He remembered how Satan had tempted Jesus to hurl himself off the highest point available, as if the demon were the purest scientist, designing the foolproof experiment. Somebody, maybe it was Milton, he thought, saw through Satan's deviousness to its very heart. If Jesus allows himself to fall to his death, he doesn't live to redeem the rest of us. If, on the other hand, he defies natural law and saves himself, he denies his kinship with us. Tricky as all hell, was Old Nick.

No, suicide wasn't the answer. There were too many things yet undone, things that he could do. It didn't matter if he never picked up the guitar again, never wrote another word. Art wasn't important, humanity was, and suffering humanity most of all. He had watched the endless parade of Bosnian children, Somali children, Mexican children, Ethiopian children, Irish children, Chicago children—always it was the children. And like everyone else, he had been devastated, not by the horror and the gore but by the selfishness and indifference of the political leaders who had allowed that suffering to occur in the first place, when it could so easily have been prevented.

Maybe that's what he could do, sign a nice fat contract with Warren Resnick, and turn all the money into some sort of one-man UNICEF. But when he thought about it, he realized that it wouldn't make any difference. There already was a UNICEF, had been for nearly fifty years, and it seemed to make not one whit of difference. The problem was that nobody cared, and you couldn't make them care, no matter how many concerts you gave, no matter how many songs you wrote, no matter how many miles of guitar strings you twisted into junk, they didn't change because they didn't listen and they didn't listen because they didn't want to change.

Better, maybe, just to retire, find some dinky hamlet in Saskatchewan, where he could talk to the moose and watch the clouds. He wondered about

Canadian clouds, if, instead of looking like Washington and Jefferson, they looked like Brian Mulroney and Pierre Trudeau. He wondered, too, whether it was the same with clouds as it was with stamps and currency—did you have to be dead before you got your cloud, too? God, imagine waking up one morning and looking at a two-mile-wide likeness of Margaret Thatcher.

The empty glass was heavy in his hand. He looked down at it, baffled by its design as by almost everything else he saw tonight. Why were shot glasses so damned thick on the bottom? Hell, for that matter, why were they called shot glasses?

That was the trouble with the world, it was full of questions, most of them insignificant, but nonetheless baffling. And those that were significant were without answers. There was a time when he had been young and naive, and believed that it was the artist's job to answer those questions. Then, when he got a little older, he believed it was the artist's job to ask them for the rest of us, and let us find our own answers. Now, in his maturity both as an artist and a man, he knew that those questions were irrelevant and the answers, assuming there were any, were worse than irrelevant—they were misleading.

Colin got up from the sofa and walked toward the fireplace, bending over to set the shot glass down on the hearth, then spreading his hands, palms outward, before the flames, feeling the warmth on his skin, the tickle of hair on his forearms as the heated air swirled around them. For a moment he thought he could see something in the flames, not so much an image of himself as an image of what he wished to be once, long ago. But no sooner did he try to focus on it than the image dissolved in the shifting slaver of blue and orange tongues.

Impermanent, he thought, that's what the artist is. His work survives sometimes, but not all of it, and it never really means to anyone else what it meant to him. He remembered talking about one of his songs, he couldn't remember which one, with Colleen once, and she had told him that the artist had no say. He made the work, then cut it loose, a message in a bottle, and whoever found it on whatever beach had the final say as to what it meant.

He had gotten mad, told her that she didn't understand, that art was not just about meaning, that it was about feeling, about tearing a slice of your heart right out through your ribs, laying it out there, still beating, hoping that people could feel the heat, feel the rhythm, let it alter the beating of their own hearts just a little, then a little more and a little more until every fucking heart on the planet was beating in time.

But Colleen had been right. People didn't care what the artist wanted them to see. They cared only about what *they* saw, and insisted on their right to see things the way they chose. Anything else was tyranny, and the artist was no more entitled than the king or the dictator to tell the rest of us what to see and feel. The most he could do was work to focus and refine his vision, narrowing it, sharpening it, until the only possible interpretation was crystal clear. It meant discipline, but it also meant sacrificing richness, and for Colin, that had been unacceptable, if not impossible. He preferred to scatter clues, let his fans follow the ones they wanted.

His songs seemed to have so many meanings that some people argued they had none at all, and Colin half agreed with them. They were aleatory constructs, he'd told an interviewer once, temporary arrangements of chance that yield glimpses of some shattered whole that can be assembled dozens of plausible and equally defensible ways.

It sounded like so much posturing now, watereddown deconstructionism, hermeneutical obfuscation. Take the real and drape it in the impossible, and let the chips fall where they may. As long as it's got a beat and they can dance do it, see if they give a shit.

But God, how he ached to be understood, an impossible dream because he did not understand himself and could not even begin to articulate what he dimly perceived in the way of teasing hints and tantalizing postulates. He felt like a fraud because he knew that some people took him to be a teacher, some sort of seer, the genius who had gone through the looking glass and lived to tell about it.

But he knew that he hadn't really made it through, or if he had, he hadn't made it back. What stared at him in the glass never ceased to baffle him, and he wondered which one was real and which was Memorex, and did each of the images wonder about the other? How did you know, after all, whether there was not someone on the other side of the mirror's surface staring at you and saying, "God, do I really look like *that*?" And who had more right to

ask the question? Were there parallel universes separated by the thinnest imaginable plane of silver?

He reached for the bottle again, nearly tripped on
the hearth as he stretched full length to grab it from
the mantel, and wobbled precariously as he bent to
refill the shot glass. Half of what he poured trickled
onto the stone, turned the slate a darker gray, and on
a whim he poured the rest of the whiskey into the
fire, watching it explode into blue-white flame for an
instant then fade away, leaving nothing but a momen-
tary hiss and a layer of white ash on the logs before
vanishing as completely as if it had never been.

When he bent to pick up the glass, he lost his balance and fell to his knees, ignored the pain in his
kneecaps long enough to down the double in a single
gulp, then threw the shot glass into the fire with all
the force he could muster and none of the accuracy
he had hoped for. The glass slammed into the mound
of embers with a dull thud, scattered a cloud of
sparks, then disappeared under the smoke and fluff
of ash, leaving just a shallow depression behind.

He fell over backward then and rolled onto his
stomach, curled one arm under his cheek, and closed
his eyes. He kept wondering if he would feel any better in the morning, as he drifted off to sleep, and
could feel his head shaking, as if the truth were some
sort of spasm that would not be denied.

- TWENTY-SIX- - -

COLLEEN WAS CONVINCED THAT COLIN WOULD STAY in the Woodstock area. "I know him. He's bruised, he's hurting, and when he gets like that, he goes back to his roots. He lived in the area for years before anybody ever heard of Colin Yeats, and that's what he's thinking now, that things were better when no one had heard of him. He can't really have anonymity, so he substitutes a *place* where he was anonymous for a *time* when he's not. More than likely, he's sitting at a table with a half-empty bottle of rye in front of him, one elbow bent, leaning on the table and holding his head up, the other arm lying in his lap."

"All right," Desmond said. "If we start with that

premise, can you narrow the geography down? We can't exactly ride through the mountains knocking on the door of every goddamned farmhouse we see."

Colleen shook her head. "Sorry, that's the best I can come up with, Mr. Desmond."

Timmy looked baffled. "I can crawl the pubs, like I've been doing, but that's been a dry hole. I don't know what else to do. Maybe make a few phone calls . . ."

"Colleen," Desmond said, "is there somebody he would go to to help him find a place to live, a friend, maybe?"

"No. No one in particular. Just musicians, but Timmy knows them all better than I do."

"What about a real-estate agent? Did he use the same person each time he bought or rented?"

"Actually, yes, he did."

"Is it somebody you know, somebody who would trust you enough to tell you where he is?"

"We can try."

"Then let's try. Timmy, you make the rounds of the clubs. I know it's an awkward time, but we can't worry about that. Roust people out of bed if you have to. Don't tell them anything you don't have to, but push as hard as you can."

"What's the urgency?" Corman asked. "Hell, the tapes have been missing for a while already. Another couple of days won't hurt."

"It's not just the tapes. It's Colin, and it's Prima-sanha. You didn't see the weapons stockpile I saw. The sooner somebody does something about that, the better off we'll all be. This guy is an accident waiting to happen. I'm afraid that the assault on Colin's

California house might just be the beginning. And you realize that it's only a matter of a day or so before the news leaks out that Colin's alive. That'll be front-page news. At best, it'll trigger a search for Colin by Primasanha's people. At worst, it might be enough to send Primasanha off the deep end. Remember Jonestown, Timmy?"

"You don't think he's that bad, do you?"

"Yes, I do. There were more than sixty people in that compound in Colorado. For all we know, there are similar numbers in other compounds around the country. From what I've been able to learn about Primasanha, he's got compounds all across the country. I have no idea how many people we are talking about, but it could be several hundred. I have to assume that there are weapons caches at each compound. If Primasanha implodes, it could make Waco look like a walk in the park."

"You don't seriously believe that people hundreds or thousands of miles apart will blow themselves up on account of this asshole, do you?"

"Yes, I do."

"Then I don't see what we can do to stop it. Once he's arrested, he can still send out the word. There might be some sort of action plan already in place in the event something happens to him. Taking him down, dead or alive, might pull the trigger on the whole thing anyway."

"I know that. That's why I've got to make a couple of phone calls. I know someone in the Justice Department. If they have a line on Primasanha's compounds, they can coordinate their efforts, move on all of them simultaneously. If the other compounds don't have weapons caches, then there's no harm done, but if they do, it might be possible to nip this thing in the bud."

"All right," Corman said, "I guess you're the boss. I just write about what people like you do. I don't pretend to understand how it all works. All I do is survey the wreckage afterward, and try to make some sense of it."

"You don't have to understand anything right now, Timmy, what you have to do is get your ass up to Woodstock and find Colin. He's the key. I'm convinced of it. If we have Colin, we have what Primasanha wants more than he wants anything else in the world."

"Except money," Corman interjected.

"Money included," Desmond insisted. "Colleen, what's the name of this real-estate agent?"

"Mitchell Realtors."

Desmond shook his head in disbelief. "Nice irony, isn't it?" He paused to light a Marlboro, and when the first wisps of smoke curled around him, he said, "All right, Colleen, since you're driving, head straight to the realtor, see if you can learn anything. Then drive Timmy around wherever he needs to go. I'll meet you at the real-estate agent in three hours. It'll take me a while to set some things up, but I'll be right behind you. If you get a lead on Colin, don't do anything about it, don't call him and don't go there. If he knows we've found him he might spook, and if he still has the muscle with him, you won't be able to stop him from bolting. Understand?"

Colleen looked numb, and Desmond took her hands in his and shook them. "Understand?"

She nodded this time. But there was no denying the confusion and uncertainty in her eyes. "I understand," she said.

"And I want both of you to understand that Primasanha's people might be doing the same thing you are. If they spot Colleen, they might follow you, hoping you'll lead them to Colin. Wait here a minute," he said, and left the room without waiting for an argument.

He was back in two minutes, a pair of small automatic pistols in his hands. He gave one to each of them. "I know this is antithetical to your way of thinking, Colleen, but we are dealing with the lunatic fringe, and I don't want to take any chances. Have you ever fired a gun?"

She shook her head. "Never."

"Timmy?"

"Yeah, I have."

"All right, show Colleen how to use hers on the way. Now get moving."

Bobby Basciano hung up the phone, resisting the urge to chew on his lower lip, because he knew that once he started, he wouldn't stop until the blood ran down his chin. He looked at himself in the mirror, the two-thousand-dollar suit suddenly tight across his chest, constricting his breathing. He felt as if someone had wrapped him in iron bands and had begun slowly to turn the screws.

He looked at his watch, wondering if he had time to get the hell out before Rajah arrived. He walked to the window, stood looking out at the gray sky for a moment, and saw that it was already too late. Primasanha's limo was already turning into the long drive. The snow was light, swirling on the wind, and little curls of it blew up off the bluestone drive as the limo descended toward the house.

Bobby thought for a minute about running out the back, but he couldn't bear the idea of running in the snow, ruining his five-hundred-dollar Italian shoes in the snow. He ran a hand through his black hair, feeling the thin sheen of oil on his fingers, and leaned closer to the glass. He was getting hives, the way he always did when things were out of control. And he could not remember a time when things were more out of control than they were now. Not ever.

He rubbed his forehead with his palm, then yanked a silk handkerchief from his pants pocket to wipe away the oil on his fingers, then rubbed his forehead until the skin burned. The limo was almost at the bottom of the hill now, and Bobby could see Gandar at the wheel, his shoulders so broad he seemed to occupy both front seats at the same time.

He patted his hip, felt the solid lump of the pistol, and wondered if he was going to have to use it. He thought he might, and tried to decide who to shoot first, Rajah or Gandar, but he couldn't make up his mind.

He could lie, of course. It wouldn't solve anything, but at least it would postpone the final reckoning long enough to get him back on an even keel, give him time to think.

But he was a lousy liar, and he knew it. He remembered the first time he had lied to his mother. She had seen right through it, as if headlines were stapled to his chest proclaiming the truth. He had told her he had found the money lying in the grass, but she had known that he had taken it from her purse, and she had nearly ripped off an ear, twisting it like the nuns did until the whole side of his head felt as if it were being torn loose.

Then she had taken the porno magazines and rolled them into a baton, smacked him across the head, and when he turned, beat a tattoo on his back and shoulders. Then she had marched him right back to the candy store, slapping him with every step until the magazines hung in tatters, tits and ass suddenly reduced to scraps on the wind, fluttering as they tore off and blew away. And Dom D'Amico had known as soon as Rose Basciano walked in that he was going to do exactly what she told him to do. It wasn't that Dom was afraid of Rose's husband, although he was. It was the woman herself, the fury in her voice, the hollow sound of that horrible thumping as she continued to beat Bobby's skull with the magazines as if it were some sort of ceremonial drum, and Bobby was only the first of two victims to be sacrificed.

He'd lied since, of course, but never to his mother, and never to his father. He couldn't lie to authority, no matter how desperate the straits, because he couldn't pull it off. Just the thought of Rose and her terrible retribution was enough to make him stammer and break out in a cold sweat. You didn't have to know Bobby Basciano at all to know when he was lying. He was more transparent than Richard Nixon.

The limo stopped and Gandar got out, opened the rear door, and slammed them both after Rajah climbed out. Rajah was in his robes again, which meant he would be on that high horse of his, taking himself too seriously, the way he did more and more often lately.

Gandar walked around to the back of the limo and opened the trunk, lifted two suitcases out as easily if they were empty, and lumbered toward the porch, his thick legs seeming not even to bend at the knee. His whole muscle-bound body tilted from side to side with each step as each stiff leg jerked forward, found purchase, and then the process was repeated on the other side of his body.

Basciano rubbed his lips, felt how dry they were and licked them nervously, then headed for the door. He was in the hallway when Rajah entered, the baleful glare already in place, the face rigid, except for the throb of one prominent vein on his left temple. It seemed to pulse and wriggle, as if something alive were trapped under the skin and trying desperately to find a way out. It would not have surprised Bobby if a small snake suddenly slithered out from under the right eyelid and dropped to the floor.

"Well," Primasanha demanded, "what did you find out?"

Bobby shook his head.

"I don't understand that, Bobby. You'll have to put

it into words." There was an edge to his voice now. It was brittle and sharp, echoing off the high ceiling and seeming to shatter into a hundred hard-edged shards that fell like hailstones to the floor. "What did you find out?"

"It . . . it wasn't him."

"I knew it! You fucked up, like I knew you would." Primasanha spun around, facing away from him now. Instead of raising his voice to emphasize his rage, he lowered it nearly to a whisper, so sibilant it might have been the voice of that snake that never quite made its appearance. "You fucked up."

Primasanha turned back. "This is the one thing that you people are supposed to be so good at, and you can't even do that right."

"I'm sorry. I—"

"Shut up. Just shut up and find him. I want him here by tomorrow morning, do you understand?"

"Tomorrow? But . . . Christ, Rajah, you have the tapes. What more do you want. What do you need him here for?"

"I need him here because I want him dead and I want to see him die so I can know that he is. I can't trust you. I can't trust anybody. You're all imbeciles."

"Why don't you find him yourself, then," Basciano snapped. "I'm sick of you and your bullshit. You wanted the tapes, and I got them for you. You wanted the man who stole them dead, and I made him dead. You wanted the men who made him dead killed, and I had them killed. I've done everything you asked, everything you wanted, and it's never enough. Fuck you, Rajah."

"You didn't do the one thing I asked you to do. The one thing that mattered most."

"I—"

"You have twenty-four hours."

- TWENTY-SEVEN- - -

THE HOUSE WAS DARK. DESMOND LISTENED AT THE door. "Hear anything?" Dan Brennan whispered.

"Just the furnace."

"You want to knock?"

Desmond looked at Brennan. "What do you think?"

"You said the men who came for you were packing. I think maybe it would be prudent to let them know we're here. I don't like the idea of getting mistaken for a burglar and getting blown away. I still have eight years to retirement." Brennan laughed. "See, I plan ahead. I want to know where I'm going to be when I finally sit down in that rocking chair for the first time."

Desmond rapped on the door. The glass pane rattled in its frame, and the sound of his knuckles on the wood echoed deep inside the house. There was no response.

"Let me try. You knock like a fucking Girl Scout." Brennan pounded on the door, rattling the glass so loudly Desmond was afraid it might shatter.

Once more, the echo came from the dark interior, but when it died away, there was no other sound. Desmond glanced over his shoulder and up toward the road, where he could see the second car, the glow of Timmy Corman's cigarette winking through the open window.

Walking around the back, Desmond noticed that there were no tire tracks in the snow. The rented Ford hadn't been moved in several hours.

"Okay," Desmond said, when he rejoined Brennan on the porch. "Let's break in. You cover me."

Brennan took up a position behind Desmond, his pistol drawn and cocked, held high in a two-handed grip. He stared at the dark glass from an angle, not wanting to give anyone inside a clean shot at him through the panel. Desmond squatted down, lock picks in hand, one glove on the floor beside him. The snow swirled around him, and the brisk wind quickly numbed his fingers.

But the lock was hardware-store standard, and it yielded to the picks in nothing flat. Desmond put a hand on the knob and shoved. The door swung open, its hinges creaking like the beginning of *Inner Sanctum*, until it banged against the inside wall, rattling the glass once more.

"Hello, Colin?" Desmond called. His voice mocked him from the gloomy interior of the house, which smelled faintly of wood smoke. He reached for the light switch on the wall, found it after groping a few seconds, and clicked it on. It was just a small bulb in an old ceiling fixture, and its illumination barely reached beyond the vestibule into the house.

"Colin Yeats?" Desmond called. Still no answer.

Desmond eased inside, his empty hands held high over his head. Once he moved past the chandelier, his shadow began to stretch out ahead of him like Plastic Man changing shape until it vanished in the general darkness deep inside the house. The smell of wood smoke was stronger now, but the house remained absolutely silent.

Brennan moved in behind him, and as his shadow oozed around Desmond, the silhouette of the gun barrel on the floor grew like Pinocchio's nose until it vanished in the gloom.

"Colin?"

Desmond, fearful the gun in Brennan's hand might be a catalyst for an unpredictable reaction, turned and whispered over his shoulder, "Go get Colleen and Timmy." He watched Brennan back away, the gun still ready in his hand, then turn as he backed onto the porch. Only then did he lower the gun, but even so, he still carried it at his side.

Desmond called again. "Colin?"

He was deep inside the room now, but the house was too dark for him to see much. Shapes of furniture, only half-formed, as if they were still in the process of coalescing, lay like mounds in the darkness.

Desmond barked a shin on the edge of a coffee table, cursed, and bent over to rub the injury. When he straightened, he decided to throw caution to the winds and moved back to the wall, felt for a light switch, and when his fingers brushed against it, he clicked it on, filling the room instantly with bright light. The shadows vanished, and the furniture seemed to have shrunk, appearing less bulky, and less ominous, in the brilliance.

He walked into the next room, clicked on yet another light, and saw Yeats lying on the floor, one arm draped over the hearthstone, the other folded beneath his head.

Moving quickly, Desmond knelt beside him, feeling for a pulse. Yeats groaned, swiped at the inquisitive hand as if it were a bug, and rolled over onto his side, curling in a ball.

There was no blood, and no other sign of injury, so Desmond took a deep breath and fell back on his haunches with a sigh. Yeats groaned again, but made no attempt to open his eyes. Desmond clapped his hands together, shouting, "Colin, wake up!"

Yeats moaned now, and his eyelids fluttered but still did not open. Desmond noticed the bottle, empty and lying on its side, and moved around the prostrate man to retrieve it. "Rye," he muttered, "just like Colleen said."

He set the bottle down against the fireplace where it would be out of the way and moved back to Yeats, grabbing him by the shoulder and shaking him insistently, almost viciously. "Wake the hell up, dammit!"

Yeats finally looked at him, his eyes narrowed to

slits against the bright light from the fixture overhead. "You look like you have a fucking halo," Yeats
muttered. "But you ain't no angel, are you . . . ?"

"Not a chance," Desmond responded.

"I know you. I sent you packing, didn't I? What
are you doing still here? Get the fuck out of here."

"First of all, it wasn't here. It was another house.
And second, you need coffee, Colin. A lot of it."

"What I need is to be left alone." He sat up then,
bracing himself with one hand on the hearth. He
stopped in midascent, looking around as if he
sensed something missing. When his eye lit on the
empty bottle against the fireplace, he laughed.
"That would explain the way my head feels,
wouldn't it?"

"Did you drink it all?" Desmond asked the question as much in wonder as for information.

Yeats shook his head. "No. I don't think so. I seem
to remember pouring some of it into the fire. The
flames were beautiful. Or maybe I just imagined it. I
don't really know."

"Not like the flames that burned your house down,
I suppose."

Yeats swallowed hard. "What the fuck do you
know about it?"

"I know that it wasn't an accident. And I think I
know who was behind it."

Yeats looked at him sharply now, but before he
could say anything, footsteps thumped on the front
porch, and his attention was diverted. "Who the hell
is that?"

"Friends," Desmond said, getting up.

"I don't have any fucking friends, man," Yeats shouted. "None, you hear me?"

Desmond turned toward the door as the imposing figure of Dan Brennan filled the entrance. Brennan moved lightly for a big man, and when he stepped aside, Yeats gasped. "Christ Almighty! Coll, what the hell are you doing here?"

"I was worried about you."

"Yeah, well . . ."

"Are you all right?"

"Hung over is all," Desmond told her.

"She was talking to me, Desmond," Yeats snapped. He struggled to his feet, bent over, and braced himself on his knees. And added, "But you're right. I am hung over. Hung over to beat the fucking band."

Colleen entered the room and Yeats spotted Timmy Corman for the first time. Yeats shook his head in disbelief. "Christ Almighty, the sixties live. So does Bird, I guess. All the old ghosts are coming back to haunt me."

"Am I a ghost, Colin?" Colleen asked.

Yeats snorted. "Sort of, I guess. No offense, but . . . what the fuck is going on? Why are you all here?"

Desmond started to answer, but Yeats cut him off. "Let her tell it. I still trust her."

Colleen moved toward him, wrapped her arms around him, and pecked him on the forehead. "You drunken little bastard. What are you trying to do, get yourself killed?"

"Hey, Coll, it ain't up to me."

"We know who it's up to, Colin," Desmond said.

"You don't know shit, man. All you know is what

you read in the fucking funny papers. But this ain't about the papers, man, it's about the *real* truth." As the only representative of the media present, Timmy Corman came in for a scathing glare, but smiled benignly back at his critic.

"Who's the big bastard?" Yeats asked, looking at Colleen.

"His name's Dan Brennan. He's a detective."

"Oh, a private eye. You like Sam Spade, are you?" Yeats said.

Brennan scowled. "Not private." Then to Desmond, he said, "You know, I like this son of a bitch a whole lot better on record than I do live."

Yeats wobbled a little, and laughed. "I felt the same way about you the last time I barged into your living room uninvited."

"He's a friend, Colin," Colleen scolded. "Be nice."

"I like to, but I'm all out of rye." He pointed toward the empty bottle, nearly losing his balance with the sudden exertion. He staggered to the couch and sat down heavily, the springs creaking under his weight. He eyed them one at a time, pursing his lips as if trying to decide what, if anything, to say. And when he finally spoke, he was the soul of hospitality. "Sit down, everybody. Sit down. There's beer and soda in the refrigerator. Especially beer." He cackled.

Nobody took him up on his offer, and he shrugged. "Suit yourselves." Once more he stared at Colleen, his face blank, as if he had forgotten who she was. "Are you going to tell me what's going on, or aren't you?"

"Of course, Colin. I'll tell you everything I know.

But not until you get some coffee in you. Where's the kitchen?"

He jerked a thumb over his shoulder, and Colleen started in the direction he indicated. He got up then. "I'll give you a hand. You can tell me what the fuck this is all about while the coffee perks." He stood there teetering. "Don't go 'way, fellas, we'll be back soon's I sober up."

Something chirped in Brennan's coat, and he patted his pockets, looking for the source of the sound. When he found it and pulled it out, the mobile phone was dwarfed by his huge hand.

"Brennan," he said. He listened, nodding. "Yeah, we got him. No, he's okay. You sure? All right, we'll wait." He folded the phone closed and looked at Desmond.

"That was Stan. He's with the state cops. Your hunch paid off, Paul. Justice got a RICO warrant. They're setting up in nine locations, and they don't want us to do anything to upset the apple cart until they're set. It'll take about an hour, Stan says."

"It'll take longer than that to get Yeats to cooperate."

"Hell, it'll take longer than that just to sober him up, looks like. God only knows how long before we can get him on board. If ever. Right now it sure as hell doesn't sound like we can."

"They're sure Primasanha is in the compound on the reservoir?"

Brennan nodded. "Stan says they been watching him for a couple weeks, everywhere he goes. They picked him up at JFK this morning. There's about six or eight people at the compound. They're not sure who they all are, but at least we got lucky on this one."

"How so?"

"It's a residential retreat, not one of those five-and-dime monasteries, or recruiting centers, whatever the hell he calls them."

"Temples, is what he calls them."

"How'd you get them to move so fast? I mean, I know from Stan that you have some interesting friends in some interesting places, but this is . . . well, let's just say that I'd like to have a few chips like that to call in."

"They had no idea about the weapons cache in Colorado," Desmond said, "but they'd been watching him for almost a year for other reasons—fraud, racketeering, so on. He was getting a little reckless. Actually, according to my friend in the Justice Department, it was Bobby Basciano who was getting reckless. Apparently, Primasanha had been putting more and more pressure on him to fill the coffers, and they were making some interesting maneuvers with the cash. The trouble is, they were moving too quickly, and they pissed off a lot of influential people."

"Took in some of the wrong rich kids, huh?"

Desmond nodded. "Yeah, you might say that."

"I still don't see how we're going to get him to give it up."

"I'm not sure we can."

-TWENTY-EIGHT---

YEATS LOOKED MORE HUMAN NOW, HIS FACE LESS flushed, and his flesh less slack. His eyes still had that drinker's glitter, but his speech was less slurred, if more elliptical, as if, in recovering from the rye, he was seeing the world from a more accustomed perspective, one in which labyrinths were the most direct routes from A to B.

Desmond was getting antsy, waiting for the call from Stan Collins. Dan Brennan was outside, watching the snow, detached and distant, trying to concentrate on the confrontation he knew was coming. Timmy Corman sat in a corner, saying nothing, taking it all in, his eyes following Desmond, his ears tuned to Colin's frequency. Only Colleen seemed unruffled.

"You mean to tell me," Yeats asked, so suddenly it sounded like an explosion in the silence, "that three people have been killed, just because of those god-damned tapes? Is that what you're saying, Desmond?"

Paul stopped pacing and faced the singer, glad to have something to focus on, to distract him from the anticipation of the call. "That's exactly what I'm saying."

"And that asshole from Jersey City is behind it all. Is that what I'm supposed to believe?"

"Believe what you want. That's my best guess."

"They're songs, man, that's all they are. Just songs. Little, orphaned ditties. They're not worth dying for."

"When you come right down to it, nothing is, really. Not land, not money, maybe love, but I doubt that."

"Definitely not love, man," Yeats said with a bitter laugh. "Trust me on that one. Definitely not love. You know the Dylan song 'Love Is Just a Four-Letter Word'? That says it all."

Desmond instinctively looked at Colleen, some protective instinct wanting to cushion her, but she was unfazed. She smiled at Desmond. "When Colin gets a little alcohol in his system, he becomes the world's biggest cynic."

Yeats laughed. "Easy for you to say, Coll." He started to pace now, hands folded behind his back, almost a parody of Desmond's earlier posture.

"You look like Groucho Marx, Colin," Corman said.

"The only kind of Marxist worth being, Ratso. You know, the thing I have come to realize as I enter the vestibule to senility and take off my boots is that fundamentally, people suck. Greed, man, that's what it's all about. That's what this is all about, greed. Primasanha is greedy. He wants all the money in the world. He wants everybody in the world to hang on his every word. He's greedy for money and for power. Griffin Records is greedy too, man. They want to squeeze every drop of lemonade out me. Peter Chandler is greedy, too. He wanted to represent everybody in the world, wanted to have everything, and if it meant fucking his clients, well, that just made it more fun. I got my own power trio, man, and it ain't the cream of the crop."

"Power trio?" Desmond asked.

"Yeah, you know. The kind of band that came along in the late sixties. Three men—one guitar, one bass, one drummer. Cream, man. Three all-stars— Clapton, Bruce, and Baker. It was all about ego. Everybody wanted to be up front. You listen to 'Crossroads' and you hear it there, everybody soloing at once, sometimes listening, mostly not. It's good music, don't get me wrong, but it was the beginning of the end. Ensemble playing went out the window. It was like what's his name, the British philosopher, Locke or somebody, says, it was the war of all against all."

"Hey, man, that's the bed somebody made, and everybody has to lie in it," Corman said. "It's the same damn thing in publishing, people paying more attention to their own careers, forgetting about the books, forgetting what it's all supposed to be about. People spending company money to buy themselves reputations and parlay them into job offers. They go to chichi parties, hang out at chic places, and kill to get a profile in *New York* or *Vanity Fair*. It's all hand waving, shouting 'Hey, look at me. I'm an editor. I'm a publisher.' In the meantime, the books go begging. Books are fucking orphans, too, man, just like songs."

"You two sound so bitter," Colleen said. "It can't be that bad. At least you get the chance to create something that matters to you. You get to leave something behind besides a stack of credit-card receipts, phone bills, and income-tax returns."

"But nobody gives a shit anymore, Coll. That's the point, don't you see? Nobody gives a shit. You read the papers around here, and everybody's talking about the twenty-fifth anniversary of Woodstock. But it's all about money and power. Hell, it's the politicians who are doing all the talking. And the promoters. 'I'll pay this if you let me do that.' 'We want this, so you have to do that.' Does anybody talk about the music? Hell, Woodstock was overblown to begin with. The music got lost even before the weekend was over. The rats were scrambling in the attic trying to figure how to wring another drop of blood from the turnip. Movies. Records. Books. Calendars. People talk about what it meant. They get nostalgic and weepy. But it was not the beginning of something, man, no golden age dawning. It was four days of mud and misery, self-indulgence reared its ugly head, and it's been a downhill slide ever since."

"You don't sound like a man who was a prophet for a generation."

"Hell, Desmond, sure I was. But it was spelled with an *f*, not a *ph*. Money, greed, that's what it was all about. I don't blame Warren Resnick. I know that he's got a job to do, that he has bosses, that he has to please them. But that doesn't mean I have to cooperate with him. Not anymore."

"What about the tapes?" Desmond asked.

"Fuck the tapes."

"What about Primasanha?"

"Fuck him, too. Fuck them all. Let them all blow themselves up and let the rats eat the corpses, for all I care."

"You know, Colin, when I was in Colorado, at the Temple of the Holy Sanctuary, I met a young woman named Samantha Alexander. You know what she told me?"

Yeats shook his head. "No, I don't. How would I?"

"She told me why she was there. She said she joined Holy Sanctuary because she admired you. You belonged, so she wanted to belong. If it was good enough for you, it must have some value."

"She made a mistake. It happens. I made one when I joined. I left. So can she."

"It's not that easy, Colin. You know it isn't. Most people are followers. Samantha certainly is. She followed you. Only she didn't realize she was following you into a lion's den."

"Snake pit is more like it, man. But it's not my problem. I didn't ask her to follow me. I think for myself, I make up my own mind. I try to do what seems right. Sometimes it is, and sometimes it isn't. If you screw up, you move on. It's like riding a fucking bicycle. If you fall on your ass, you have two choices. You can walk away or you can get back on. I always get back on. You're trying to run some guilt trip on me, Desmond. But if she listened to my songs—I mean really listened—she'd know that what they're about, every last fucking one of them, is thinking for yourself, making your own decisions, using your own eyes and ears to examine the world. I was not a preacher, forcing my message down somebody's throat. I didn't even *have* a message, man. That was the point of my songs. There *are* no messages. Like William Blake says, there's innocence and there's experience. And that's all there is. You get the latter trying to defend the former. It's a losing battle, but those are the ground rules. Everybody has to play by them."

Desmond was about to respond when the front door opened. Dan Brennan waved for him to join him outside. Closing the door behind him, Desmond asked, "What's up?"

"Stan's there. Pete Fischler, from the state cops is there, too. They want to know if we're coming or if they should just go ahead and take the place down."

"I'd like to find out if the tapes are there," Desmond said. "We're talking about a fortune. If the tapes can be saved, we have to try."

"Short of asking Primasanha, I don't know how we do that, Paul. It's either that or hit 'em quick and hope it goes down easily. Then we can search the place."

"But if it doesn't . . . ?"

Brennan shrugged. "Then I guess Griffin Records loses a bundle. Worse things could happen."

"Let me try Yeats one more time. I think he's getting close to coming around."

Brennan laughed. "The last time I was inside, it sounded to me like he'd just as soon put a match to the fucking things and roast weenies over the flames. But go ahead, give it one more try. I'll tell Stan we'll be there in forty-five minutes. It's a half-hour drive, so you don't have much time."

"Thanks, Dan. One more shot, that's all I want." He looked up at the sky, felt the tickle of snowflakes on his eyelids, and took a deep breath. It was what he loved about the Hudson Valley, the genuineness of the winter, the way it came early and stayed late. The progress of the seasons, each one clearly marked from the others, and unlike so many places in the country, it had all four of them. Just like it was supposed to.

He went back inside and found Yeats sitting on the hearth, a cigarette dangling from the headstock of his acoustic. He watched as Yeats tuned it by ear, adjusting the low E twice before he was satisfied with the sound of a chord. Yeats smiled at him. "I guess I've been giving you a hard time," he said.

"I'm a big boy, Colin. I can take it."

Yeats sped through a few blues runs, then broke into the old Reverend Gary Davis tune "Come Back, Baby," bending the strings to wring every last bit of feeling from them. His fingerpicking was magnificent, and the steady rumble of the bass notes made it obvious why Yeats was so picky about the low E.

"The song's appropriate," Desmond said.

Yeats looked at him with a puzzled expression. "Why's that?"

"Let's talk it over one more time. Isn't that what the song says."

"You know it?"

"By Reverend Gary and by Dave van Ronk."

"You surprise me, man. Most people nowadays don't have any idea about the old blues guys. Reverend Davis, Mississippi John Hurt, Sleepy John Estes, Son House—those motherfuckers could *play*, man. You know, it's all the same. People think Kenny G is a jazz musician because they never heard Charlie Parker or Jackie McLean, let alone Sidney Bechet or Chu Berry. You know, when I was a kid, the white radio stations, which meant most radio stations, played Pat Boone instead of Fats Domino when they played 'Ain't That a Shame.' It's supposed to be better now, but the way it seems to me, the good black musicians are still out in the cold. The only real difference is that inane black music gets played now on black radio stations. You still don't hear Charlie Parker or John Coltrane. Hell, man, New York, the Big fucking *Apple* doesn't even have a real jazz station. The closest one is in Newark, and it's listener-supported."

"People don't care. They'd rather hear Kenny G. Kenny G doesn't challenge anybody. He's not dangerous, like Parker or Coltrane or Miles. He's comfortable."

"Yeah, well . . ." Yeats did a fancy run, then another chorus of the old blues thing, flawlessly picked, his head bobbing in time to the steady bass line. "The best art is always dangerous, man."

"You're dangerous," Desmond pointed out. "And not just to Rajah Primasanha."

"I'm not dangerous to him, man. He's irrelevant."

"No, he's not. He's dangerous, too. Colleen told you about the guns, I assume."

Yeats nodded.

"Well, think about it, that man has hundreds, maybe thousands of followers. And he's leading them down the primrose path. Some of them followed him because of you. And that's significant. Because the reason great art is dangerous is that it takes responsibility, it forces people to see how things are, and dares them to change."

"People don't want to change, man. That's why *I'm* irrelevant."

"But you're not. You can't be, or Primasanha wouldn't care so much about getting rid of you."

Yeats shrugged it off, but Desmond bored in. "You have a responsibility, Colin. I'm not talking about the tapes alone, although I am talking about them. But if there's anything you can do to get Primasanha out of that compound without a fight, you ought to do it. There are other people there, and for all you know, some of them are there because of you. If we can prevent an armed conflict, we have to do it."

"You're wearing me out with that shit, man. I already told you that I—"

"I know what you told me. But I don't believe you. Nobody could play with as much feeling as you just did if he didn't care, and care passionately. You're hurt, I know that. You're angry, and I don't blame you. But you are *not* indifferent and you are not powerless."

Once more Yeats sought refuge in the strings. He bent over the guitar as if he were whispering to it, and the guitar whispered back as his fingers flew over the strings, caressing them, and suddenly the sound died away altogether. He set the guitar down gently and got to his feet.

"All right, man. What do you want me to do?"

"Colin . . ."

"It's all right, Coll. Desmond's right. I have responsibility here, and I can't slough it off."

- T W E N T Y - N I N E - - -

THEY HAD TO WALK NEARLY A QUARTER OF A MILE TO avoid tipping off those in the compound. Stan Collins flagged them down and led them along the snowy lane as he filled them in. "Looks now like there may be eight people inside, but we can't be sure. Your boy Primasanha is there, Paul, and so is one of my boys."

"Bobby Basciano?"

Collins grunted. "You betcha. The rest of them appear to be Primasanha's palace guard. Beefy fucks, too."

"What about other people? Women and children?"

Collins shook his head. "Nope. Not as far as we

can tell. The problem is, we got a hold of the builder, and he says there's a regular bunker underground, whole bunch of rooms, connected by tunnels. He told Captain Fischler that twenty or thirty people could live down there, and have room for a party, too. If anybody's down there, we got real problems on our hands. A fistful of hostages would make this real messy real quick. I suppose the situation's the same at the other locations."

"Any way to get inside the underground section without going through the house?"

"Always thinking, aren't you, son? As a matter of fact, yes, there is. There's a tunnel in from the road, all the plumbing and wiring is underground and leads into the cellar. The conduit is big enough for a man to move around in, and we've already sent three men down. They're at the hatch that leads into the building."

"And?"

"And nothing. We've been waiting for you and the star of the show to get here. Couldn't take a chance on entering the building, because if the men are seen, there's no turning back. Washington is watching this one real close. . . . Waco and all that has made them kind of timid."

They reached a fieldstone wall, wrought-iron gates set in six-foot-high pillars blocking the road. But the gate was unlocked. Desmond saw the severed chain that held the gates closed lying on the ground, half-covered by new snow. Three men were crouched behind the wall. Over it, Desmond could just make out the main house. A separate garage, big enough to house half a dozen cars, was connected to it by a breezeway. Two other structures, both of them cottages made of the same rough stone as the wall and the main building, were on the other side of the compound.

Stan ducked down, even though it would have been all but impossible to see him from the house, and Desmond and Brennan followed him. After introducing Brennan and Desmond to Fischler, Collins asked, "Well, any bright ideas?"

Desmond looked at the house, peering over the stone wall like Kilroy. He was worried about the possibility of hostages. The palace guard and Bobby Basciano would have to worry about themselves.

Ducking down below the top of the wall, Desmond moved in close to Fischler. "How many men do you have altogether, Captain?"

"Six, counting myself and the three men inside. We were told to make this small, and we're doin' our best."

Desmond nodded. "Counting Stan, me, and Dan, that gives us nine. Numerically, we have the edge, assuming there's no one else inside that we don't know about. But they have plenty of cover. And we're hampered by having to coordinate with the other locations."

"We have a satellite link to handle that. I'm in touch with my office by phone, and they're plugged in. Sixty seconds' notice is all they need, if we want to move simultaneously. But from what Stan, here, tells me, you got an idea that might make things a whole lot simpler."

"Yeah. It's a long shot, but it might work. I have Colin Yeats with me, and I think he's somehow the catalyst for this whole situation. I think Primasanha has gone around the bend, primarily because he's obsessed with Yeats, and getting even with him. My guess is that Primasanha was behind the destruction of the house in California."

"You want to use Yeats as bait, is that it?"

"Something like that."

"I don't know about that. Anything happens to him, big star like that and everything, Janet Reno'll have us all made into cigars and chain-smoke us. Does he know what he's getting himself into?"

"He knows," Desmond said.

"Run it past me, see how it sounds."

"I figured the thing to do is try to get Primasanha out of the house. If we can get him to agree to a rendezvous with Yeats, we can pinch him and then move in on the others. With the boss already gone, they'll be more likely to give up without a fight."

"This guy's no fool, from what I hear. You think he'll go for that?"

"What have we got to lose? Even if it doesn't work, we're no worse off than we are now. He'll have no idea we're out here."

Fischler thought it over, tapping his hands on the snowy stone of the top of the wall and humming. "What the hell, maybe it'll work. Like you say, it won't do no harm."

Suddenly the compound was flooded with light. In the bright glare, they could see the front of the house quite clearly, even through the swirling snow.

"Uh-oh," Fischler muttered. "What the hell is happening now?"

As if in answer to his question, the front door of the house opened, and two men appeared on the patio. They headed toward the garage, and one of them waved his hand across his midsection. In response to the gesture, one of the garage doors rumbled open. Desmond borrowed a pair of binoculars and watched the men. Floodlights were mounted at both ends of the garage, a third in the middle, and the men were outlined in profile. He didn't recognize either one.

"Where the hell are they going?"

The two men disappeared into the garage. A door slammed, and a wash of red light spilled into the snow as someone stepped on the brakes of a vehicle that Desmond could not see. The sound of an engine cranking up, then catching, echoed across the compound, and exhaust swirled out into the snow. A second garage door now shuddered up, and a panel truck backed out into the snow. As the truck cut to its right and stopped for a moment, Desmond saw the same Holy Sanctuary logo that had marked the security Jeep in Colorado.

The truck now moved forward, headed to the house, and pulled up by the broad steps leading down off the patio. The driver opened the door, and Desmond could see his face now in the pale interior light. It was Basciano. The junior mobster climbed out of the van and went back into the house.

"The fuck is going on?" Fischler hissed.

"I think I know what's in that truck," Desmond whispered.

"Your tapes?"

He nodded.

A second vehicle appeared now. It was a Dodge Caravan, and after backing out of the garage, it rolled up behind the panel truck. The garage doors, either operated from inside the house, or by remote control, descended one after the other, with a rumble that was audible over the sound of the idling engines.

"We can't let them leave," Fischler said. "We got people all over the country waiting on us. If Primasanha comes out of the house, we're going to move."

He was right, and Desmond didn't argue. Fischler got on the comm pack and raised the men in the tunnel. "Looks like they're getting ready to leave, guys. Have the hatch ready to move. We can't let them get out of here."

Desmond heard the squawk of the comm pack, the officer's voice tinny and blurred. "We're ready to roll," it said.

Fischler said, "Stan, you better get those civilians out of here. Take them back up the road and keep them there." Collins nodded and moved back away from the wall, where Colin and Colleen were in huddled conversation among the trees.

The front door of the house opened again, and Dan Brennan moved in alongside Desmond, tapped him on the shoulder, and when Desmond turned, thrust a Kevlar vest at him. Brennan was already wearing one of his own. "Better put this on, Paul," he said.

Desmond struggled out of his coat, slipped into the vest and pulled it tight, then fastened the Velcro tabs. He didn't bother putting his coat back on. Brennan handed him an M-16 assault rifle. "You know how to use this?"

Desmond nodded. "If I have to."

Bobby Basciano reappeared on the patio, and several men streamed out the door as he held it open. The lights inside the house went out, and Fischler said, "This is it." He clicked open the comm link and said, "Tommy, they all seem to have come out the front. They're leaving. You guys move. Now! Come on out the front, onto the patio. I'll hold as long as I can."

He grabbed a bullhorn then and squeezed the button. He checked along the wall to make sure the men had spread out and were not exposed. When he was satisfied his men were ready, he watched the house. The men on the patio were moving toward the van, and Basciano closed the storm door, then jumped down to the ground and climbed into the driver's seat of the panel truck. The bald pate of Rajah Primasanha gleamed in the security lights for a moment as he bent to open the passenger door of the panel truck.

"If you're not ready, say so now," Fischler whispered, pressing the earphone into his ear a little more tightly. There was no objection.

The bodyguards were in the van now, and Basciano's panel truck was just starting to move. Fischler held his ground, not wanting to reveal his presence until the three men in the house made their appearance.

Desmond felt odd, knowing that similar scenes were now unfolding in a dozen widely scattered places, but he pushed the thought aside to concentrate on the events under his nose. He believed that the tapes were in the panel truck, but he couldn't be sure. They must have been planning on moving them, probably to Mega Sound. He glanced over his shoulder, looking for Colin Yeats, but the singer was lost in the shadows with Stan and Colleen.

The front door of the house burst open just as the van began to roll. The floodlights exploded again, filling the air with the swirl of snow, and the panel truck roared into high gear. Fischler fired a flare into the long drive, where it exploded in white heat, cascading sparks and sending the panel truck veering around it and into a tree. The radiator burst and steam gushed from under the hood.

Through the bullhorn, Fischler barked. "Police! Stop your vehicle and surrender!"

The van ignored the command, rolling over the sizzling flare and throwing its wheels into sharp relief for a moment. "Slow them up," Fischler barked, and a burst of automatic weapons fire sprayed the lane a few feet ahead of the careening van. The driver was trying to zigzag, but the lane was narrow and the snow cut down on his traction. The van skidded to a halt, slammed into reverse, and did an abrupt K-turn.

Desmond was moving toward the wall, Dan Brennan right behind him. The panel truck still hissed, and so far there was no sign of life. He wondered if Basciano and Primasanha had been injured, perhaps even rendered unconscious, but he didn't want to wait to find out.

Desmond leaped over the wall, Brennan following,

and suddenly darting past him. For a big man, Brennan had surprising speed. The passenger door of the panel truck suddenly gaped open, and the dome light in the cab showed Basciano slumped over the wheel. The windshield was a tracery of cracks where something, probably his head, had struck it.

Primasanha backed away from the van, but Desmond angled through the trees, moving to cut off his escape route as Brennan bore down on him.

There was no firing behind him, and Desmond was relieved. The bodyguards, surprised by the small assault team, must have surrendered. Primasanha saw Brennan coming and reached into his parka. Brennan raised his rifle. "Don't move," he said.

But the guru ducked to his right behind a tree, still fumbling in his coat pocket. His right hand reappeared, an automatic pistol clutched tightly in it, and Desmond launched himself through the air from ten feet away, driving his shoulder into Primasanha's back and sending him sprawling. The pistol flew into the night, and Desmond locked one arm around the guru's neck. Dan Brennan reached the struggling men, hauled Primasanha to his feet, and trained his rifle on his midsection.

Desmond grabbed his own rifle from the snow, and Brennan moved in to cuff the guru. He was none too gentle, but Primasanha said nothing. Brennan shoved him back toward the open area in front of the house, and Primasanha stumbled along, shifting his shoulders to keep his balance on the slippery footing.

The bodyguards were all lying facedown in the snow, under the watchful eyes of Fischler's tac squad. One by one, they were cuffed, and Prima-sanha was ordered to take his place on the end of the row.

Desmond and Brennan then moved to the panel truck. Basciano was still groggy. He leaned on the steering wheel, moaning. Blood oozed from several cuts on his forehead, but he was able to climb out of the truck unassisted. "Should have been wearing your seat belt, asshole." Brennan chuckled, dragging him toward the other prisoners.

Desmond smelled gasoline and realized the truck's tank must have ruptured. He raced to the back and yanked open the doors. In the dim light from the house floods, he could make out several large cardboard cartons lashed to the walls of the truck. He climbed in hurriedly, tore one open, and reached inside. Using a small penlight, he found himself staring at a mountain of cassettes and tape boxes. He fished several out and examined them. They were all neatly labeled, and each one was part of the missing horde. He started unlashing the carton when a shadow spilled into the truck. He turned to see Colin Yeats standing at the rear of the van.

"So," he said, "you found them after all."

"Yeah. I guess they're all here, but . . ."

Yeats climbed up into the truck and peered into the carton while Desmond played the light over its contents. "Yeah," he said. "Yeah. So people died for this stuff, huh?"

Desmond nodded.

"Stupid. So fucking stupid." He backed out of the

truck and dropped to the ground. "You better get out of there, Desmond. The gas tank is leaking."

"I know. Give me a hand, and help me get the tapes out."

"I don't think so."

Desmond turned to stare at him in disbelief. He saw the cigarette in Yeat's mouth, the Bic lighter in his hand.

"What the hell are you doing? Are you crazy?"

"Feel like a smoke, Desmond."

And in that instant Desmond knew what Yeats was planning, and he knew, too, that he'd better move fast. He dove out of the truck as Yeats spun the wheel on the lighter and took a drag on the cigarette clamped in his teeth.

Desmond caught him across the midsection, but Yeats didn't care. He flicked the cigarette in an arc over Desmond's shoulder. As the two men sprawled in the snow Desmond heard the dull thump of the gasoline igniting, and started to scramble to his feet. Yeats clawed at the ground, gained a stumbling crouch, and sprinted after him. The two men stood side by side, staring at the flames licking at the rear of the truck.

The rumble of the truck's gas tank erupting shattered the silence and flaming gasoline sprayed in every direction.

Yeats sighed. "Don't worry, Desmond," he said. "I'll tell Warren you found them." He moved away, found Colleen, and draped an arm around her shoulders. Together, they walked up the snowy lane until they were beyond the reach of the orange glare from the burning truck.

Primasanha howled at him in rage. "You bastard. I'm not through with you yet, Yeats."

Colin Yeats never turned, and he said nothing. The hiss, pop, and crackle of the burning tapes was more eloquent than any words, and he knew it.